Brain Fever

Brain Fever

Peter Holdroyd

ISBN:-13: 978-1081581480

DEDICATION
To my cherished granddaughters, Aimee and
Hannah (who modelled for the cover photograph)

CHAPTER 1

Cat Mitchell jerked awake and gazed into the sleeping face of Alan Crossley. Hot and in need of a shower, she slipped out of bed, careful not to wake him.

Later, showered and wearing a terrycloth bathrobe, the aroma of fresh coffee in her nose, she perched on a stool at the breakfast bar, dropped bread into the toaster and poured her first cup of the day.

The bread erupted from the toaster and she scraped low-cholesterol margarine on it. Her coffee was cooling and she drank it all before refilling her mug from the cafetière. She pulled her laptop computer towards her from beside the bread-bin and booted it up. The email program loaded itself and collected the overnight postings, most of which went straight into the Junk Mail folder from which she would dump it unread.

One sender's name caught her eye. Craig Jordon. She shivered. What was he doing, writing to her twelve years after leaving her and going to Canada? The kitchen door opened and Alan walked in, barefoot, and rubbing sleep from his eyes. He'd slung a red checked shirt on over a pair of boxers. He rubbed his face, hand rasping on stubble.

Her eyes fell on the email from Craig, the man who'd been her first real love – and lover. She quickly opened it to read.

Her thoughts turned to the unexpected proposal she'd received last night from Alan Crossley. She was puzzled by her reaction: they'd been living together all through the summer; they didn't get on each other's nerves – though when she'd agreed to the cohabitation, she'd feared they would; and there was no reason why they shouldn't marry: no impediment, as they say. Both single – now that Alan's divorce was final – both earning good money, he as a Fellow of Mid-Yorks University, an archæologist, she as an osteologist, often called in to examine ancient skeletons unearthed at archæological digs.

Interests in common – what more could she ask for?

On the other hand, she thought, she didn't need a man – was perfectly capable of putting shelves up herself, if she needed any more, and as for children... well, women were having babies in their *sixties* these days, so no worries there, then. So why, she wondered, had she simply smiled and told him she'd like time to think about it, instead of happily accepting?

Passion was a temporary emotion you could find with many men: but the *right* man had to have potential to provide more than that, otherwise a marriage could be pretty dead after the novelty had worn off. Of course, passion had its place, and as a girl, the idea of a man loving her madly and passionately had filled her head and her heart. It had taken until she was in her final year of post-grad study to realise what a stupid, childish fantasy that was. These days, she was usually too busy to mix socially.

She rarely met men outside the orbit of her professional life. In so circumscribed an existence, she should be grateful that any half-way presentable man thought enough of her to propose. So why not jump at the opportunity Alan had presented her with?

But of course, she didn't *need* a man in her life, though she liked having Alan around.

"Anything interesting in the post?" Alan asked, pulling bacon and eggs from the fridge and adding them to the mushrooms and baked beans he'd already got out.

"Not yet," Cat replied, thankful that he couldn't see the email before her on the laptop's LCD screen. It was from Craig Jordon.

Dear Cat, I know this may come as something of a surprise, my writing to you after all this time, but something's come up and I need your help.

She felt a confusing mixture of warmth that he needed her, and indignation that he'd more or less ignored her for twelve years.

Mum and Dad have been killed in a road accident, and I need to come home to sort out their estates. And there's the business, too, I don't know who's running that at the moment, but I hope it's someone who knows more about horses than I do.

She felt momentary sorrow for the loss of his parents. They'd been nice to her while she and Craig had been going out together, and once or twice since, when she'd seen them on shopping trips to York or Skipton.

I know it's a bit of an imposition, but is there any chance you can meet me off the Toronto flight at 09:30 your time, tomorrow, and take me up to Holt Carr. I could get a taxi, but I need to talk to you. Leaving in an hour and will be thoroughly jet-lagged when I see you. Best, Craig.

What cheek! she thought. No, he could get a taxi like everyone else. She clicked on the Reply button and started to write. Her eye fell on the date and time of his message. Hell! It was yesterday. So that meant he was arriving *today!* She looked at the kitchen clock, radio-controlled and therefore always right.

"Christ!" she exclaimed as she realised he'd be landing in an hour.

Alan looked up from the cooker. "What?"

"I've got to go out. Meet someone at the airport."

"Who?"

"Somebody I knew years ago. Been out of the country since then. Arriving this morning," Cat gasped as she shut down the laptop and hurried into the bedroom. There was only just time to make it to Leeds and Bradford Airport. She grabbed a clean pair of jeans and green long-sleeved jumper from her wardrobe, and pulled a brush through the wildness of her natural curls until she believed them tamed enough for her to appear in public. Finally, she applied light makeup and forgot to kiss a startled Alan goodbye, as he was sitting down to his usual plateful of fried food. She disliked cooked breakfasts, and was glad she wasn't going to have to watch him eat his way through another one. She got behind the wheel of the silver estate car she kept in the garage beneath the apartment block and headed out of York towards Yeadon.

*

She'd seen the plane land half an hour before, rocking in the currents of air forced upwards by the undulating folds of the landscape below the glide path. Early morning sunshine reflected from the pools of overnight rain-water and dappled the concrete façade of the terminal building as clouds scudded eastwards. People were beginning to emerge, some carrying bags, others pushing trolleys, looking for taxis.

She saw him. To her surprise, she recognised him instantly. Older, of course; bronzed and weathered – she knew practically nothing of what he'd gone to Canada to do but guessed from his appearance he led an outdoor existence. She wondered if he'd recognise her as easily. She checked her appearance in the mirror, flicked her pony tail which had been squashed against the head-rest of the car seat, and got out to wave at him.

He stared at her for a moment before his face split into a grin which briefly caused her heart to pound. He pushed his trolley-load of bags towards her.

"Cat! Thanks for coming." Craig parked the trolley and came up to her.

She was still surprised that she had recognised him as soon as she had seen him, when he'd hardly featured in her thoughts for so long. He leaned forward and kissed her lightly on the cheek. To her amazement, her body reacted in a way which she hadn't expected after all this time. It took her breath for a moment.

"Craig," she gasped at last, "it's taken you long enough to remember me."

He looked at her in some surprise. "Course I remember you, Cat."

His voice sounded as tanned as his face, his Yorkshire accent overlaid with a Canadian drawl.

"Recognised you at once. You look just the same."

She detected an impulse to blush with pleasure at his compliment and told herself not to be so girly. "I'm sorry, I should have said how sorry I am to learn about your parents."

"Yeah, it was a bit of a shock when the solicitors managed to find me to tell me."

"I – I guess it would be," she said. "Let's get your stuff in the back of the car," she said, opening the rear hatch. There was enough space for him to cram his two suitcases in beside the bags, boxes and equipment she normally kept in there. She closed the vehicle, and they bumped into each other as he unthinkingly went for the right-hand door at the same time as she did.

"Sorry!" he said, 'spent too long among left-hand-drive cars."

She was aware of the unintended pressure of his body against hers as she shrugged and sat behind the wheel and waited while he went round to the nearside. She navigated away from the terminal building onto the Skipton road, heading for Holt Carr.

"In your email, you said you needed to talk to me," she reminded him when they were clear of the airport traffic, heading towards Poole Bank, and she had time to think of other things.

"Yeah. I wanted to know how you are, and what you're doing."

"You could have asked me that any time in an email or by phone."

"I wanted to see you – you know, face to face."

"I'm flattered I'm sure," she said. She was annoyed with herself for jumping to do what he asked after all this time.

"And I wanted to apologise for not being in touch since I left."

She glanced at him wondering if his mien supported his words, which certainly sounded sincere. Possibly.

"You think you can clear off for twelve years then come back and simply apologise for not keeping in touch? You think that's all you have to do?"

He stared out of the window at the rising moorland before turning to her. "It's a start. I know it's not enough."

She drove in silence for a few minutes. "I don't even know what I'm doing here," she told him. "I only got your email this morning, and it was too late then to tell you to get a taxi."

"I appreciate your picking me up." He hesitated. "No wedding ring, I see."

"No." She took her eyes off the road long enough to look at him. "You?"

"Not married. Never."

She was surprised, and told him so.

He grinned, in a way that brought back memories. "Not too many girls in the north of Canada."

She glanced quickly at him, all broad-shouldered, trousers stretched by his muscular-looking thighs.

"I'm sure what there are were falling over themselves to meet you."

He glanced at her, teasingly. "Of course... but I prefer Yorkshire girls. It's the difference between home-grown and supermarket. The First Nations are nice people, basically friendly but they're not my type. That ruled out most of the indigent population."

She waited a moment. "But? I feel a 'but' coming on?"

"Well, I never signed up as a monk."

She pursed her lips. Perhaps she had pried further than she should, but she was interested in his answers.

"What do you do in the frozen north?" she asked.

"Spend a lot of time on my own, chipping bits off old rocks," he replied. "I had a promising new spot in my sights when I was held up – first by a grizzly bear that was trying to make up its mind if I was a threat or lunch – and then by the solicitors calling my cell phone."

"Doesn't happen often, then?"

He shook his head, his eyes scanning the landscape either side of the road. "No. And a caller with an English accent is even rarer. My boss, Gerry Ancrom, usually waits for me to ring him because he knows how difficult it can be sometimes to answer a phone. It was in my rucksack, and I had to get my glove off to get it. It's so cold up there that if I'd touched the barrel of my rifle, my fingers would have stuck to it."

"You had a rifle?" she asked, surprised.

"Believe me, you don't go out there without one," he said. "If the grizzly had decided to have me for dinner, I'd have had to shoot it. It's kill or be killed in the wilds." He grinned at her.

She caught sight of his white teeth in the mirror.

"What are you doing these days?"

"Forensic Anthropology. I study bones, ancient and modern," she replied.

"Study them?"

"Usually to determine age, cause of death, or the sex of the skeleton. And I do a little tutoring at the University."

"Sounds interesting."

"It is."

"Did you have that in mind when you decided to stay here and finish your PhD?"

"Careful, Craig: you almost make it sound as if the last twelve years of no contact were my doing."

She turned off the road up the track which led to Holt Carr, the old stone farmhouse where Craig had been born and brought up. He asked her to stop short of the yard, by the gateway in the dry-stone wall. She turned off the engine. He chewed his lip.

"The last twelve years of no contact were something we both wanted."

She turned to him, scandalised. "Rubbish! You were the one who wanted to go swanning off to Canada. I didn't send you away."

"No, you wanted to stay and finish your post-graduate studies."

"I only had another year to go for my doctorate!" She sounded angry even to her own ears. "Don't you dare try laying off any blame for ending our relationship on me. It was *you*, doing what *you* wanted to do."

"And you."

"I could have gone to Canada any time." She took a deep breath. "All right! I know I wanted to finish my PhD here, but I could have travelled anywhere after that."

"You could have finished your PhD in Canada, if you'd wanted," he retorted.

"You never hinted that I should."

"I didn't think I had the right."

She stared at him, anger threatening to overwhelm her self-control. "What do you mean? We'd been going out together for six months."

"I know that! But we'd never spoken of a long-term commitment and I thought you probably wouldn't want one while you were still sorting out your career. So I didn't feel I could ask you to give up everything and come out to Canada – even after you'd finished your studies."

She pursed her lips again, not daring to respond. They sat in silence for a moment before he opened the door.

"Do you mind if I go on from here alone?" he asked, climbing out of the car.

Cat unlocked the boot with the remote catch. "No. I have to get back to York anyway."

She waited until he closed the hatch, then turned the car in the meadow in front of the house and drove down to the main road. She had to admit to a grain of truth in what he said. There had been no talk of commitment, but that wasn't to say she hadn't considered it. Why was she even worrying about matters which had lain dormant for twelve years? Why should she think even this much about Craig, who'd left her, when back home in York, there was loveable, loyal Alan, as kind and considerate as any man could be. He'd never have disappeared without a word for twelve years then suddenly decide to get in touch again out of the blue. He'd have maintained contact – Hell! He'd have taken her with him. Bloody Craig! Damn him!

*

It was still only eleven o'clock when she got back to her apartment. Alan had washed up before going out, but had left the dishes stacked in the drainer. It was another minor irritant: she liked to keep the place neat and tidy, but Alan had brought his more relaxed attitude to such things with him when he moved in. She carried her laptop computer out of the kitchen and balanced it on her knee while she laid out comfortably on the settee. She waited while it went through its boot-up routine. There had been another email requiring her attention, apart from Craig's, this one from her bosses at the University.

Dear Dr Mitchell, we've been asked to provide expert assistance to an archaeological project taking place near Skipton. We understand that human remains, thought to be Bronze Age, have been unearthed at HCAP. I would remind you that taking part in fieldwork is a condition of your contract with us. You should expect to be on detachment until Christmas. It should be noted that while the University will fund overnight accommodation at a suitable nearby hotel, should you decide to live in the site marquee which houses the other members of the team, no overnight subsistence will be payable. You should report to the Site Director, Dr D Pountney, at your earliest convenience.

It was signed by 'Pompous' Piggott, head of her department. No-one else but him would have used the phrase, "at your earliest convenience". No doubt, she thought, another wonderful money-making scheme for the uni. And what was HCAP? Typical of Piggott not to mention it, or assume she knew. She picked up her phone and called Piggott's secretary.

A moment later, she closed the connection and shook her head in bewilderment. Why did things always seem to happen in threes? Alan's proposal, Craig's reappearance, and now the fact that she was being sent to work on his doorstep, on the Holt Carr Archaeological Project.

*

Craig had made a quick tour of the ground floor of Holt Carr before going back into the hallway to collect his bags and carry them upstairs. He instinctively made for the bedroom which had been his until he left home. Dumping his bags, he glanced quickly around, to see that the large print showing a mountain range somewhere, depicted in pastel shades of pink, blue and purple with snow-covered upper slopes, which he'd so enjoyed looking at all that time ago, was still adorning the wall opposite his bed, where he could wake up and see it first thing each morning.

Memories flooded back: long-ago Christmases, when his father – normally the most staid and conservative of Yorkshiremen – would assume the portly and jovial guise of Father Christmas and hand out presents to Craig and his younger brother, William, who'd been born with a defective heart, and died when he was eight; Mother playing Schumann on the upright piano in the lounge... The list went on.

And then there were the memories of Cat. Six months when he hadn't realised how lucky he was to have her. Grey eyes which could sparkle with fun, darken with desire and shine with intelligence and curiosity. He'd been right earlier, when he'd told her how little she'd changed in the time he'd been away. What a fool he'd been! From what she'd told him in the car, he guessed that if he'd asked her to join him in Canada, either when he went or after her final year at uni, she might well have agreed. He'd misread her heart, and paid heavily for it.

The pain of parting had taken a while to sink in. He'd intended keeping in touch, but realised that it would be like continually scratching away at an open wound, every time it began to heal over. A clean break was the only way, he thought. In time, things would get easier, and Canada offered him a fresh start. Or so he'd thought. Whitehorse and Dawson City had their share of young women, but although he'd dated some, he invariably found himself measuring them against his memories of Cat and finding them wanting. In his mind, she grew into an image of perfection against which the real-life, flesh-and-blood, girls he met really stood no chance.

His job took him away from civilisation for long periods. He learned to look after himself in the wild, shoot straight when it counted, and pan for gold. He was tasked with finding commercial-sized mineral deposits, which he did successfully, but there was nothing in his contract which prevented him from a little private enterprise with a gold pan whenever he found himself beside a promising stream. The amount of gold he'd amassed had grown over the years and he'd converted it for the most part into investments. Somewhere in the house, he supposed, would be the rings and jewellery he'd had made for his mother, and on his right hand there was a signet ring. But the rest provided a steady income, as long as stock markets were buoyant.

His introspection was interrupted when the front door opened.

"Craig? That you, son?"

He tried to place the half-familiar voice. "Mr Stalland?" he asked uncertainly, heading for the stairs.

As he descended, he recognised the man who owned the neighbouring farm.

"Aye, lad," said the old man. "I'm sorry for tha loss. Thy parents were good people, and they shouldn't have gone yet, I'm thinking."

"No. Come in."

"I've got me boots on, so I'll keep off t'carpets, just come through to t'kitchen." Stalland stepped gingerly so as to minimise the amount of farm dirt which fell off his boots, and Craig followed him into the big room.

"Let's put the kettle on," he said, picking it up and holding it under the tap.

"Nay, lad, I'm not stopping. I'm sure tha's lots to see to. I just came to tell thee, I've been looking after the 'orses for thee, and they're all right and tight."

"Thanks very much, Mr Stalland," said Craig. "The fact is I don't know enough to look after them: there's a big gulf between mineralogy and animal husbandry. I need someone to work for me."

"You're keepin' t'business on, then?"

"Aye," replied Craig, slipping into the local dialect unconsciously. "For now, anyway. I haven't thought what to do beyond the short-term."

"Well, you could do worse than get my son in to take care o' t'orses."

"Simon? He still around? Do you think he'd want to work here?"

"Aye, he lives over in Nidderdale now, but I think he'd jump at t'chance of working here."

"I don't know," said Craig, chewing his lip. "He might not want to work for me."

Stalland waved the air dismissively. "Ah, you're thinking of the spot of bother you boys had? What is it? Ten years? Twelve? All water under the bridge. Simon's married now, and got a couple of kids."

Craig looked relieved. "Well, if he's good with horses, and he would want to work here, I'd be glad to have him."

"They call him the 'Orse Whisperer o' Pateley Bridge," said Stalland, tapping the side of his nose with a gnarled forefinger. "I'll tell him you're interested."

"Thanks."

"Aye. Any road up, I'll be off. I'll carry on looking after t'animals until Simon turns up.'

"I'm very grateful, Mr Stalland."

The old man waved in the air again. "Nay, tha's no cause. Thy parents were good enough to me and the wife afore she died. You owe me nowt."

Craig wondered if Simon really would have put the 'spot of bother' they'd had behind him. Stalland let himself out, and Craig went back upstairs to finish his unpacking. He decided to move into his parents' more spacious bedroom, and took his luggage through. He looked around. The place was both familiar and unfamiliar. He guessed it was just as they'd left it on the morning they'd been killed. He ought to feel terrible grief at their loss, and yet he'd rarely seen them in the time he'd been away so he couldn't in all honesty say he missed them. In their room, he felt closer to them, and that would have to do.

The flight had robbed him of around six hours of sleep. He figured if he were to lay on the bed, he'd not open his eyes for a week. He stifled a yawn, dumped his bags, and went back downstairs to begin his search of the house.

CHAPTER 2

The telephone rang. Craig woke with a start and glanced at his watch. He'd slept all through the night until nearly noon. He answered the call and found himself talking to the Yorkshire Archaeological Service.

"Mr Jordon? I'm Sarah Brewster. I've been trying to contact you for a couple of days now, so I'm glad you're in."

"I've been in Canada."

"Ah, how nice. Holiday?"

"No. Working there."

"Oh. Look, I'm sorry to hear about your parents."

"Thank you."

"It must have been a horrible shock."

"It was."

"Did you know they gave us permission to conduct a dig on your land."

"Oh. Did they? Where?"

"Behind the house, on top of the moor. They're digging up Viking artefacts." She sounded quite excited.

"Right," said Craig, still too jet-lagged to take much interest. "And you are ringing because...?"

"Ah, yes, well, we've found some burials, so I was just letting you know that there's an osteologist – a specialist on human remains – on the way, so that will be one more person on the site, from tomorrow."

"How many others are there?"

"There's a team of four; Doctor Dave Pountney is team leader, and there are three students. I'm sure if you go up to the site, they'll be pleased to show you what's happening, and what they've found."

"Okay. Thanks for letting me know." He hung up. Tiredness had overtaken him after William Stalland's departure, and even now, his body was convinced that it was around six o'clock in the

14

morning. Two hours later he woke again. He showered and shaved, and feeling better, went downstairs to find something to eat, and begin a list of things needed to replenish supplies.

An hour later, fed, shopping list written out and appointment made with his solicitor, he put on his green waxed jacket and set off to walk up the steep track leading to the moor top. Just beyond the traditional cairn of stones piled up by walkers over hundreds of years to mark a high point of the moor, was an area marked off by tapes. To one side was a large marquee, facing an area about a quarter the size of a football pitch where the thin turf and topsoil had been removed. Just under the surface were jumbled lines of stones, among which a man and a pretty woman, who both looked to be in their twenties, were squatting, wielding trowels and brushes. A few yards away another man, about the same age, was breaking the ground surface with a pickaxe and shovelling the spoil into a wheelbarrow. As Craig watched, a bespectacled man in his mid-forties, wearing a check shirt and khaki shorts emerged from the marquee through its open side, facing the dig, and hopped across the stones to where the girl knelt. Craig walked around the tape towards the archæologists. The girl glanced up and saw him, causing the man to look in the same direction.

He straightened up. "Morning."

"Hi," said Craig. "Are you Doctor Pountney?"

"Dave Pountney, Site Director."

"Craig Jordon. I guess this is my land since my parents died." They shook hands.

"I was sorry to hear about that. They were both nice people and very interested in the dig."

Craig nodded then indicated the site, wanting to change the subject. "What have you here?"

Pountney's face lit up with enthusiasm. "Let me show you. Come over to the tent. Just don't walk on the stones and you'll be okay," he added as Craig stepped over the tape on to the site.

15

A pair of long trestle tables had been set up in the marquee, their surfaces covered in plain white paper. Plastic trays had been arranged on them in ranks, each one containing similar artefacts: pottery in some, pieces of blackened stuff in another, and in one, a few white fragments.

"Ah," said Craig, "I heard you'd found some bone."

"Oh? Those are dog ribs. Viking man's best friend, and buried with him. How did you hear we'd found human ones?"

"Your office phoned: they told me you're being sent an, uh, osty-o, uh?"

"Osteologist. Good." He slipped his spectacles off and polished them with a tissue he dragged from a box on the table. "The really good news is that we think we've found an articulated skeleton. There's what we think was a burial site just a few yards outside the settlement here. It's a bit difficult to be sure, but we think the stones which should have covered it have been picked up over the years by people walking this way, who've added them to the cairn up there." He nodded in the direction of the pile of stones not far up the moor. "And where there's one, there could be others," he concluded, staring out of the tent.

"Cairns?" asked Craig, puzzled.

Pountney turned back to him. "What? No, burials."

"Ah. Sorry. What's this black stuff?" Craig asked, pointing at one of the other trays. Pountney became animated again.

"That, my friend, is shoe-leather. It's a fantastic find! Very little Viking leather is found – except, of course, at York: they found quite a bit there – so we're very fortunate. The type of soil here has helped to preserve it."

Craig was beginning to feel overwhelmed. "Well, I'm glad the dig is going so well. If there's anything I can help with, just let me know."

"Thank you," said Pountney.

"This is really quite fascinating. If it's all right, I'd like to come back later and see what's happening."

"Any time, Mr Jordon," said Pountney, as Craig waved and set off back to Holt Carr.

Pountney returned to the trench.

"Who's the dish, Dave?" asked the female student when he reached her.

He grinned. "Name's Craig Jordon. The new landowner. Odd, though, he sounds American. But seems a nice chap. Now... any more bones or boot leather?"

"Hope he'll be back. No, nothing just yet, but I think those stones over there may mark out a hearth. What do you think?"

*

Cat had found the morning very unsettling. Craig's arrival had stirred long-buried memories – long-forgotten hopes, too. The first thing she knew for certain was that she couldn't accept Alan's proposal now. She spent what remained of the afternoon preparing what she'd need for the next few weeks or months of fieldwork. It was a part of her job she always enjoyed: there was a wonderful feeling of camaraderie among the archæologists and other experts, like herself, and above all, there was the opportunity to put her skills into practice. Alan arrived back from the university around five. One of the things she liked about him was that she found him very easy to read. From the look on his face, he had news. She waited while he pulled off his shoes in the tiny vestibule and hung up his jacket.

"Darling," he said, beaming, "you are looking at a new star of the small screen."

She smiled at him whilst thinking what a corny line that was. "You're going to be on television?"

He nodded enthusiastically. "Yes. The company that makes those archæology programmes have asked me to join their regular panel of experts for the next series. I'll get a retainer, plus a proper fee for any episode I appear in."

She smiled again. "You'll be wanting an agent next."

He chuckled. "Funny you should say that..."

"Don't tell me you've got one already?"

He grinned. "No. I'm an academic, remember; not supposed to have a business-like thought in my head." He shrugged. "Maybe I should think about it?"

"Maybe – if your contract is renewed."

"Contract?" he repeated, looking horrified. He smacked his forehead with the palm of one hand. "You mean I should have a contract?"

For a moment, Cat was alarmed too. "You don't have one – " Then she saw the sparkle in his eyes that told her it was a wind-up.

"Gotcha!" he said.

She acknowledged his success. "When does it start, this burgeoning TV career of yours?"

"I'm already booked for a programme later this month."

"Good," she said, deciding this was as good a moment as any to tell him a little about her day. "I'm going to work on site for a while. Could be up to Christmas."

His face fell. "Oh? Doing what?"

"They've started unearthing bones at a dig near Skipton. So I'll be doing my thing for science, like you, but without the television cameras recording my prowess for posterity."

He grinned again. "Jealous, Cat?"

"Oh, green-eyed, I'm sure."

Something seemed to have occurred to him in the silence while she was deciding whether to tell him her decision. He sat next to her on the settee, his expression serious.

"About what I asked you last night," he said, "I wondered if you'd made up your mind. The thing is, of course, that with my career prospects taking an upturn, and yours taking you away into the wilds of Wharfedale for months, we probably couldn't get married until next year."

She rested her fingers on his hand. The time had come.

"Alan," she said. Something in her tone of voice must have told him what was coming because his face fell again. "What?"

"Just at the minute, I don't feel able to accept your proposal." She stopped, unsure whether to elaborate on that, or offer him some ego-massage.

"Oh," he said, seeming obviously crestfallen. The fact that he didn't seem more disappointed made her even more certain that she was right to turn him down.

"It – it's just not the right time for me to be thinking about marriage."

Not the right time for an image of Craig, tall, tanned and fit, as he'd emerged from the airport terminal building, to come into her mind, either.

He drew his hand away and leaned back. "Do you want me to move out?"

She considered it. "I'm going to be away for some time, so it's not as if we'll be seeing much of each other. I don't mind if you stay here while I'm gone."

"Your flat-sitter?"

She grinned. "If that's what you like to call it." She felt a need to soften the blow. "Look, I haven't said no, I've just said, not at the minute. Not this year. We've lived together comfortably all summer, and I don't mind if we carry on like that. Just... I think we need some time apart, and thanks to our jobs, we're going to get it."

He nodded gravely. "Thanks for saying that, Cat. I think I'll look out for a place of my own, but somewhere which would do for newlyweds and their first child – just in case you change your mind."

She nodded. "If that's what you'd prefer," she said.

He stood up and looked down at her for a long moment, his lips pressed together in a thin line. "Tennyson was right." She narrowed her eyes, figuring out what he meant. She nodded when she guessed. "You mean, 'Better to have loved and lost'? That one?"

"'Than never to have loved at all'," he concluded in confirmation.

"God, Alan! It makes you sound pathetic, and I never thought you were that. You should try Samuel Butler's version of it: 'Better to have loved and lost, than never to have lost at all.' It's perkier." The minute she stopped she wished she could unsay it.

His face darkened. "I see. I'll think about being perkier," he said. He went into the vestibule and pulled on his shoes. As he grabbed his jacket he glanced back at her through the open doorway. "I think I'll dine out tonight. I don't know when I'll be back."

The door closed behind him. Cat stared at it for a moment, then took a deep breath. The apartment suddenly seemed very empty. It seemed like the end of another part of her life.

*

Victoria Stalland busied herself with the washing-up, going through the automatic process while her mind was on another matter: she was trying to decide whether one of her ribs was broken or merely cracked. Whichever, it certainly hurt every time she leaned over the bowl or picked up a heavy saucepan. She gritted her teeth, determined not to advertise her pain to her husband who was leaning against the jamb of the open door watching her and sipping from a bottle of vodka.

"Will you dig up some more potatoes this afternoon?" she asked him without looking round.

"Aye."

She wanted to ask him why he'd started hitting her. He'd been a good husband until about two years ago, when he'd lost his temper with the man employing him to look after his stable and been sacked on the spot. Although he'd found a new job quickly, word had begun to circulate that he was unreliable and disrespectful. He was sacked again and again, if he didn't walk out of a job before

20

being dismissed. And then, a year ago, he'd hit her for the first time. And now she'd learned she couldn't ask him anything about the change in his behaviour without earning another beating, so she kept quiet.

There were the children to consider as well. She was frightened they'd discover what was going on. She knew she should do something about it, but didn't know what. If she did nothing, there was always the possibility that Simon would start beating the children, and she'd have to do something about him then. Surely better to pre-empt the situation. Whatever she did , the children would be left effectively fatherless.

The telephone rang. She turned to see if he would answer it, since it was mounted on the wall near his shoulder. He didn't move. She dried her hands on the towel and moved towards the door, expecting him to stand aside. He didn't and she had to squeeze past him, causing a sudden increase in searing pain from her injured rib. Fighting to control her breathing, she answered the phone. She listened a moment then held it out towards him.

"It's for you, Simon. Your father."

He took the receiver from her with a grin. "Dad?"

She escaped into the kitchen again, closing the door: she knew Simon didn't like anyone eavesdropping on his telephone conversations, though again, that was something that had never bothered him until relatively recently. She went to the sink to finish washing up the dishes. Her friend and neighbour, Jo Box, had recently taken delivery of a dishwasher, describing happily how it saved a lot of time standing at the kitchen sink. Victoria had tentatively approached Simon about getting one, but he had brushed the idea away on the grounds of cost. If he had been the person doing the washing-up, she thought, he might have felt differently.

There had been a time, when they'd first met, he couldn't do enough for her.

She'd been a student nurse at the Infirmary, and he had been recovering from a head injury sustained in a fight. After his discharge, they had started seeing each other, and she had fallen pregnant quite quickly with Louise. Although it had surprised her when Simon proposed, she'd been pleased and relieved about it, since even in the enlightened nineties, the Yorkshire Dales folk tended to look down on single mothers. But now, after all these years, she knew her marriage was, to say the least, shaky.

He still seemed to dote on his children, but Victoria, now with no living relatives, felt increasingly isolated and alone. She heard Simon hang up the telephone. The kitchen door opened and he came in. "Well, there's a thing! I've been offered a job."

Victoria turned towards him. "Where? Doing what?"

Simon swung the arm which held the bottle, not noticing when it splashed her. "Well, that's the joke, you see, you'll never guess!'

'What?' she asked, brushing at the spots of vodka with her hand.

'Looking after some horses. There's a feller in Wharfedale as needs someone to look after some brood mares. My old stamping-ground, you could say.' A warning-bell sounded in Victoria's head. "Didn't you have some trouble over there, about a woman?"

Simon swung the bottle again, but this time she was ready and avoided it. His face took on a crafty look.

"Aye. That's the funny part, though. The bloke as wants to employ my services is the one as half-killed me." He swallowed some vodka and muttered, "Mebbe he'll wish he'd succeeded if I go back there."

Something in his tone sent a shiver through her. "It was a long time ago, Simon," she said. "The

22

job's your sort of thing, by the sound of it," she added, trying to sound bright in an attempt to keep his mind on the positive track.

"Aye, it is." He stood away from the door frame against which he'd been leaning. He seemed suddenly to sober up. "So, then, you think I should take it?"

"It would be nice to have a bit more money coming in. Did your father mention the wages?"

"Forgot to ask."

"Well, go over there and ask the man in person. Harder for him to be mean if you're standing in front of him." She had a thought. "I take it he knows it's you who's applying for the job?"

"So my daddy said," replied Simon, whose use of the diminutive informed Victoria that he was already quite drunk. "Do you want to go this afternoon?" He stared at her intensely with what she fancied as suspicion before nodding. "Aye."

"Perhaps I should drive you?"

"What?" he began angrily, but then caught sight of the bottle, now empty, in his hand. "Oh, bugger!" he muttered, and threw it at the old stone sink where it shattered, chipping the surface.

"Oh Simon!" she exclaimed before she could stop herself. His mouth turned down, his expression meaner. "Don't hit me, Simon – please!"

He chewed his lip for a moment.

Victoria glanced at the clock on the wall. "I'll just slip into something better to wear," she said, hoping he might take the hint himself: she didn't dare suggest it to him. He stared at her without saying anything, then went into the living room and slumped in the chair. Victoria got a dustpan and brush out from under the sink and carefully swept up all the broken glass, wrapping it securely in two plastic bags before putting it in the bin. Then she went upstairs to change.

*

Bloody woman! He didn't know what had come over her in the last couple of years – always moaning, always complaining, and, getting sex out

23

of Victoria was like getting blood from a stone these days. Not like when he'd first met her. Innocent, but bloody keen. So innocent, he'd discovered she hadn't even had the sense to use protection – and her a nurse! She'd been up the duff in no time, and it was only because he was a well brought-up lad with a conscience that he'd proposed to her. She'd settled into the comfortable, housewife-and-mother routine just fine, getting knocked up again within a year or so of having Louise. After Mark, it seemed she'd found out how to stop having more, which was a pity, because he enjoyed the idea of getting her pregnant.

Since he'd lost his job – well, several jobs – she'd got more withdrawn. She spent a lot of time encouraging him to go out and find work, and not enough taking care of his other needs. He didn't need to go looking for work – as witness the phone call from his dad.

Work came looking for him – the Horse Whisperer of Pateley Bridge. He laughed, staring up at the ceiling and wondering what was keeping her. He knew about the soubriquet, and wondered if Craig Jordon did. The idea of working for – no, *with* – Craig was challenging. He'd need to make sure Craig and Victoria didn't spend time chatting: he'd allowed her to believe that Craig had taken unfair advantage of him in their fight. It wasn't true, but it had had a big influence on the way she had felt about him. It wouldn't do if she were to hear – and believe – Craig's version of events. He didn't want her discovering he wasn't quite the hero she'd believed him to be. No point in muddying that particular pond.

*

"Simon! It's been a long time," Craig said, holding out his hand. Simon took it with just a moment's hesitation, then smiled briefly.

"Craig. How-do."

"Pretty good. And who's your driver?" he asked, turning to the woman climbing out from behind the wheel.

"My wife." Craig walked round the car and shook her hand. "Craig Jordon," he said.

"Victoria Stalland." She smiled.

He thought she had certainly once looked pretty but was now a little careworn. Her hair was tidy, but beginning to show a few strands of grey. Her smile was timid, and Craig found himself wondering why. He became aware that he was being watched by an unsmiling Simon.

"I expect your father told you I need someone to look after the horses?" he asked.

"Yes," said Simon.

"He said you were very, very good with them."

"I am." Craig glanced at Victoria who was standing apart from them, her eyes cast down.

"Is he?" he asked her, attempting to bring her into the conversation. He was surprised when she looked up, shooting an almost fearful glance at Simon before licking her lips and smiling tentatively.

"Oh, yes. None better." As she finished speaking, she dropped her gaze again and remained standing there passively. Simon shot her a glance which Craig would have described as venomous. Trouble between them, he thought, if he reacts like that to an innocuous remark. Turning towards the house, he led the way into the kitchen.

"The thing is, would you be prepared to work for me?" he asked, when they were seated in the warmth from the Aga.

"Depends," said Simon. "What would you expect me to do?"

"Out there is a maternity ward for brood mares," said Craig indicating the new stable block across the yard at the rear of the house. "We take in mares from the time they're covered by the stallions, and look after them until they foal. Some time after that, the owners come and take them away."

"Would I be doing this alone or have you got some help in?"

Craig hadn't thought about employing others. "If you find you need help, I don't see any reason why we shouldn't get some."

"I see." Simon's face closed, and he dropped his gaze..

Craig understood it was a move designed to up his wages. "If you would consider the job," he asked, "what sort of salary would you be looking for? I can tell you that I don't have much capital just at the moment, and it will be a while before the estate is sorted out, so for a few months at least, the going could be quite tough – for all of us."

No self-respecting Yorkshireman would have failed to claim poverty in this situation, and despite his years in Canada, Craig was a Yorkshireman through and through. Simon named a figure. From the almost concealed tightening of her clenched fingers by Victoria, sitting silently at the far end of the table, Craig guessed it represented a very high level of remuneration, so he pretended to think about it for a moment or two. Eventually, he offered half the amount. Simon seemed offended. The argument went to and fro until they agreed a figure close to two-thirds Simon's original proposal. All three of them seemed to feel they had achieved a satisfactory outcome. Craig noticed an expression of relief flit across Victoria's face at the conclusion of the deal.

"Have you seen the animals? Let me show you what's what," said Craig, leading Simon out of the house through the kitchen door. Victoria followed in their wake, across the yard to the large stable block and covered yard in the field beyond it. She glanced at her watch, and unclipped a mobile phone from her belt. Simon turned to her at once. "Who're you calling?"

"Jo," she said, turning to address Craig. "I just have to ring my neighbour to ask her to look after the children. You carry on."

"Okay," said Craig, "we'll be in the stables. Join us or wait in the warm." He smiled, nodding towards the kitchen, before both men turned and walked up the path.

*

Victoria headed for the kitchen as her phone made the connection to Jo Box. She had summed up Craig quite quickly when she first saw him as a thoroughly nice guy. It was hard to believe he had taken unfair advantage of Simon.

"Jo? It's Victoria." She quickly obtained her neighbour's agreement to pick up the children from school and rang off before she had to endure any searching but well-intentioned questions. She suspected that Jo had an idea that all was not well between her and Simon.

She lowered herself carefully into one of the two old leather armchairs set either side of the Aga, gritting her teeth as her rib reminded her that she needed to take care. She didn't realise she'd fallen asleep until Craig and Simon re-entered the room. She came quickly awake and pushed herself out of the chair, causing the pain to stab her in the side again.

"S-sorry," she stammered, trying to keep her breathing under control. "I must have nodded off."

She watched Simon, but he seemed unconcerned.

Craig smiled. "No worries. You must feel comfortable here, and we were rather a long time." She glanced at the short-case clock on the wall. She'd been asleep half an hour, but it was obvious that she'd needed it. She felt better. Even the ache in her side seemed duller. Perhaps the bones were healing.

Simon held out his hand to her. "Right, lass, tha can drive us home. Dad's going to put the horses to bed today and I'll be back in the morning."

She almost took his hand, but stopped herself when she thought that if he jerked it, it would almost certainly set her ribs off again. She realised that Craig had seen her hesitation. She felt a blush steal into her cheeks as she turned and headed for the door, expecting that Simon would follow her.

At the car, he paused, looking Craig in the eye. "I'll not let you down."

"It's good to have you on side," Craig said.

Victoria hoped desperately that the sentiments boded a peaceful relationship. Simon's expression, as she glanced at him in the driving mirror on the way home, did not fill her with confidence.

CHAPTER 3

When Simon arrived at Holt Carr the next morning, he could see no sign of Craig and the house seemed closed and quiet. Catching up on his beauty sleep, he thought. He made his way to the new stable-block and found his father in there.

"Hello, son. Thought I'd make a start, but now you're here tha can get on with earning thy money." He handed Simon the door key. "Drop in later if tha wants a cup o' tea," he added, and left the building.

Simon glanced at the horses. There were, he knew, nineteen of them, with five empty stalls. All the animals, both mares and foals, looked settled so he decided to have a good look round the place without Craig being present. There was a tack room at the far end of the block, which contained one of the family's older battered leather armchairs – one corner of which was propped up on an out of- date Yellow Pages, presumably in place of a castor. He pulled a litre bottle of vodka from his coat pocket. He'd noticed on his earlier visit that there was a small fridge, intended for milk, and he put the bottle inside. There was a sink in the corner, with a wall-cupboard above it, which held mugs and a small supply of coffee, tea-bags and sugar, and a couple of plates. A long, low fitment ran along the wall opposite the door, below the long, stout pegs which were designed to hold saddles, blankets and bridles. In the bottom of one of the cupboards below the fitment, he found a shotgun and a box of cartridges. He was surprised the barrels of the gun had been sawn-off, making the weapon illegal, but guessed it had been intended for use at close range, probably for rats and foxes. He peered closely at the cartridges, which looked as if they might have been hand-filled. He shrugged, putting everything back where he'd found it. The floor was covered in linoleum and the room was lit by a single overhead bare bulb. Well, he thought, hanging his jacket on a hook near the door, it would do. He stood in the doorway, looking out past the stalls.

There was a lot of horseflesh, and considering half of it was about to give birth, it was going to take some looking after. Mares had no more idea than women about giving birth in daylight hours. He figured he could find a couple of schoolgirls who'd look after the horses for him in exchange for the opportunity to ride some. He chewed his lip. It wouldn't do to ride any of this lot, he thought. He wondered if Craig would let him buy a couple of hacks. Maybe three or four. He decided to go and ask. He got as far as the yard door and saw Craig emerge from the kitchen and head across to the old stable-block, which was now being used as a garage. He moved quickly on an intercept course.

"Craig!"

Craig stopped and turned. "Hello Simon. I was just off into town – Skipton. Do you need anything?"

"Aye. P'raps some milk?"

"Sure."

"And I want to get a couple of girls in as can 'elp wi' t' 'orses. I reckon I could get 'em real cheap if I could offer 'em summat to ride on. Like a couple of hacks. Maybe we could get, say three or four. Do a bit o' riding yourself then, eh? The 'osses'd be cheap. Can't ride the mares in foal. What do you think?"

"How much are we talking about?"

"A few 'undred. Mebbe five. We can sell 'em on when we've finished wi' 'em." Craig thought about the matter for a moment, then nodded. "Okay. Three hacks. I'm no horseman, but you and two girls... Okay. Will you see to that?"

"Aye," nodded Simon, pleased.

"Well, gotta go," said Craig. "Shopping and solicitors. You know what it's like."

"Aye," said Simon again, watching as Craig continued to the garage, before turning and heading back into the stable-block.

*

Craig climbed into the Land-Rover. As he drove it out of the garage, he glanced to his right and saw the young female archæologist running down the field. She waved at him, obviously wanting to talk, arriving breathless and flushed. Her legs were long but the rest of her shape was concealed by the bulkiness of her clothing. He opened the window.

"Hello. Something happened?"

She smiled, shook her head, still panting. "No, no problem. Just wondered if you could give me a ride."

"Where to?"

She was recovering her composure. "Where are you going?"

"Skipton."

"That'll do. Do you mind?"

Craig shook his head, smiling. "No. Hop in."

She ran round the vehicle and clambered up into the passenger seat.

"Hold tight, this first bit's bumpy," he said as she settled herself into the unyielding but functional seating and clipped the seatbelt on. Reminded by this, he fixed his own, then set the vehicle on the track down to the road. She gripped the handle in front of her as the four-wheel-drive lurched over the uneven surface.

"Do you do much off-road driving?" she asked.

"I have done, back in Canada."

"Oh, is that a Canadian accent?"

"I think it's Canadian Yorkshire," he grinned.

"What were you doing in Canada?"

"Looking for mineral resources my company can exploit."

She thought for a moment. "Like gold? Did you find any?"

"Occasionally. The Stampeders – that's the folk who travelled from all over Canada and the States

31

to the Yukon in eighteen ninety-eight – pretty-well cleared the gold out of that part of the world."

"What else did you find?"

"Well, I guess the biggest find I've ever made was an outcrop of oil shale further east. The company got enough oil out of that to make quite a few bucks."

He risked a quick glance at her. She was pretty, bright, and very fit. He'd noticed her feminine curves when she had eased the seatbelt between her breasts.

"I'm Jemma, by the way," she said.

"Craig."

"I know. I saw you at the Dig."

"Ditto." He spent the rest of the journey, in gradually increasing levels of traffic, adjusting to driving on the left.

"You should come to our camp one evening," she said, breaking what had been a long silence.

"Are you all camping on the moor?" Craig asked, surprised. "When it's fine. If the weather gets really bad, we find a B & B."

He drove on, wondering if he should offer them the use of the empty bedrooms at Holt Carr. There were probably enough. The emptiness of the place pressed heavily on him, especially in the night. He found it difficult to focus through eyes which had suddenly misted with tears. The Land-Rover hit a stone at the side of the road, and bounced them around. He grabbed the wheel and braked.

"Sorry," he mumbled, wiping his eyes with the back of his hand.

His passenger looked at him, concerned. "Are you okay?"

"Yes. I'll be all right. Just need a minute." He felt foolish. The girl rummaged in a pocket and pulled a clean but slightly creased tissue out. She offered it, and he accepted gratefully. "Sorry. I was just thinking about my parents. I'm still trying to get used to the idea of not having them around."

She nodded sympathetically. "It must be awful losing either of them, and to lose them both together must be absolutely devastating."

"I've not been home that often in the twelve years I've been away. Now I'll never see them again, but life must go on." He suddenly had a thought and turned to her, concern in his voice. "Did I hurt you, when we hit the rock?"

She blushed prettily. "No. I'm okay."

"Good. Let's get on, then."

He parked in the middle of Skipton. They arranged to meet at the vehicle in two hours, then he went in search of the offices of his solicitor. Two hours later as he leaned against the Land-Rover, waiting for his passenger, his head was spinning with the ramifications of Inheritance Tax, transfers of equities and other assets, probate, and one major problem: a large loan, secured on the house, used to finance the building of the indoor exercise arena, built on the opposite side of the yard facing the new stable block.

The debt was overdue. He'd been to the bank after leaving the solicitors and they'd confirmed the amount outstanding and politely invited him to give them some idea when it would be paid off. He'd not been able to name a date, but had given them a cheque drawn on his personal account as an 'earnest of good intent'. They'd sniffed a bit, but accepted it.

He saw Jemma at last, weaving towards him carrying two heavy supermarket bags. Craig unlocked the tailgate door. She smiled apologetically.

"Sorry I'm late. Been waiting long?"

He shook his head. "No. No problem. Stocking up for a siege?"

"It's amazing what an appetite you work up grubbing about in holes in the ground," she said.

"You don't sound to be complaining," he said.

"Well, no. You work the calories off, so it's no problem – eat, drink and be merry, just be sober in the morning."

"Is that what Mr Pountney tells you?"

"Doesn't have to. I think it's written into the contract somewhere. He's a nice old man actually. I've worked with worse."

"Shall we get some lunch? If I recall correctly, the White Horse over by the Market Place does good food."

"Okay." They walked across the ancient site of the market, to the public house. Since he had last seen it, the old building's interior had had a face-lift. They settled down, each with a pint of local real ale, and a large dish of fried sausages in onion gravy with mashed and creamed potatoes. On a cold day, it lined the stomach with extremely tasty insulation.

"So, are you studying anything apart from archæology?" he asked her.

"History of Art," she said, giving the phrase capital letters.

"Give me a clue here: it's about old paintings?" he asked.

"It covers all the fine arts," she replied.

"How come you're taking that if your real interest is in a scientific subject? Surely archæology is more akin to forensic science than the fine arts?"

"I'm not a one-track person," she said. "Are you?"

"I read earth sciences, specialising in mineralogy and petrology."

"Is there a difference?"

"One's the study of minerals, the other the study of rocks."

Jemma gazed at the logs glowing redly in the cast iron fire grate. The impression given by the open fire, the old oak beams and the smell of old ale and smoke felt good

"I expect it's very cold in Canada," she said, hugging herself, 'must make today feel like high summer."

"It's cold all right, and you spend long periods alone, but I never feel lonely. It's very much a case of pitting yourself against wild nature – red in tooth and claw – but the landscapes are incredibly beautiful."

She watched his face for a moment. "It's an unusual choice of occupation, if I may say so, for a Yorkshire lad."

"I've always been drawn to mountains – perhaps it's being born here, within spitting distance of the Pennines – but I mean the biggies – Everest, Kilimanjaro, the Eiger, the Matterhorn, Mont Blanc."

She chewed a mouthful of food and swallowed. "Have you climbed any of them?" she asked.

"Not so far. You can't just pack your bags and jet over to Africa or Nepal or wherever. You have to arrange an expedition, or join one. And to be allowed to join one, you have to be good. I'm not sure that, in terms of climbing technique, I'm good enough. I don't have to do so much that is really difficult in my job: after all, if it's difficult to get at, it's costly to extract, so you would have to find a really valuable mother-lode for it to be worth the effort."

His face had unconsciously lit up as he spoke. Jemma was fascinated. She found that sort of enthusiasm, which made a dream seem real, very attractive in a man. She found herself considering him sexually. He was broad across the shoulders, narrow at the waist, and tall enough to cause a crick in the neck if she had to spend long looking up at him. His thighs, it seemed to her, stretched his corduroy trousers almost to breaking point.

Her thoughts caused her cheeks to flush. She had to remind herself that he was considerably older than the men she was usually interested in. The age difference didn't matter to her, but he would probably be returning to Canada soon, and that would be that. In any case, she wanted to finish her education, and had her eye on a job with one of the county archæological units dotted around the UK. So, on the whole, she concluded rather reluctantly, this fish would have to go back

in the pond. But perhaps not just yet. Not...
unsampled.

*

Back on the road, they were heading out of town
along the valley road towards Holt Carr. The
subject of Dave Pountney had been raised again. It
was obvious Jemma thought of him as having
possibly gone to school with Methuselah.

"I didn't think he was that much older than
me," said Craig.

"Depends," she said. "How old are you?"

You can't beat a direct question, he thought.
"Thirty-five," he said.

"I'm twenty-two," she said, "in case you were
wondering."

"Well, I guess Mr Pountney is only about twice
that."

"Well, he acts a lot older. I think somewhere
there's a Mrs Pountney who spends her days
knitting and baking scones, and wondering when
he'll be coming home."

"You know this, do you?" he laughed.

"Not for a fact. But he hardly ever leaves the
site, and he's totally absorbed in the work. If he *is*
married, his wife doesn't see much of him."

"It might be a marriage made in heaven, then,"
he suggested, amused.

"When I marry, I don't want my husband
disappearing for weeks on end." She hesitated a
moment before adding, "I want him handy." She
grinned.

"I'm guessing that'll not be so he can unblock
the sink and clean the bathroom."

"Do I look the kind of girl who needs a man to
do that?"

"Not really, but I don't dare go further."

She smiled, dimples forming in her pink
cheeks. "I can tell what you're thinking."

Craig harrumphed. "I don't suppose you're
different from any other woman," he said, lifting
one eyebrow. This time, she laughed. She looked
away and the dimples made a brief reappearance.

He decided to change the subject. "Did you find the bones?"

"No. Dave did. That's one thing about him: he likes to get his hands dirty like the rest of us. Some Site Directors think it's somehow beneath them, but Dave prefers digging. He's great to work with."

"That's good," said Craig. "What happens to them now?"

"Oh, we've got this whiz-kid coming over from York. Knows all about old bones."

"Are there any more to be found?"

"The chances are that there's a burial ground near the settlement. After all, they had to put their dead somewhere."

"Quite."

"We'll be digging some test pits where we think the burials might be. The soil's so thin in places that they'll be quite quick to do."

*

It was mid-afternoon when they arrived back at Holt Carr.

"Fancy a cup of tea?" asked Craig.

"Sure. Thanks."

Jemma carried the shopping bags across the yard and dumped them on the floor just inside the farmhouse kitchen. Craig put the kettle on before sitting down at the table She took a seat opposite him. He rested his arms on the table. "I've been wondering whether to offer Mr Pountney the use of the spare rooms here for all of you. Do you think that might go down okay, or am I sticking my nose in where it's not wanted?" Jemma considered for a moment. "It's up to you. Personally, I quite enjoy sleeping under canvas, but I guess when the weather's bad, it would be nice to have to come only this far for a solid roof. If you have a shower, though, that might make the place a whole lot more desirable. Sometimes we don't get to wash too well, too often."

"Ah!" said Craig. "Take a shower any time; there's plenty of hot water."

"I'll tell 'em when I get back. I take it you meant that as an invitation to us all?"

"Of course," said Craig. The kettle boiled and he got up to make the tea.

She didn't waste time on hers, cooling it with a lot of milk and drinking it quickly before picking up her carrier bags. As she stepped out of the door she turned back.

"Come up to the camp for a barbecue – about half-past seven. Bring a bottle," she said.

Craig smiled. "Okay, thanks. See you then!"

He went back into the house and washed the cups out. One thing he learned during long periods in the mountains when he'd had to be self-sufficient was not to let housekeeping jobs pile up. Besides, he preferred his surroundings clean rather than dirty. He whistled a little tune. His domestic interlude was ended when the telephone rang.

Drying his hands, he went into the hallway and picked up. "Craig Jordon," he said.

"Ah, Mr Jordon, I'm Major Clarkson at Appleby."

"Major: what can I do for you?"

"You have a mare of mine, close to term. Now I gather you've just recently taken over the business?"

"Yes."

"Well, I wondered whether your knowledge is up to that of your parents."

"You heard that they were killed in a road accident?"

There was a brief silence. "Yes. Sorry. So who's looking after the bloodstock?" The major's real concern was obvious.

"I've employed a man called Simon Stalland. I'm told he's very good." Even if it was his father who said so. "No complaints so far."

"Ah. Young Stalland. Well, I agree, he *was* very good. Not sure now."

"Can you lose that sort of skill?" Craig asked.

"Well you wouldn't think so, but I gathered from m'friend, Angus Linklater, that Stalland has developed something of a problem with the demon drink. Loses his temper a bit too easily these days, as well."

"Oh," said Craig. "Well, so far – he's only just started working here – he's been fine. No signs of being drunk on duty, or temper. But I'll keep an eye on him. Was there anything else?"

"Mmm. So, you're intending to carry on?" asked the major, after seeming to brace himself.

"It hadn't occurred to me not to," replied Craig.

"Hmm. Right, then. Must go. Cheerio."

The line went dead, leaving Craig staring at the phone.

*

By the time Simon decided to pack in at the end of his first day, he was hot and tired. Worse was the fact that he was getting one of his headaches. The one time he submitted to Victoria's urgings to see a doctor with them, he'd been told they were "probably migraines', and prescribed tablets. They had a very limited effect. In the two years since that diagnosis, the headaches had become nauseous, and on one occasion in the car he had been unable to focus on the traffic.

As he had been drunk at the time, this did not surprise him, though he was frightened by the experience. He'd gradually devised his own form of treatment, involving codeine tablets and copious amounts of vodka. Depending on how much of each he took, he either stayed awake, but drunk, and the pain lessened, or he fell asleep. Sometimes, the pain was so acute he would bang his head against a wall.

When it finally stopped, he would be left feeling weak, reflecting sourly that the source of the pain was exactly where, during his fight with Craig twelve years before, his forehead had made contact with the kerb. He went into the tack room and opened the fridge. He took out his bottle of vodka and unscrewed the cap, taking several mouthfuls of the potent spirit before replacing it. He dragged his waxed jacket from the hook and pulled it on as he felt the effects of the alcohol begin to surge through his body. He switched off the light, then remembered whose electricity he was saving. With a curl of his lip, he flicked the switch on again, turned and left the building.

He spun the wheels of his Toyota pickup on the hard ground and snaked it down the track and through the gate onto the lane leading to the road. The noise of the diesel engine screaming in too low a gear brought a vicious smile to his lips as he wrenched the wheel straight and sped homewards. By the time he reached his house, the headache was ripping through his skull. All he wanted was darkness and quiet: what he didn't want was Victoria on the doorstep, with a smile on her face, asking him how his first day had been. The snarl on his lips as he turned to face her in the light killed her smile instantly.

"What's wrong?" she asked, her arms crossed over her chest protectively.

"I've got a headache. Get out of my way!"

He pushed his way past her, buffeting her against the door jamb and, ignoring her cry of pain, groped his way upstairs. After drawing the curtains, he collapsed on the bed, in the blessed darkness. Pain thundered in his skull, pounding with every beat of his heart. He forced himself to open the cabinet beside the bed and pull out the bottle of fifty-seven per cent vodka he kept there. Somewhere in the back of his mind, he knew that the only times he'd hit Victoria was when he was drunk, and he knew there was a risk that if he drank, he might hurt her again; but he also knew that if he drank enough, he would pass out and finally be free from the terrible, tearing, pounding pain. No contest, really: he lifted the bottle to his lips and began to drink deeply.

*

Victoria felt the back of her head tentatively, and found her fingers smeared with blood. She closed the door and very slowly slid down the wall until she was sitting on the floor. The pain in her ribs had started up when he pushed her, and now her head hurt.

Wearily, wincing as every step caused her ribs to complain, she climbed the stairs to the bathroom, where she pulled off her top and washed her wound under the shower. This really couldn't continue, she told herself.

The tears came – softly, and then in profusion. Racking sobs rocked her, and she hated her own weakness. Slowly, she pulled herself together and got dressed. She blamed Simon's drinking, suspecting he consumed more than he admitted, more than she guessed.

Half an hour later, she looked in on him. Her hair was bound up in a towel, and her head still hurt from the cut. He was sprawled across the duvet, snoring. The bottle, with some vodka still in it, was on its side on the floor. She automatically picked it up and placed it on the cabinet. She let herself out of the room, closing the door quietly, her face empty of emotion. The children were watching a show on television. Mark looked round as Victoria came into the room.

"You all right, mum?" he asked.

"Yes. Just decided to wash my hair."

"Is dad all right?"

She sighed. "He's tired. He put in a long day today, and it's a longish drive between here and Holt Carr. Don't disturb him: he's asleep."

"Okay."

Mark turned back to the television. He and his sister exchanged glances. Victoria, standing behind them, noticed. *They knew*, she realised, with a sinking heart. She hesitated to bring the matter out into the open. More than anything, she dreaded the break-up of her family, and feared what Simon might do if forced to confront the effects of his behaviour. Her attention had drifted, and when she looked back at the children, she found Louise watching her. The girl turned away quickly and stared at the television. Victoria made a decision: she couldn't keep the children out of the situation any longer. She sat in the settee behind them.

"Louise, Mark, I need to talk to you."

She tried hard to stop her voice wavering as she spoke. The children turned away from the television. Victoria wished they had turned it off, but children, she'd long-ago decided, were more able than adults to tune out extraneous noises – though she also suspected they liked to keep the programme running so they could tune her out instead if they lost interest in what she was saying.

"This isn't to go outside this house, okay? I don't want everyone knowing. Is that agreed?" Victoria began.

The children nodded.

"Your father is not well. You know he has these headaches? Well, lately they've been getting very, very bad." She took a deep breath. The children were gazing at her with rapt attention. "And sometimes, he drinks a lot – a lot more than he should."

Both children dropped their gaze. They'd noticed, Victoria thought.

"The thing is, when someone gets very drunk, they can do things they wouldn't usually do." Louise looked up, her face serious.

"You mean like when he hits you."

Victoria felt her heart thump. She'd thought the children hadn't known *that*, hadn't seen. Tears sprang to her eyes, and for a moment she couldn't speak. She nodded, sucked in another deep breath.

"Let's not make a big thing of it: yes, your dad has hit me a couple of times – a long time ago – but he didn't hurt me." A white lie. He'd broken her heart even though until now he'd not broken any bones. She tried a smile, but it faltered pathetically, incongruously, with tears running down her cheeks. The children glanced at each other again, before first Louise, then Mark, crept

42

onto the settee, either side of her, put their arms round her neck, and laid their heads on her breasts.

Just at the age you expect them to get all bolshie, she thought, they can do this! She felt such love for them, her chest so tight she could hardly breathe for a moment. She put an arm round each child and closed her eyes, her welling love for her children overcoming the painful consequence of holding them close.

CHAPTER 4

"What a nice man!" Jemma said teasingly, as she helped Craig unload beer, wine and glasses from his Land Rover. "You will be invited again."

"Oh, good," he replied, "and that's before you've sampled the stuff."

"I work on the basis that it's the thought that counts: that way I can stand a bit of disappointment if the goods themselves don't quite live up to expectations. But if the label on that case is correct, you've brought real ale from the local brewery, and that'll go down well here." He followed her into the marquee where they stacked the cases against one wall. They grabbed a beer each. Mike, one of the other two students on the dig, put a compact disc into the team's laptop computer and filled the air with the sound of classic jazz and blues. The evening passed pleasantly with Jemma encouraging all the men to dance, though they would only perform one at a time, with her – even Dave Pountney, who looked sheepish even while he attempted to keep up. When a slow track was played, she grabbed Craig and snuggled up against him. He enjoyed the moment. Not long after they'd eaten, he found himself struggling to keep awake. "Sorry, Jemma," he said, "but I'm falling asleep. Still suffering from the jetlag." She reached up to whisper in his ear. "Is your offer of a shower still on?"

"Yes, if you want one."

"Dancing makes me hot. I probably stink."

"I'll give you a lift down to the house."

"I'll just get my things," she said, and ran to the curtained-off compartment at the rear of the marquee where she slept. She returned clutching a toilet bag and a towel, and they left the party which was now winding down. The temperature had fallen while they had been warm in the big tent, and there was an autumnal chill in the air. They were shivering when they opened the kitchen door of the farm house. The warmth from the central heating and the big Aga cooker which drove it was very welcome. Jemma made a beeline for it, leaning against it with closed eyes and hugging herself with the voluptuous pleasure as the warmth spread through her.

"Want a coffee?" asked Craig.

"That would be great," she said, smiling.

"Before or after?"

"Before or after?" she echoed.

"Your shower."

"Ah! Yes. After, I think. Where's the bathroom?"

"Follow me," he said, and opened the door into the hallway. Moving ahead of her to turn on the lights, he pointed upstairs.

"First door on the left," he said. "Thanks."

She ran lightly up the stairs and he enjoyed the sight of her long legs in the tight-fitting jeans as she mounted each tread. After she turned at the top of the stairs and disappeared from view, he went back into the kitchen to make the coffee. He heard the water running down the shower drain and imagined her, naked. While the coffee brewed in his cafetière, he made himself comfortable in one of the armchairs near the fire and drifted off to sleep. He woke up slowly, suddenly becoming aware that she was seated in the other chair, nursing a mug of coffee and watching him. When she lifted her gaze to his face and found he'd woken, she glanced away.

"Would you like yours, now you're awake?" she asked.

Craig sat up straighter and grinned. "Thanks, yes please."

She walked over to the Aga, collecting a mug on the way. "How do you like it?"

"Just as it comes."

45

She filled his mug and brought it back to him.

"Thanks for the shower," she said. "I borrowed the bathrobe, just until I've properly dried off."

"It looks good on you," he said, smiling.

She looked away. "Where'd you learn to make coffee?"

"In Canada. There's a knack which most of us in England haven't quite got. Do you like it? Have I got the knack?"

Jemma perched on the arm of his chair, allowing the bathrobe to fall away from her knees. "I'd say, you definitely have the knack, Mr Jordon."

"Would you like to try it for yourself?" he asked, resting his mug on the floor. She did likewise and swivelled her body until she faced him.

"Very much, sir," she said.

"Let's stop being so formal," he said, reaching as he did for the belt of her robe, and pulling it slowly loose. She was naked beneath it, and leaned towards him. They held each other's gaze until she turned her head and closed her eyes at the last moment before their lips met. She relaxed against him. Somehow, he took her weight, standing up seemingly without effort, and carried her up to his bedroom.

*

Afterwards, she watched him kissing her body, her lips, her fingertips. Craig was still breathing heavily from his exertion, and she just loved the way he was so strong before and so weak afterwards, even if the "weakness' was largely illusory.

"Did you learn that in Canada, as well?" she asked when she could speak. Her body glowed and she felt warm and very comfortable.

"Mostly," he admitted. "You have to do something to keep warm in the colder parts."

"A few more sessions like that and you'll own my soul," she said, smiling.

He raised himself on an elbow. "Our coffee will be getting cold. Are you staying the night?"

"You want rid of me, do you!" She feigned hurt. "What part of "are you staying the night' suggests to you that I want rid of you?"

"Well, you've had your bit of fun. I bet even in Canada they've heard of "wham, bam, thank you, ma'am"."

"They only phrase it that way because "bam" wouldn't rhyme with 'sir"." She grinned. "Well, what's sauce for the goose..."

"Yeah. Now, are you staying?"

Jemma sat up and kissed the tip of his nose. "No, I think I'll go back. We have this person coming tomorrow, so Dave will want all hands on the burial site from the crack of dawn."

"Sure," said Craig, resuming the clothes he had shed, while she went to the bathroom to retrieve hers. After Jemma had returned to the site, he stripped off his clothes and stepped into the shower. Little pools of water remained from Jemma's use of it earlier, and he fancied he could detect the clean smell of her body lingering in the air. He soaped himself all over with shower gel, and wondered when and if they might repeat their unexpected hour of passion.

He had not intended to have sex with Jemma when he had first met her. She was pretty and he had appreciated her slender figure – what man wouldn't – her cheerful personality, and especially her obvious intelligence, but in the first place, he was still feeling the loss of his parents, and not really looking for a female with whom to begin a relationship, and in the second place, she *was* quite young. Somehow, during the evening, chemistry had played a part in bringing them together. He was glad it had, with hindsight. It had been a long time since he had slept with a woman, and the experience had reminded him of delights he had almost forgotten in the stresses of the past few days. He slipped into his rumpled bed and was asleep within minutes.

*

47

The following day dawned with bright sunlight from a cloudless sky and a crisp chill in the air. Cat stared at her bedroom wall bright with the light of the low sun reflected from the distant Rose Window of York Minster. Only at this time of the year were the angles just right.

She stretched, taking advantage of the extra space available to her since Alan had moved out. She wondered where he'd gone, but told herself he was old enough to look after himself. There were still some of his things he'd told her he'd come back for.

She'd expected to shed tears when he'd told her he was going. The fact that she didn't made her more convinced than ever that she had done the right thing in not accepting his proposal. The radio alarm turned on and for a few minutes she listened to news of world affairs before swinging her legs out of bed and padding across the planked floor to the bathroom in her bare feet, wearing a pair of winceyette pyjamas which she'd taken care never to wear while Alan had been living with her. They were ideal for keeping warm during a November night, but not exactly the sort of thing you'd want a lover to see you in.

The thought brought Craig to mind. She stepped under the jets of warm water. Afterwards, she dressed in warm clothing for what she guessed would be a few weeks in chilly temperatures. She really should be more annoyed with Craig than she was, she told herself. On the face of it, not contacting her at any time for the past twelve years should, by most measures, be unforgiveable, the sort of behaviour which should put him beyond the pale... But she couldn't deny she gone to the airport and picked him up, and she'd felt a promise of the old magic when he'd touched her, and – well, the fact was, she just was not angry. Rather the opposite; she was looking forward to seeing him again. Feeling like that was dangerous. She was well aware that he might not feel the same way, and she ran a severe risk of being hurt again.

She'd been scarcely more than a naive girl last time he'd hurt her, but now she was a woman in full command of her life, with experiences and wisdom to fall back on and cushion the effect, if it were to happen.

She packed a couple of suitcases while consuming her usual coffee and toast breakfast. It was not the sort of start to the day her Scottish Presbyterian mother would have considered suitably sustaining but she was used to it now, having decided some time ago that a fry-up was not something she could face first thing in a morning. With breakfast out of the way, she checked for emails before shutting down her computer and slipping it into its carrying case. She washed up her breakfast things, aware that the draining board was unusually bereft of the frying pan and large plate Alan would have used.

At last, everything was put away. The apartment looked clean and tidy. A black leather Pilot bag contained all the readily-portable kit she was likely to need. Juggling that, her computer and the suitcases, she made her way down the stairs to the front door of her small maisonette to the basement garage and loaded them into her car. Ten minutes later, she had negotiated the tight corners and narrow streets of York and was leaving it behind.

A shock awaited her arrival at Holt Carr. As she drove slowly through the yard towards the trackway up to the dig, Simon Stalland emerged from the stables, leading a pregnant mare. She hadn't seen him since the night, over twelve years ago, he had attacked Craig and herself just after they'd left a bar in the old part of York. He'd come at them with a blacksmith's hammer and while he hadn't attempted to strike *her*, Craig had been lucky to escape serious injury. He stopped and stared at her. Tethering the horse, he came towards her car. She thought about driving on but decided to see what he had to say.

"What you doin' here, Cat?" he asked.

"Come to work at the excavation on the moor," she replied. "And you. What are you doing here?"

"Your old flame knows nowt about 'orses."

"And you?"

"'E's employing me to run his daddy's horse farm. I'm good with horses, I am."

"It's good... It's good that you and he have got back together again."

"Oh, we're good buddies again. That's right and tight."

"You recovered all right from the knock you got?" His eyes moved over her. She was glad she was well covered-up. "You mean when he half killed me?"

"I mean when you fell over and hit your head."

"If you say so. I recall it differently. But yes, I was okay – it'd take more than a bang on the head to do me any serious harm."

"I'm glad to hear it," she said, and it surprised her that she meant it. He glanced up towards the moor top. "So you're going to be around for a few days, eh?"

"Could be. They found some old bones they want me to look at."

"You know about them, do you?"

"It's my job these days."

"Aye. Tha were allus a bright girl," he said in his thickest accent.

She realised he was deliberately playing the role of the ignorant yokel and decided it was time to go. "I expect I'll see you around from time to time."

"Aye. Any time you'd like a ride, come and see me. I'm sure the young master won't mind – he can have one any time."

The double entendre did not escape her. She had the feeling that Simon had changed and was no longer the entertaining and carefree man she had once, before meeting Craig, fancied herself in love with. There was something darker about him now. Something which made her skin crawl.

"Thanks. I'll let you know," she said and let the clutch in gently, so that he had to move away from the car. She closed the window and let out a breath, pointing the vehicle towards the moor. Keeping the big car on the narrow track demanded all her concentration and effectively took her mind off the conversation she'd just had. As she parked by the large marquee, Dave Pountney paused in his efforts, straightening up painfully after spending a lengthy period kneeling or bending. He climbed out of his trench and made his way across to where Cat was getting her stuff out of the back of the estate.

"Great to have you with us again, Cat," he said.

"Hi, Dave. You have some bones for me to look at, I understand."

"Yes, but would you like some coffee before getting stuck in, or shall we get to the bones at once?"

She smiled at his enthusiasm. "Let's do both. We can look at the bones while we drink."

"Excellent suggestion. Follow me."

He led the way into the marquee. Cat followed, bringing her laptop and the Pilot bag. Dave made some coffee and showed her the finds while they sipped the strong hot drink. After looking at all the other trays and photographs of the bones *in situ*, which gave Cat a good idea of the archæological context, she pulled a pair of latex gloves from her bag and picked up a fragment of bone, about nine inches long. One end was broken and jagged, the other was unmistakably the end of an ulna which fitted into a humerus at the elbow. She looked up and smiled at Dave.

"Did you hope it would be human or animal?" she asked.

"Oh, human. Please say it's human!"

"Okay, Dave, it's human."

"Bless you, my dear," he said, grinning broadly. "I must just tell the others."

As he turned towards the flap which did duty as a door, it was pushed aside and Jemma entered.

"Hi," she said quickly to Cat, then turned to Dave. "Dave, we've got a skull."

"Ah! Excellent. The day gets better, even if you have stolen our thunder."

"What?" she asked. "Just that Cat here has identified the bones as human."

"One of them," said Cat, quickly scanning the smaller pieces in the tray, "but the others look to be human, too."

"Great," Dave said. "I should introduce you: Cat, this is Jemma; Jemma – Cat."

"Hi," said Jemma again. "I guess you're our osteologist."

"Yes. Are we going to see your skull?" asked Cat.

"Oh, yes! This way."

Jemma led the three of them across the site to her trench, in which Mike and Diarmuid were crouching either side of a smooth crowned piece of bone. Cat was ushered up to it and the young men moved to allow Jemma to carry on gently teasing the earth away.

"Is it male or female, doc?" asked Diarmuid.

"I'll need to see a bit more – the brow ridges above the orbits are a good guide," Cat replied.

Jemma brushed away soil to begin to reveal the eye sockets. "That enough for you, Cat?" she asked.

Cat lightly ran a finger above the upper part of the orbits – the lowest part of the forehead – to confirm what she could see.

"I think you are unearthing a woman, Jemma," she said. "The brow ridges in a male are much more pronounced: female skulls, more gracile."

"Are you going to give her a name?" asked Dave.

Jemma thought for a moment.

"She's the oldest lady I've ever found. I think she should be called Lucy, after the fossil skull found in Olduvai Gorge in Africa."

"Lucy she is," said Dave. "Think the lads and I should get on. You okay here, Cat?"

"Yes, thanks."

"You're a free agent. Examine what you want to. I'd like the bones we already unearthed to be fully identified at some stage."

"That's okay. I'll do that now." She turned to Jemma. "When you've finished unearthing Lucy, will you let me know before you start lifting the skeleton? And if you find any more interesting burials, tell me please."

She returned to the marquee to do some serious work on the bones already found, while the rest of the team settled back into their stride, discovering more secrets of the ancient settlement. By the end of the day, most of Lucy's bones had been lifted from the ground and were laid out on a table all to herself in the marquee. Jemma was watching as Cat made a record of the bones in her computer. Lucy's pelvic bones had confirmed her gender. Furthermore, there was evidence she'd given birth. Cat had examined the bones unearthed earlier and decided that they had probably come from a person around twelve to fifteen years of age, but without the skull or pelvis, it was difficult to be certain about the sex of the person – or persons: there was at present no guarantee they were from just one burial. It was too dark to work outside and the three men came into the marquee to clean up.

"Anyone fancy going to the pub, to celebrate?" asked Mike.

"It's a fair distance," said Dave.

"I'll drive us, if you like," said Cat. "I don't want much to drink."

"Sounds good to me," said Mike.

"I'll ask Craig along," said Jemma.

Cat glanced at her. She wasn't sure she wanted to be anywhere near Craig while she still had ambivalent feelings about him. On the other hand, it wasn't as if they'd be alone.

"Do you think he'd want to go drinking with a bunch of archæologists?"

Jemma grinned. "I reckon if *I* ask him, he will."

Cat looked at her and realised the girl had a crush on Craig. Maybe the feelings were reciprocated.

"Oh, right. You two are an item, yes?"

Jemma's blush told her all she needed to know. Half an hour later, Cat drove carefully down the track to the farm house, where Jemma hopped out and went to collect Craig. She found herself studying the pair of them as they made their way back to the car, silhouetted against the kitchen lights. A distinct twinge of jealousy slithered through her like a knife, proving to her that even after all he'd put her through, she still had feelings for him – feelings she had better keep to herself, preferably suppressing them altogether. Diarmuid and Mike had gamely volunteered to sit in the Rover's luggage space, leaving the rear seats for Jemma and Craig, whilst Dave sat in front alongside Cat. Jemma opened the door and climbed across the back seat.

"Cat, this is Craig," she said blithely, as Craig ducked into the car. He turned to Cat and the smile froze on his face. Oh, no, thought Cat, don't make it obvious we know each other. But Craig had other ideas.

"Cat! I heard an osteologist was coming. Never guessed it'd be you."

"Hi, Craig," she said, hoping she sounded indifferent to him.

Jemma was looking from one to the other, puzzled. "You two know each other?" she asked.

Craig turned to her. "We're old friends. From before I went to Canada," he explained.

Cat put the car into gear and moved off, careful not to look at him. She caught sight of Jemma in the rear view mirror and saw the curiosity on her face. She reached the bottom of the track, where it met the road. "Is the Mucky Duck where I left it?" she asked with forced brightness.

The three younger archæologists looked at each other, puzzled as there was no pub of that name but Dave Pountney guessed.

"Ah, you'll mean the Black Swan. Yes, it's still there."

If he had thought the atmosphere in the car was strained, he gave no hint. Cat drove in silence and parked in the pub's yard. She was wondering how the evening would go. She certainly didn't feel in a celebratory mood, but she would make an effort for the sake of the others, who were relying on her for a ride back to the camp. Dave offered to buy a round. Mike went with him to the bar and the other four sat at a large table. Jemma had seated herself opposite Craig, whilst Cat sat at the end of the table, as far away from him as possible, trying not to show much interest. She thought he looked a little uncomfortable. Jemma, seeming oblivious of the tension between Craig and Cat, spoke to him.

"We found a fairly complete skeleton today, Craig. Cat reckons it was a female of about thirty years of age – right, Cat?"

Cat looked up, met Craig's eyes, looked down at her beer, then back at Jemma. "Yes, that's right. Jemma found her and called her Lucy."

"How can you tell she was female?" asked Craig.

"The brow ridges, just above the eye sockets, are almost non-existent on females. Still marked on men—"

"It's a throwback to their Neanderthal ancestors," said Jemma.

"—and the sciatic notch on the pelvic bones. It's a different shape on females, because it has to allow for the passage of a baby down the birth canal," Cat added. "It's a better indicator than the skull."

"What about when you find neither skull nor pelvis?" Craig asked.

"You can sometimes tell from the thickness of the major bones, like the humerus, radius and ulna in the arm, or the femur, tib and fib in the leg. If the person did a lot of heavy work, there might well be signs of it on their spinal vertebrae.

Someone showing signs of injuries on almost any bones might well have been a warrior and probably male. I'd expect to find more signs tending to the same conclusion, though."

Cat felt better talking about her own subject and gradually recovered some of her animation and the enthusiasm she'd felt earlier. Although she kept to just the one pint of beer, the others drank more freely and it was a merry group which sang boisterous renditions of old rugby songs to while away the journey back. At Holt Carr, Cat stopped to let Craig out. She caught sight of Jemma and it seemed to her that the girl was expecting to go in the house with him, but Craig merely kissed her lightly on the cheek and said goodnight before going indoors alone. Jemma's face told Cat what she had suspected – that she and Craig were sleeping together. Except that tonight, for some reason, he had chosen not to.

She guessed the girl would be feeling very put out and resentful: she knew she would have been had the situation been reversed. Jemma put a brave face on her disappointment and looked at Cat.

"I guess we're going to be sharing the ladies' room in the marquee," she said.

"If it's going to be too crowded, I can sleep in the car. I've done it before."

Jemma shook her head. "No way. You're one of the team, so sleep with us. We'll manage, there's room."

Cat realised Jemma didn't want her feeling alienated and was grateful. She smiled. "If you're sure. I wouldn't want to feel I was crowding you out."

"Believe me, it can be so cold up there, you'll be glad we're sleeping close to each other."

Cat drove the big car up the track to the dig. They were glad to get into the marquee, which was at least warmer than the outside temperature. Mike, who seemed to have appointed himself chief cook, offered to make some coffee. The women sipped the hot drinks and decided to take the mugs with them and get into their sleeping bags, not wishing to linger in the chill. Within half an hour, four of them were asleep, Diarmuid snoring gently and Jemma wriggling from time to time. Only Cat lay awake, wishing she was back home.

She should have realised that Craig would interest any single woman. She was just a bit surprised at the difference in age between him and Jemma. Surely an attractive -year-old would have preferred men nearer to her own age? The thought depressed her. Added to it was the knowledge that she had let Alan go out of her life because she'd allowed herself to entertain some nebulous idea that now Craig was back, he'd want to take up where he left off. Perhaps, if she was honest with herself, she would have to admit that the minute she'd seen Craig Jordon's name on the email, she'd shied away from a settled future with Alan Crossley.

In an instant, all the little things he said and did she'd once thought so endearing were suddenly unattractive. Even his hirsute legs. She would have to be careful not to let anyone, especially the young woman in the adjacent sleeping-bag, suspect that such an idea had planted itself some place from where it refused to budge. She liked Jemma and didn't want to cause her hurt, seeing herself at that age, enjoying what life put her way, with a strong focus on her career and future. And tomorrow, there might be more bones. There was always her work to keep her positive and help her ignore the disappointments life threw her way.

CHAPTER 5

"What time do you call this, lad?" William Stalland asked in as neutral a tone as he could manage when Simon arrived an hour late the next morning.

Simon scowled resentfully. "I overslept. Did Craig call you in?"

"No. It's fortunate that I was just beyond the wall and heard some of the horses kicking up a fuss. I came over to see what was what. When you weren't here, I thought it would be as well to get on with the job." He stopped and peered at his son's face. "You all right, Simon? You've got a big red mark on your forehead."

Simon's lips turned down into a scowl. "It's nothing. Just banged my head against the steering wheel."

William looked over his shoulder at the new dent on the front of Simon's pick-up. "Have you had an accident?" he asked, concern edging his voice.

"No. Yes, well, just a little one. No damage."

Simon rubbed his left arm which, with his left foot, had ceased to work without warning, causing him to swerve into a gatepost at the side of the road. He'd recovered the use of both limbs in a few minutes, but he wasn't about to tell his father about the loss of control, which would have betrayed his weakness.

"Anyway, I'll get on with it. Thanks for stepping in."

William Stalland held out the fork he'd been using to shift the bedding without further comment. Simon took it, concealing as best he could a tremor in his left hand which had remained since the incident, and watched his father stride out of the building without a backward glance. He bent to the task of cleaning out the stall.

*

On the moor above Holt Carr, Cat had woken when she heard one of the men crawl out of his sleeping bag. She still felt tired as she pulled on her jeans, thick socks, boots and heavy cable-knit sweater and went to the gas ring and put the kettle on. Today, she had to continue the tedious but vital business of cataloguing and recording all the data needed so that the bones could be taken back to the lab for further detailed study. She turned and stood by the long trestle table bearing the skeleton which had been carefully reassembled. Jemma came to stand beside her. She looked at the bones for a moment, keeping her eyes down.

"Tell me about you and Craig."

Cat glanced sideways at her, noting the younger woman's even features in profile. "What's to say? We went out together for a few months, then he went to Canada."

Jemma turned to face her. "Did you love him?"

Cat forced a chuckle. Best, she thought, to be straight with the girl. "Yes. How could anyone not? How about you?" she asked, sounding less interested in the answer than she really was.

Jemma didn't reply as quickly as she'd feared. "Well, he's nice and we get on well," she said, with a touch of uncertainty in her voice, "but I don't know that I would want a man that much older than me as a long-term fixture, if you see what I mean."

Cat couldn't help defending him. "He's not old—!"

She almost bit off her tongue, knowing how revealing her reaction to be. Jemma lifted an eyebrow. Cat gave up pretending any further interest in the skeleton. "Let's go outside."

The two women left the tent and strolled away from the site towards the cairn.

"There really isn't much else to say," said Cat. "Craig and I were briefly in love – I think – but not so much that when he got the chance of a job in Canada, he took it." She sat down on a large slab of limestone.

Jemma sat beside her. "You know Craig and I are having a fling?"

"I guessed."

"It's not serious. We're just enjoying ourselves. I think he's been a bit starved of female company."

"Probably," said Cat bleakly.

Jemma seemed to hesitate. "Are you and Craig still in love with each other?" she asked.

Cat looked round at her, one eyebrow arched in wry amusement. "You like to go for the jugular, don't you?"

Jemma shrugged. "Just thought we ought to know where we stand." Cat stood up and gazed at the moor slanting down on three sides into the valleys of the rivers Wharfe and Aire. A hawk of some kind – she wasn't good at identifying birds, especially at a distance – hovered a few hundred yards away, suddenly folding its wings and plummeting earthwards. Cat was fascinated. At the last moment, it extended both wings to act as air brakes until it almost stopped. It plunged into the tight-packed heathers and seconds later, it powered it up and away with some small creature held captive in one talon. She thought of Craig seeing such sights quite often in the northern wilderness of the Yukon Territory.

"The answer is no," said Cat sounding more certain than she felt. There was absolutely no reason to think otherwise... and yet every time she saw him or heard his voice, a persistent and rebellious part of her responded positively. It was something she was finding increasingly difficult to ignore, but she knew she must. Jemma seemed to be giving her time to change her mind.

When she didn't, she said, "If you're sure about that, okay?"

Cat shrugged. "Okay."

Jemma seemed reasonably happy with their agreement. "Better get back to camp or Dave will be moaning."

"Yes," said Cat, getting to her feet. "Let's go and unearth some more bones."

*

"Twelve years ago, there was a bit of trouble," Cat began. "I'd been going out with Simon – we'd been friends since school. He wasn't like he is now. He used to be much more fun to be with. He's changed a lot since I last saw him. Craig was his best mate: they were quite competitive, and they were always trying to score points off each other." She smiled at the recollection as they reached the cairn. "Simon was always proud of his strength, while Craig was more inclined to study, though he was pretty good on the rugby field and could beat Simon in a sprint."

She sat down on a large rocky outcrop.

"Anyway, I found I preferred Craig's company to Simon's and when I told him, he became very jealous, and one evening he attacked Craig and me." She glanced up at Jemma. "He was apprenticed to a farrier at the time, and I think it was one of those long-handled hammers they use to beat red-hot iron."

Jemma nodded.

"Anyway, Craig fought him off, but in the process, Simon went down and banged his head against the kerb. Lost consciousness. We sent for an ambulance, and he was in hospital a couple of weeks with concussion and cracked ribs. I lost track of him after that. Craig and I continued seeing each other for a few months, then he got a job in Canada and I went on to post-grad studies."

She looked up into Jemma's eyes. "Never saw him again until I collected him at the airport a couple of days ago."

Jemma had also found a rocky outcrop and perched on it. "Did you go back to Simon?"

Cat raised an eyebrow. "No. In any case, Simon had got one of his nurses pregnant, did the decent

61

thing and married her. I got on with my studies and... here I am as a result. Are you doing post-grad at the minute?" she asked in an endeavour to turn the subject.

"Yes," said Jemma, standing, but not quite as ready to talk about something else. "Are you going to start seeing Craig again?"

Cat shook her head. "Of course not. We hardly know each other after all this time." She did not dare to let Jemma see her face lest it give away her uncertainty.

*

Craig might have been surprised at having his immediate future decided by Cat and Jemma. He had had to deal with a dilemma the night before when they'd got back from the pub. Had Cat not been present, he'd have had no hesitation in suggesting to Jemma that she might like to "take advantage of the facilities in the house", but in fact, he'd found himself thinking about Cat.

He knew that it wasn't right to sleep with Jemma if his heart, and his thoughts, were somewhere else. He figured the situation was only temporary. He hadn't asked, but he supposed that Cat was in a relationship with someone else, and in any case, she'd still seemed cross with him when she'd brought him home from the airport. So obviously, she wasn't interested in rekindling what they'd once had... but he knew he was. Or would have been. The fact that he was always aware of her presence, and she was often in his thoughts amounted to a "blip".

He would meet someone, he felt sure, who would excise Cat from his mind. Jemma, he knew, was not that woman, though she was a step in the right direction. He guessed that she thought of him in much the same way. Despite that, he felt privileged that she'd decided to have a fling with him. He decided to walk up to the archæological site. Simon was out in the yard by the time he was ready to go. Craig paused to admire the mare

Simon had on a leading rein. "Morning, Simon. A fine animal, that."

"Aye, she is. Are you sure you don't want to ride? It's not that bad if you go gently."

"The cowhands in Alberta used to say you can't call yourself a rider until you've fallen off a few times, preferably breaking a bone. I'm afraid I rather took them at their word. Took ages for the ribs to heal."

Simon enjoyed the thought. "This isn't Alberta. This is your own horse farm in the Yorkshire Dales." He looked defiantly into Craig's eyes, as if daring him to comment. "I've bought the hacks – you'll be getting a bill. And I put the word out for a couple of girls who know enough about horses to be able to help me look after them and exercise them. We should have 'em in the next day or two."

"Fine. Will you be able to manage until then?"

"No problem. Now how about we get you up on one of these hacks? They're well-behaved to the point of lethargy."

Craig was tempted. He was putting off the visit to the site as much as possible. "Okay, but you'll have to go steady."

Simon grinned. "No problem. Let's go and saddle a couple up."

He walked the horse round and Craig followed them into the stable block. Fifteen minutes later, they each led one of the hacks, both mares, bearing saddles and bridles out into the yard. Simon positioned Craig's animal adjacent to a mounting block and held her steady while Craig got on her back. He looked down at Simon.

"Shouldn't we be wearing riding hats?"

"Them's for cissies," he said with a lop-sided grin. "You'll be all right. I'll be reet beside thee." Simon mounted his own mare lithely and they walked the horses out of the yard side by side, along the path which led gently up the moor in the direction away from the dig site. They came to an old stone quarry from which the Victorians had extracted sandstone to build their towns in the dale below as well as the farm houses and barns in the surrounding countryside. Craig remembered his father telling him that Holt Carr House itself had been built with the stone from this quarry. Disused for many years, the edge of the quarry wall was unprotected. The rotted posts of an old fence around the rim lay partly covered in moss and heather. His horse stumbled in a fissure near the edge and leapt back away from the danger. Craig held on, knees and ankles cramping for a moment, but afterwards feeling quite pleased that he'd not been thrown. Simon had watched impassively, a strange gleam in his eyes. They'd walked on past the quarry and moved up to a trot before they turned and headed back to Holt Carr.

"Right," said Simon when they got back into the yard, "next time, we'll both go a bit further and see if we can't get you cantering and galloping. You'll like that – very exhilarating."

"I think I need to remember the old adage about not running until you can walk," said Craig.

"Well, you've been walking, so what's left?" asked Simon.

There was something in his grin that Craig didn't like. He remembered one of the things that had led him to avoid a close friendship with Simon when they'd been at school was that Simon seemed to enjoy putting others down, and often used what he called practical jokes to do it. Craig directed the horse back towards the stables and swung his leg over her to dismount.

Having firm ground underfoot after the ride felt strange, in the way that land feels unsteady after a period spent at sea. He was also beginning to discover that the stress on his thigh muscles caused by keeping his knees clamped against the animal was quite painful even for a fit man like himself. He grinned, ruefully. Simon took charge of the horses and Craig walked painfully over to the Land-Rover. He heard Simon laugh gratingly inside the stable block and it was not a pleasant sound.

At the dig site, Craig climbed stiffly out of his Land-Rover. Jemma was kneeling in her trench in the burial ground and walked over.

"Hi," he grinned.

Jemma looked round, studied his face and returned the smile. "Hi. You all right?"

"Never better. Apart from aches and pains in places I'd rather not mention, from riding. Found anything this morning?"

"Bits of pottery. I think there's another foot over there," she pointed, 'so that's where I'm heading next."

"Mind if I watch?"

"No."

Craig was aware that Jemma's attitude was markedly cooler than it had been. "I'm sorry about last night," he said.

She stopped work and turned towards him. "What about last night?"

"I meant to ask you indoors, but frankly, Cat's being present caused a certain amount of confusion. Silly really, as I realised later. We used to go out together?"

Jemma nodded.

"It was years ago, but it suddenly all seemed like yesterday. I guess it's the time I spent away in Canada seems to count for nothing now I'm back home. Of course, I realise she's not the same girl I left and will have moved on, as we all do. I was just being foolish and thoughtless and I hope you won't hold it against me."

She smiled. "A very good speech. Actually, Cat told me about you and Simon. From what she said, I think you're right: she has moved on."

He stood up, glancing at his watch. "Sure. Uh, I can't actually stay. I need to do some shopping. See you later – I don't lock up, so help yourself to the shower – any of you – if I'm not around."

He turned and made his way back to the Land-Rover, feeling much better.

*

Jemma watched him go, her lips pursed, wondering how much he believed of what he'd told her. How much did *she* believe, come to that. Oh, sod! she told herself, was it worth worrying about? Craig was a great lover and they could have good times together until the dig finished. He was not making any moves on Cat, nor she on him, so why shouldn't she, Jemma, make a little hay? She'd need another shower later, so why not take it when he was around? She was smiling again as she turned to the toe-bones sticking out of the trench floor.

*

Cat withdrew from the doorway of the marquee. She'd seen Craig and Jemma talking and she had experienced an unwelcome tightening of her chest. She had sternly reminded herself that Craig was a free agent and they had nothing but some ancient history linking them. It was clear that he retained nothing of his affection for her and he could hardly be blamed for that after twelve years.

She was looking down at Lucy's remains and suddenly found her vision blurred. Angry with herself, she brushed the unwelcome tears from her eyes. Really! she thought, I am not the kind of girl who cries! Move on, get a grip!

She gathered her strength and forcibly pushed herself back into professional mode, resolving not to think about Craig any more. She allowed herself one more gusty sob before getting back to the job of cataloguing the bones. Behind her, Dave Pountney had been about to enter the tent when he had seen her private sadness and had waited until she got over it before coming in with a tray of finds. He put the tray down on another table, speaking without facing her.

"Are you okay?"

She looked round, startled, her eyes still misty, but she blinked furiously and shook her head. "I'm fine, thank you."

"Right," he said, still sorting through some of the items in the tray and not looking at her. "It's just that, if you want to talk to someone, privately... I like us all to be happy and I can see something's upset you."

"I'm fine, Dave. Don't be concerned," she said, touched that he should be so understanding.

*

Simon watched Craig drive off to Skipton. He had a little time free, and it occurred to him that there was no-one in the house. He decided to look around it. Checking his entry into the place was not witnessed, he took stock of the kitchen before moving through the stone-flagged hall into the living room. Here, he gazed around, taking in the collection of photographs on top of the piano. The largest was of Craig in academic gown and a mortar-board, clutching his degree.

Simon's lip curled with disdain. He hadn't been clever enough to get to university, and besides, he wouldn't have wanted to go. He preferred using his hands, even though it hadn't been until he was working with the farrier that he'd discovered his knack with horses. He thought of himself as tougher than Craig, and the fact that Craig had put him in hospital was more to do with his cheating and devious method of fighting than a matter of strength. Simon figured he needed to get even with Craig for that night, and he was determined that this time, Craig would be the one being carted off to hospital.

He found Craig's laptop computer set up on the table. He was not very conversant with small computers like this: there was one at home which was mainly used by Louise and Mark, but it was a bigger, desktop type. He recognised the power switch and, not having any definite purpose in mind, he switched on. He soon found himself looking at the same sort of screen he knew from the machine at home. There was a mouse on the table beside it. Craig's own log-in was password protected, but the "Guest' login admitted him without a problem. He opened a web browser and watched as the screen showed a box labelled *Insert search term*. He thought for a moment and typed in *Yorkshire* and clicked on the box marked *Search*. In a second, the screen informed him that there were over seven million references to Yorkshire and listed the first ten. He had never used a search engine before and was amazed at the amount of information it could retrieve and how easy it was to use.

Before he could try another search, he heard the kitchen door open and close. He froze for a moment, then switched the computer off and dived behind the settee as footsteps came into the hallway and passed the door. The steps seemed for a moment to pause and he held his breath, his eyes squeezed tight shut and his head again beginning to thump. At last, whoever it was went up the stairs. Moments later, Simon heard the shower begin.

He slipped from his hiding place and out of the house, back to the stable-block. His heart was pounding and his head was aching badly. Suddenly, his vision began to blur. He recalled that he'd experienced similar symptoms on an increasing number of occasions, including that morning before he lost the use of his left arm and leg.

A feeling of nausea swept upon him. Every time he moved his head he felt his gorge rise. Very carefully, he felt his way into the tack room with his eyes closed, found the chair and sat in it, squeezing his eyes shut with frustration. He felt in his pocket for the tablets he normally kept with him but was unable to find any.

He rifled the drawers and cupboards in the tack room, not sure what he was looking for, until rewarded by the discovery of three old sachets of Equipalazone, an equine pain-killer. He took his vodka from the refrigerator, tore open a sachet and poured it into the bottle, shaking it until the powder dissolved, then gulping several mouthfuls of the doctored spirit. He groaned in his agony.

What was matter with him? Could these headaches, this double vision, really be caused only by migraines? According to the doctor he had consulted some years before, it was all perfectly possible and there was no real cure. Things had to be really bad for him to visit the surgery. He lay back with his eyes closed and waited for the drug to kick in.

He slept for close to an hour. When he awoke, his vision had cleared, his head still thumped, but tolerably, and the horses were getting restless. He needed to take them out for some exercise. As he guided two of the animals on leading reins outside, he saw one of the students coming out of the house, a rolled-up towel under his arm. He waved. Simon glowered at him, annoyed that he'd been so close to catching him using Craig's computer.

Diarmuid shrugged and walked back up to the camp.

CHAPTER 6

A few days later, half an hour after school had finished, two girls arrived at Holt Carr. Craig answered the door to their knock. One of them was wearing an old fleece and shapeless jeans, the other a pair of tight-fitting jodhpurs and a sweater. This one stepped forward.

"I'm Kelly and this is Susie. We're here to help Simon with the horses. Are you Simon?"

She tilted her head slightly, causing her ponytail to swing. Craig noticed that she was wearing makeup, with shadowed eyes and glossy lips, in contrast to her friend who watched him shyly.

"Uh, no. I'm Craig Jordon. Simon's in the stable block. I'll show you the way."

He stepped outside and led them along the front of the house to the yard where the track from the main road came round, giving access to all the outbuildings and the moor beyond. As they rounded the corner to the rear of the house, he pointed out the stable-block and explained what the business was about.

"So all your horses are pregnant mares?" asked Kelly.

"Yes, unless they've recently given birth. There are some foals here, mostly waiting to be collected by their owners."

Simon saw them and walked across the yard in time to hear Craig. "Tha needs to invest in a few decent stallions, Craig, then we could 'ave a right-old knockin'-shop for 'orses." He grinned. "And offer a complete service, as you might say."

"Ladies, this is Simon." Craig introduced them.

"I'm glad you're 'ere," Simon said, "we 'ad a new arrival last night and the stall needs cleaning out and new bedding ready for the next..." His voice faded as he led the girls into the stable block.

*

At the dig, Cat and the archæologists gathered round Dave Pountney as he outlined the timetable for the rest of their time there. "Not long to go now, people," he said, "and there's lots needs doing."

"There's still a lot of the site we haven't looked at," said Jemma. "We'll look at the GPR again, and see if we can decide an order of priorities. What we can't do in the time will have to be left for another time."

Cat knew that that meant for ever. Every dig she'd been on had been left unfinished because the budgets ran out, and every time there had been the same trite sentiment, that what was left would be looked at 'another time'. A radar sweep or a magnetic survey to try to identify the full extent of whatever remains there were often had to suffice, and they didn't always manage to get that. There was never enough money to finance the completion of the digs, and the same would undoubtedly apply to the Holt Carr site.

When Dave had finished outlining his plans, she turned and went into the marquee, followed by Jemma who went to find the charts produced by the ground-penetrating radar.

While Cat worked on a newly-lifted skeleton, taking measurements, examining the surface of each bone, looking for signs of disease and injury, Jemma began poring over the charts. A moment later, Dave came in and joined her. Craig had not been near the site for several days and whilst Cat had availed herself of the shower facilities in the house, she had done so deliberately when he was out. Although she maintained publicly there was nothing between herself and Craig, every time Jemma went down to the house when Craig was at home, Cat experienced what was undeniably a twinge of jealousy and was annoyed that she was not indifferent.

She wished that whatever remnant of her and Craig's relationship still lurked in her heart would leave her in peace. The result had been a series of unhappy nights and dour days. She had tried to be stern with herself and demanded of her heart if any man was worth the ache. The answer was not what she wanted, nor was it unexpected. Her only defence was to concentrate on her work to the exclusion of all else. Jemma noticed her introversion and suspected the cause.

Craig was not similarly troubled and showed no signs of regretting their relationship, and Jemma knew its days were numbered anyway, according to her own rules of engagement. In the meantime, Craig was too handy to pass up, and Cat had stuck to her declared position of having no interest in him.

Jemma decided to be as discreet as possible about visiting him so as to minimise any upset to Cat's feelings.

*

"Eh, tha's got a fine action." Simon was watching Kelly as both she and Susie worked at brushing the mares' coats. Kelly had taken off her tunic top and Simon feasted his eyes on her nubile figure as she bent and stretched at her task. Once or twice, he caught her glancing at him from the corner of her eyes, so he had little doubt that some of the performance was for his benefit.

She grinned. "I bet yours is pretty good," she said, with a smirk that said she was aware of the flirtatious nature of their conversation.

"Aye, well, I've "ad a bit more practice than thee."

"I should think so," she said, sweeping the brush in arcs against the horse's flanks, "an old bloke like you."

She flicked a glance at him again and next time the brush reached the end of its travel, she dropped it, bending to pick it up. He saw her glance at him again and he smiled to himself. He wondered if she'd be as easy as she seemed. Susie seemed years younger than her friend. Her chubby face, and obvious lack of sophistication aroused no interest in him whatsoever. She was good with the horses, he'd noted, but was totally uninterested in him as a man. Kelly, on the other hand, had made efforts to engage his interest, and succeeded. Simon watched her, flaunting her curves for his benefit, and tried to decide the best way of getting her alone.

*

Kelly noticed his interest in her and felt flattered. She fancied Simon, liking his "outdoorsy" appearance and manner. She enjoyed teasing him, which she did as often as she could contrive it. Simon didn't wear jods himself, but his jeans fitted quite snugly. She wondered how interested she could get him before he tried to put her off by pointing out he was old enough to be her father. She wondered what sex would be like with a real man. She'd allowed the boys at school certain liberties with her breasts, but had stopped short of letting them put their penises inside her, despite their promises to pull out at the crucial moment. Somehow, she knew that if she ever let Simon get that close to her, there would be no stopping him from going all the way. The thought frightened her and fascinated her, at the same time. Susie, she knew, was determined to push ahead with her exams rather than worry about boys – or men, in Simon's case – so they didn't spend much time talking about him. Kelly found her friend's disapproval amusing and redoubled her efforts on the horse, making sure she did a lot of bending and stretching for Simon's benefit.

*

There had been a time, Victoria recalled, when Simon had been a loving and attentive husband. She determined to try and remind him of happier times when they sat down to dinner that evening. He'd been unusually taciturn on his return home, showering and changing with scarcely a word. Victoria couldn't be sure what sort of mood he was

73

in. The four of them sat down to a Toad-in-the-Hole, which was something he usually liked.

She smiled. "Simon? Do you remember when Mark was born?"

He frowned at her. "Aye. So?"

"I was just thinking how thoughtful and... loving... you were. I still remember the flowers and the Belgian chocolates." He stared at her, the frown still wrinkling his brow.

"Aye?"

She didn't know what else to say. "It – it's just something I was remembering. Happy times."

"Is there some sort of message in that for me?" he demanded. "Is it supposed to excuse this... this *shit* you've served up?"

He seized his plate and threw it and its contents on the floor at her feet. Victoria whimpered. Louise and Mark stared at their parents. Simon got to his feet and pulled her up out of her chair. The yank on her blouse set off the pain in her ribs, which had been quite slight during the day when she could take care not to stress them. She moaned. He dragged her out of the kitchen, up the stairs, and threw her on their bed. She guessed his purpose when he unfastened the belt holding up his trousers.

"Simon, no! Please, don't. My ribs are still sore. They're getting better. Soon, Simon, but not just now – please!"

"Shut thy noise!" he told her, roughly unzipping her trousers and pulling them down.

Victoria concentrated on not screaming while he mounted her, concerned that the children should not become involved. She shut her eyes, trying to shut out the pain he was inflicting on her and the sight of his face, screwed into rage.

He climbed off her at last. She lay there, tears of shame and hurt spilling down her cheeks, while he pulled his trousers on and turned to leave her. At the door, he stopped and looked back, all emotion gone.

"Now get downstairs and clean up t' mess on t' floor. And cook summat better."

Unable to speak, she nodded.

"Tonight!"

She swallowed. What could she cook for him in this state? He slammed the bedroom door behind him, and she slowly reached for the trousers he'd torn off her. She needed to clean herself up in the bathroom, but every slight movement caused stabbing pain in her side. She sobbed, and even that hurt. If she could only get through the night, tomorrow, she'd get the bus to the Accident & Emergency department at the local General Hospital, a few miles beyond Skipton. She could always tell them she'd fallen off a ladder. Downstairs, she heard the front door slam, and guessed that Simon had left the house. Biting her lip to keep from screaming, she managed to pull her trousers on and stand up. Every step was painful, but she made it to the bedroom door at last and began the slow descent of the stairs. It took her a full ten minutes, resting on each tread while her ribs settled again, before starting them off again as she took another slow step. When she eventually reached the kitchen and pushed the door open, Louise was washing up, Simon's plate had been picked up and put in the bin, and Mark was drying. They stopped as they saw their mother.

Louise's cheeks were streaked with tears. Mark looked ready to cry, too, and seemed to be fighting manfully not to. The sight of them tore at Victoria's heart. She pressed a hand over her lips to try to control her response, but she couldn't prevent her own tears from rolling down her cheeks and across the back of her hand. She knew she should do something to stop the violence. She feared what would happen if she did: tonight, Simon hadn't hit her, he'd merely wanted to have sex. If she stirred up trouble for him, there was every reason to believe he'd really go for her, the first opportunity

75

he got. She leaned against the wall, fearing the effect of sitting down on her ribs.

"Did your father say where he was going?" she asked Louise.

The girl paused in the act of pulling the plug out of the sink and looked over her shoulder.

"Down the pub." She stared at Victoria before asking, "Mum, why does daddy hit you?"

"He didn't hit me."

"You screamed a lot."

Victoria bit her lip. She must have screamed despite trying not to. But what to say? *Mummy and Daddy were just making love?* She shook her head. What he'd done was rape, pure and simple, and it had frightened her.

"He hurt my ribs," she temporized.

"But he hit you when he broke your ribs. Why?"

"I..." She stared at her daughter helplessly. "I don't know."

"Are you going to tell the police?"

Victoria shook her head. "No. If I do that, daddy might..."

"Hit you again?"

That, and throw her out of the house without a penny, and without the children. She nodded. Louise finished wiping down the draining board while Mark put away the last few things. "Why don't you go to bed, mum?"

"I can't. Your father wants me to cook him something new, that he likes. I don't know what..." She found herself dissolving in tears. Louise watched her for a moment, then beckoned Mark to her side and they left the room together. A moment later, Victoria heard the front door open and close, and for a terrifying moment, thought Simon had returned. She edged away from the door to the far end of the table. The pain in her side was abating so she could breathe easier, without every breath stabbing her. She waited for him to come in. Whatever he did when he found no food, she would just have to put up with it. She closed her eyes and for the first time in a long time, she prayed. It was the only thing left for her. She prayed for release, for deliverance, for her children and herself. She heard the door burst open and screamed. She opened her eyes and saw her neighbour, Jo Box, staring at her open-mouthed.

She rushed forward, and Victoria backed away, protecting her ribs with her hands. Jo saw the movement.

"Victoria! What's happened? What's the matter with your ribs? Oh, God. Let me get an ambulance."

She unclipped her mobile phone from the belt of her jeans, but before she could dial, Victoria laid a hand on her arm.

"Please, don't. It would only upset him more."

Jo stared at her for a moment, then clipped the phone back on her belt and put her arm round Victoria's shoulder. "So it's true, what the children said. Simon's been attacking you?"

"Yes... No. He was drunk."

"Drunk or sober, it makes no difference," growled Jo. "How long as it been going on?"

Victoria slumped into one of the kitchen chairs, wincing as she felt her ribs stab her again. "A couple of years," she whispered. "It's been getting worse."

Jo touched her side. "Has he hit you here?"

Victoria nodded. "I think I've broken a couple of ribs. It's taking ages for them to mend."

"You mean *he's* broken a couple of your ribs."

Victoria shrugged

"The children said he's just dragged you upstairs and hurt you again. Is that true?"

Victoria glanced at Louise and Mark, still in the doorway, listening wide-eyed. "It's all right now, children. Go and watch television and shut the door, please."

When the two women were alone, Jo turned to her again. "Did he force himself on you?" She indicated upstairs with her thumb.

Victoria nodded. "But if you say anything, I shall deny it."

Jo shook her head. "You're a fool if you do. Nothing will stop him, short of putting him away or your leaving him."

"He used to be a good man. I'm sure he could be one again."

"He's got a taste for it now – power. I'd be surprised if he gave that up without come form of coercion." Victoria shook her head. "You don't understand: if I left Simon, or if he went to jail, what would we live on? This house is in his name, and we'd be turfed out."

"Do you not have any savings?"

Victoria laughed sourly. "You've got to be joking – on what he gives me? I don't know whether I've got the bus fare to get to the hospital tomorrow."

"Let me get you an ambulance tonight – it'll save you the cost," Jo grinned.

"No, thanks. If I go tomorrow while he's at work, he'll not know. If you got an ambulance here, everybody in Nidderdale would know. He'll be annoyed, but I really must get my ribs looked at. They were healing, but I think he's broken them again."

Jo put her arm around her comfortingly. "Oh, poor Victoria! You've got to let me help you. I'll take you to the hospital tomorrow."

Victoria felt tears start to flow and she reached for the paper kitchen towels to mop them. "Thank you, Jo. I'll make it up to you."

"You'd better let me do the school run as well. You just concentrate on your own comfort. Now, what about tonight? We've got a spare room." Victoria felt panic and sat up. "No, no! I couldn't do that. Simon would go mad. I'm supposed to be cooking him some dinner anyway."

"I thought you'd had your meal?"

"Yes, well, he didn't like his."

Jo box sighed in frustration. "Victoria, that's his hard luck. Where is it? In the fridge?"

Victoria smiled damply. "No, he threw it on the floor. The kids cleaned up. I expect it's in the bin."

Jo's lip curled in satisfaction. "You wait here, my girl."

She got up and went to the bin. The remains of Simon's dinner were on top of the other kitchen waste, interspersed with pieces of shattered plate. "Got an old plate anywhere?" Jo asked.

Victoria, bemused, pointed at a cupboard. Jo took out a plate, and used her hands to pile it with as much of Simon's devastated dinner she could easily find in the bin, not bothering to remove ceramic splinters and an old teabag. She put the unwholesome mess down on the table, away from Victoria, washed her hands, and sat next to her friend.

Victoria laughed weakly. "And now what?"

Jo grinned with feral satisfaction. "Now, my girl, we wait for his lordship to deign to return home, and we make him eat it." Victoria laughed aloud this time. "You can't do that! He'll kill us. He'll kill me, the minute you're gone."

"No he won't." Victoria shook her head in disbelief.

"How can you be so sure?"

"Because the alternative I offer him will be something he'll enjoy even less than forcing some of that down," she said, pointing at the plate. Victoria stared at her. She heard the outside door open and close. Footsteps approached the kitchen.

"Time to see if you're right," was all she had time to say before Simon had taken two steps into the room and pulled up short at the sight of Jo Box.

"Hello, Simon," she said. "Victoria and I have had a little talk. Sit down!"

She waited while he sat and his eyes fell on the plate that contained the remains of his dinner. He stared at it as he realised what it was, and glared at Victoria.

"Don't look at her, Simon! I did that." He swivelled his gaze to his neighbour. "Seems that you had a tantrum earlier, and threw your dinner on the floor like a baby."

79

His scowl deepened and his face grew mottled with growing anger. Victoria dreaded the moment when he would explode, but at the same time was fascinated by the way Jo was handling the situation.

"So, like a baby, you have to learn to eat what's put in front of you. The sooner that's eaten, the sooner you can have something else, like breakfast tomorrow. If you haven't eaten it by the time you come home from work, just think what it's going to look like in a few days. Now, eat it!"

He glared at her and stood up, but she gave him no chance to refuse. "Eat it, or I get the police here, tonight."

She lifted a hand from her lap so he could see her mobile phone was gripped in it. "I have only to press this button, and they'll be here. Now, eat your dinner like a good boy."

Simon made a strangled sound, staring from the phone, to Jo's face, to Victoria, and to the plateful of ruined food. Victoria put her hand over her mouth, certain he would attack both of them. Jo put the phone to her ear. And suddenly, Simon sat down. Staring at Jo, he pulled the plate towards him. "I need a knife and fork."

"Use your fingers. Like a baby."

He leaned towards her. "Fuck you, Jo Box," he hissed. She copied him, leaning forward.

"Lay a finger on me, and it'll be the last thing you do until you get out of hospital. Eat!"

Victoria tried valiantly to hide her astonishment when he sat back. He stared at the ruined Toad-in-the-Hole, then began to pick at it, pulling the teabag and pieces of splintered plate out with stubby fingers. Both women watched in silence until he had eaten. Afterwards, he burped.

"You can wash it up now," said Jo.

Slowly, Simon got to his feet and took the plate with its detritus over to the sink. Watching her, he opened the door and threw both the remains and the plate into the bin in a small act of defiance. "Obviously, you need a bit more training, Simon. I said wash it up, and next time I tell you to do something, you do it."

She glanced at Victoria who was watching, mesmerised. "And if I hear of your putting one finger where it shouldn't be, saying one inappropriate word to Victoria, I *will* call the police. Do you understand?"

His eyes flicked from one to the other. He nodded.

"Good. I mean it, Simon. You used to be a much nicer bloke. Time you found him again if you don't want to lose all you hold precious."

She turned to Victoria as she stood up. "The walls are thin, Victoria. Just say if he breaks his word. And come round tomorrow."

Victoria stood up as well. She felt fear rising as she wondered what he'd do the minute Jo had left them. Jo put her hand on her arm. "You'll be all right, dear." Victoria followed her along the hall and closed the door behind her. She heard Simon's footsteps approaching and waited for his hand to fall on her. When it didn't she turned and watched in surprise as he mounted the stairs without saying a thing.

CHAPTER 7

Cat was finding it difficult to maintain her air of indifference to Jemma and Craig's relationship. It seemed to her that Jemma was spending every spare minute down at the house, ostensibly showering, but obviously making love as well – even the longest shower didn't take the length of time she was away.

She knew Craig was at the house, and announced that she was going to take a shower. Jemma was on her knees in a new trench when Cat collected her toilet bag and some clean underclothes and set off down the track. More than anything, she wanted to stop the feeling of pain every time Craig and Jemma set eyes on each other with *that* look, and figured what she needed was practice at being near him without letting the fact bother her. Familiarity, she figured, should breed contempt. Or something. , all those years ago.

As soon as she'd decided he wasn't the man for her, he'd ceased to have any effect on her at all, and she had never thought about him in his absence... It had even worked while Craig was away in Canada. And the memory of him, emerging into the morning sunlight at the airport... It popped into her mind unbidden with regularity. That, and his kiss. Even now, she experienced an echo of the feeling it had engendered. Much more of this sort of thing, she told herself severely, and the shower would have to be a cold one.

*

Craig found himself glancing out of the kitchen window whenever he was in it, in the expectation of seeing Jemma striding down the path. He was surprised to see Cat. He knew she'd used the shower, because Jemma had told him that all the team members had. But usually, it was when he was out, as if she was avoiding him. He opened the door as she reached it.

"Hi, Cat."

For a moment, she stared at him, then seemed to straighten her shoulders. "Hi. I... wondered if I could use the shower."

"Of course." He stood aside to let her enter the kitchen, and caught the scent of her as she passed him. She stopped when she reached the Aga and turned to look at him.

"You have no idea how good it feels, to have this warmth," she said with a grin.

"Oh yes I do," he said. 'remember, I'm used to being up to my neck in snow and ice, even in the middle of summer."

"Oh, yes." She looked down.

He wiped his hands on the tea-towel he'd been holding. She looked up before the pause could become too awkward.

"Right. I – I'll go and shower," she said, with a flicker of a smile, and moved towards the hallway.

"Shall I make us some coffee for when you've finished?"

She looked round at him again.

"I'm very fussy about my coffee," she said, "I brought my own for up there." She nodded towards the dig site.

"Then I shall put my best coffee-making skills to work, and you can assess my coffee, Canadian-style."

"You never used to like coffee."

"There are times when a decent cup of tea is hard to find but wherever you are in Canada and the States, there's always somebody supplying coffee. I learnt to love it out of desperation for a hot drink, and then I learned to make it."

She was amused. "All right. But I'll tell you if I don't like it."

He nodded. "Of course. I shall expect you to apply a scientific approach, without prejudice, in return."

She laughed. "Of course."

While she was gone, he busied himself with a cafetière and his choicest blend. When she reappeared, her hair wrapped in a towel and wearing a clean shirt and jeans, the scent of coffee filled the room and her nose twitched appreciatively.

"Smells nice," she said.

He nodded. "Yup – and so does the coffee," he said, grinning.

The smile disappeared from her face. "Craig! Don't!"

"What?"

"Don't do that. That... flirty thing. I'm not your girlfriend, Jemma is."

He raised both his hands. "Sorry. Didn't think."

She studied his face for a few moments before relaxing and sitting in one of the old armchairs. He poured two mugs of coffee.

"How do you like yours?" he asked.

She told him, and he brought the drinks over and sat in the other armchair. Both were placed where the heat from the Aga could still be felt. She tucked her feet up onto the cushion and picked up the mug. She sniffed delicately, then drank a mouthful, like a sommelier tastes a fine wine. And smiled.

"Pretty good," she said. "And let me assure you, that's an encomium, coming from me."

He bowed his head. "I'm very honoured, I'm sure." He kept the conversation on the safe ground of her work, and when they'd finished their drink, she rubbed her hair gently with the towel and brushed at the tangle of curls, whose colour was lightening as they dried.

He watched as she teased order out of chaos in the process so different from his own, and found himself wishing their history had been different. Perhaps if he hadn't been so determined to leave the country; perhaps he should have tried harder to persuade her to go with him... All over and finished with, he thought. What's done is done, and a lot of water has passed under the bridge in the last twelve years. But not without leaving a mark.

*

Cat walked slowly back to the encampment at the dig site. It allowed her time for thought and time for her hair to finish drying in the breeze. In one way, the experiment of her visit to Holt Carr had been a disaster. She had wanted to exorcise the feelings she apparently still had for Craig, on the grounds that he belonged in her past, and that they should both have moved on since he'd left.

As things had turned out, she'd been aware of his interest in her from the moment she'd arrived. She could smell him as he stood back to allow her to walk into the kitchen. His scent was a heady mixture of soap and aftershave that seemed to suit his "outdoorsy" life in the Canadian wilderness. She'd felt that special tingle that signified a man her body fancied, even if her mind was desperately keen to set him at a distance, and had been glad of the excuse of the Aga's warmth to explain the flush in her cheeks. The shower was just what she'd needed, letting her feelings subside.

Afterwards, back in the kitchen, she'd commented on the wonderful aroma of coffee filling the place. And Craig had taken it as a cue to flirt. It almost undid the calming influence of the shower. Telling him off helped. Obviously, it was just a momentary slip, and they'd spent the time sipping their coffee talking about her work and the other archæological discoveries on the moor.

She'd brushed at her drying hair, trying to sort out the tangle of her curls, thinking that something so mundane, so practical, would further disenchant him, and indeed, he made no further remark that she could interpret in the same way as the earlier one.

Then she'd got up to leave, and he'd unwound himself from his armchair in a movement so naturally lithe and sinuous it had made the breath catch in her throat. She felt the tension rise inside her, and fought to keep any of these effects from being apparent.

Another nose-full of his scent, as he held the kitchen door, left her thinking she could do with another shower, but somehow she managed to get out of the house without his seeming to notice her inner disturbance. So – disaster then. She'd wanted to prove to herself that Craig was consigned to the past, and all she'd proved was that he still fancied her... and, if the truth were told, she still... well, perhaps it was safest to say that there was nobody she liked better.

But he was involved with her friend, and she'd declared she had no interest whatsoever in Craig. Jemma was younger and prettier, if she was honest – if you liked blondes. And she hadn't met a man yet who didn't.

*

Cat was leant over a trestle table in the marquee, brushing bones clean, taking measurements and keying them into her laptop. Jemma came in, closing the entrance flap behind her to keep in the heat from the portable gas heaters.

"Anything I can do to help?" she asked. "My back's beginning to ache with all that crouching down in the trench." She put one hand behind her and knuckled the bones of her lower vertebrae to relax the muscular tensions in that region.

Cat looked up at her and smiled, pushing the bright light over the trestle table up further, so she could see past it.

"Volunteers always welcome," she said. "Can you take the remains of V-double-O two-six and begin to clean them up for me?"

"Sure," said Jemma, picking her way through the boxes towards the one indicated by Cat, identified by the code written on its side in black felt-tip marker.

They worked quietly together, both concentrating on the delicate bones, while scurries of wind whipping across the moor outside was almost the only sound.

"Doing anything special for Christmas?" Cat asked.

"Haven't really sorted it out yet. I mean, it's six or seven weeks or so away," replied Jemma. "Have you planned your Christmas already?"

"Hah! My Christmas doesn't take much planning," said Cat. She straightened up and brushed a curl out of her eyes. "I expect I shall be invited to share Christmas dinner with my parents. Usually they pair me up with the Christmas Fairy so the seating plan's easier."

Jemma grinned. "Better than being paired up with a Christmas Tree Star."

Cat laughed. "No, not a Christmas *Tree* Fairy, just the Christmas Fairy. It's my cousin Jimmy, who came out at Christmas dinner a couple of years ago. Caused the sort of stir mum could have made use of when she was making the Christmas Puddings. Bit conservative, my parents – with a small "c"." She brushed another straying curl away and straightened her back.

Without warning, the tent flap was pulled open and Simon came in.

"Hello," he said.

Cat registered the smell of horses clinging to his waxed jacket. Jemma and Cat glanced at each other before looking round at him.

"Hello. Can we help you?" asked Jemma, sensing that Cat didn't want to become involved in a conversation with him. She was in any case nearest to him, whilst Cat was standing on the other side of the trestle table.

"I wanted to talk to Cat." Simon stood just inside the flap, his face flushed and his hands clenching and unclenching, apparently with nervousness.

Jemma judged that he wasn't looking particularly dangerous, but she wasn't about to leave Cat alone with him.

"Carry on. I'll just be getting on with my work."

His hands flapped agitatedly. "I want to talk to her alone."

Cat stopped trying to look busy and shook her head at Jemma, indicating that she could leave them. The younger woman dried her hands then, giving Simon a wide berth, she walked past him out of the tent. He took a few steps nearer to Cat.

"What do you want to say to me, Simon?" she asked. "I'm busy, you know. Lots to do."

"Aye, well, I – I feel a bit uncomfortable."

"I think I can identify with that. I'm as uncomfortable as hell," Cat retorted.

He shuffled up to the table and stood still, arms by his sides, an overall air of dejection hanging over him. Now he was in front of her, she remembered seeing him earlier, standing in the doorway of the stable-block, watching her as she'd left Holt Carr House. "The fact is, I feel bad about the way I treated you, Cat."

She turned her head slightly and frowned, studying him through narrowed eyes. "No. No, I don't understand that. You didn't treat me any way which requires apology."

"I must have done, to drive you away."

"We are talking about twelve years ago, aren't we?"

"Yes. I must have driven you away and I didn't mean to."

He took another step closer to her, so that he was touching the other side of the table.

"You didn't drive me away. Don't worry about it. It was me: I decided you weren't the right man for me. I must have phrased it badly, though, to cause what happened afterwards."

"I was blinded by jealousy." He suddenly reached across the table and gripped her left arm near the elbow. "You were always the girl for me— "

Cat used her right hand to try to loosen Simon's grip, which tightened in response.

"—and you're the only girl I've ever truly loved."

Cat pried at his fingers, but he casually caught her right hand in his left and pulled her towards him.

"Simon! Let go of me," she commanded.

He ignored her.

"The only girl..." he repeated.

"Simon! Let go!" Cat said, raising her voice.

"But Cat, I love you," he said.

"You have a wife and children," she retorted.

His grip was beginning to leave red marks on her flesh and she was reminded how very strong he was. But he flung her away from him in seeming disgust. The table rocked causing a collection of metatarsal bones in a plastic tray to fall to the floor.

"She's not like you," he said.

"Simon, please understand: we do not have a relationship. Not since school and – and a bit after. We have both moved on."

She came round the table, because she was concerned for the safety of the brittle bones laid out on it and she needed to get him away from them. He moved to block her.

"But didn't it all mean something?" he protested, reaching for her again.

This time she was too quick for him and avoided his grasp. "Simon, please go now. I've told you my position and I shan't be changing my mind."

His brows lowered in a frown and his mouth took on a sullen expression. She had a split-second's warning that he was going to do something and hastily backed away. He was blocking her route to the door so went the only way she could, towards the rear of the tent, where the sleeping areas were. His expression became a knowing and sly grin.

"You're only kidding, aren't you, Cat? Just finding a nice soft place to lie down with me, eh?"

Cat suddenly lost her temper. He obviously wasn't going to be convinced by rational argument.

"Simon! Go away and get out of this tent!" she cried.

He continued to approach her, blocking her every attempt to get past him, until she felt the sleeping bags blocking further retreat. His grin broadened.

Behind him, Jemma appeared inside the tent. "What's going on?" she demanded.

He turned round, startled. "Nothing to interest you—"

As he spoke, Cat took advantage of his distracted attention to slip past him, running towards Jemma. Simon turned and saw her.

"Cat! We haven't finished!" he growled

"I think you have," said Jemma. "You're in my sleeping quarters and you have no right to be there. It's time you left."

"Yes, get out!" cried Cat, beginning to shake.

Simon found himself confronted by two angry young women, between him and the exit and decided to abort his purpose. With a snarl, he pushed them out of his way and stormed out of the tent. Cat and Jemma turned to each other and simultaneously expelled the breath they had been holding.

"Are you okay, Cat?" asked Jemma, rubbing her arm where Simon had shoved it.

Cat was breathing heavily with relief. "Thanks to you!" she said. "I don't know what got into him – he never used to be like that. Wouldn't take no for an answer."

"What was he thinking?" asked Jemma, leading Cat to a comfortable pile of beanbags where the team would sit during off-duty times. "He was being stupid. Seemed to think we would be an item again if only I'd forgive him."

"He's an idiot! I'll make some tea."

"What I crave is coffee. I have some real stuff, I'll get it."

Cat climbed shakily to her feet and went in search of strong Arabica and her cafetière while Jemma boiled a kettle.

*

Simon needed a drink. He passed Kelly, grooming a foal, and slunk into the tack room, retrieving his vodka laced with Equipalazone from the fridge. He took a slug – he was finding it quite effective in relieving his headaches – and turned to watch the girl through the open door. He ran his eye over her taut figure as she bent and straightened to brush the animal's hide. He was furious with Cat for rejecting him after he'd made the effort to tell her his feelings.

If Craig had not hospitalised him, and therefore put him in the way of meeting Victoria, history would have been different. Cat would have come back to him when Craig left and they would have been happy ever after. He rubbed his hardness as he watched Kelly moving.

Was she, he wondered, another little tease? A girl who would make a lad fancy her, then dump him for someone else when someone else came along. Probably. They were all the same, women. He wondered if Kelly realised what effect she was having on him – and whether she'd mind if she did. He suspected not.

He sipped thoughtfully at the adulterated vodka, watching her. When she wasn't moving, her hands made little stroking motions, and from time to time she would glance at him from under her eyelashes. He was fairly sure she was doing everything she could to engage his interest. He tried to imagine Louise, in a couple of years' time, doing something similar but couldn't. She'd been better brought up than Kelly, he assured himself.

He knocked back another mouthful of the strong liquor and replaced the bottle in the fridge before picking up the keys to his truck. It might be early, but he was going home.

91

CHAPTER 8

Simon climbed in his truck and drove down the track to the road. At the junction, there was a car approaching, but he figured he could beat it. He let in the clutch, but the diesel engine took longer to accelerate than he'd thought and the car he was racing was much closer than he'd expected by the time he pulled in front of it. The driver sounded his horn in righteous indignation, but Simon merely swore and pressed on. The car tailgated him almost all the way to Skipton where Simon turned north.

Leaving the town's by-pass, he swept past a school, marked by lines of parked cars outside, where parents were picking up their children. He did not slow down, nor did he notice a marked police car containing two officers observing the scene.

The sudden blare of a siren just behind him drew Simon's attention to the rear-view mirror. The blue flashing beacons and the sight of the two yellow jacketed officers made his heart sink and brought his mind back to more immediate matters. He pulled over and awaited the inevitable. He watched as an officer climbed out of the nearside of the car and approached his passenger door. Simon leaned across and unlocked it. The policeman opened it and leaned in.

"Did you know you just drove past a school, sir?" he asked.

"Yes," Simon replied.

"I've stopped you because you seemed to be driving very quickly, considering there were lots of children around. I'm not convinced you'd have been able to stop if one of them had run across the road."

"Yes. Well, they didn't. Look, I'm in a hurry. I've got a headache. What's the problem?"

The policeman had noticed an empty half-bottle of whisky which had slid partly under the passenger-side seat. He sniffed, but couldn't detect a smell of the spirit in the car or on Simon's breath. He pulled the bottle out.

"This yours, sir?"

Simon barely looked. "So?"

"Have you been drinking, sir?"

"That bottle's been there a long time, empty," said Simon, but the copper noticed the evasion. "But have you been drinking something else, sir? Vodka, for instance?"

"Why do you say that?"

"It's a popular drink with drivers, sir. They think we can't smell it on their breath."

Simon made the mistake of cupping his hands over his mouth and breathing into them, to see if he could smell the vodka he'd had earlier. The police officer grinned without humour.

"How long is it since you had a drink, sir?"

Simon thought quickly, glancing at his watch. "An hour, mebbe," he said, in the belief that exaggerating the time would be somehow better.

"Would you like to step out of the car, sir and come round to the side of the road."

"Why?"

"I have reasonable grounds to believe that you have been driving a motor vehicle on a road with alcohol in your body. I require you to provide a specimen of breath for analysis."

Simon shut his eyes for a moment, then slowly got out of the car. A few minutes later, he was staring at a red LED on the breath-test machine and hearing that he was being arrested on suspicion of driving under the influence. He was taken to the police station, where he was tested again on a much larger and more accurate machine. After a pause of a few seconds, a small strip of paper like a till roll emerged from a slot.

The sergeant operating it tore it off and read what was printed on it.

"Thirty micrograms, sir. Just below the limit."

Simon allowed himself to breathe again.

A warning about drinking and driving later, he found himself outside the police station. They had been very apologetic about being unable to ferry him back in a police car and had given him directions to a taxi stand. Inwardly furious and unable to afford a taxi, he set off to walk. He reached his car long after all the school-children had gone home and the street lights had come on, and drove home sober. His headache was getting worse.

By the time he reached the house, his mood was foul. His head was aching badly, thumping away just behind his temples. Mark and Louise were in the living room, watching a boy band on the television. The overloud drumbeat and twanging lead guitar seemed to slice through Simon's skull. He put his hands to his ears in a vain attempt to shut out the sound and screamed at the children to turn off the noise. Victoria came out of the kitchen.

"What's the matter? What's going on?"

Simon was rubbing his head with both hands, his face screwed up as if trying to shut out the world. His lips were drawn back and teeth bared.

"It's the noise. I can't stand the noise. My head...!"

"Let's go into another room," she said, "there's no need to shout at the children."

He locked both hands together and pulled them down on top of his head, at the same time moving it from side to side. He slid his hands down into the nape of his neck and brought the elbows up, tight in against his cheeks. The muscles in his neck stood out as he put them under tension.

Victoria watched him. "Simon, I think you should go and see the doctor again. I'm sure these headaches are getting worse."

He uttered an incoherent cry of pain and rage and turned to leave the room. He tripped over Mark's sports kit, abandoned on the floor when he came in from school, lost his balance and struck his head against a small table by the door. Victoria went to him. A trickle of blood seeped out from under his hair, but before she could say anything, he had pushed her away from him and lurched out of the room, up the stairs. In the bedroom he lay on top of the quilt. He grabbed it and squeezed, but it did not alleviate the pain. In desperation, knowing somewhere deep down that it was bad for him and made him violent, he reached for the bottle of vodka he kept in the cabinet. Anything, he felt, was preferable to this throbbing, persistent pain. He drank a quarter of the bottle and as it took effect, he at last experienced some relief. All he wanted was to be left alone until the headache and the vodka both wore off.

Victoria came into the bedroom and found him sprawled across the quilt.

He looked round, bottle in hand. "What do you want?"

"Simon, we have to talk," she said gently. He put the neck of the bottle to his lips and swallowed a deep draught. "What about?"

"You know what about: losing your temper – and the vodka doesn't help."

He got off the bed at the far side and walked round it towards her. She saw the expression on his face and was suddenly afraid.

"Simon, sit down!" she said, holding her hands out in front of her, to ward him off. His brows came together and he glared at her. He brushed her hands aside with the bottle. "There's nowt to talk about. You know I get these headaches and nowt touches 'em. They drive me mad and the only relief I get is when I drink myself to sleep."

"I know that, Simon," she said.

"Well then! Shurrup! I've heard enough."

"What I'm concerned about is the effect losing your temper is having on the children. They're frightened of you."

"Well, you'd better talk to them, then!"

"You need to talk to them, to reassure them – and not when you're drunk," she said.

He stared at her for a moment. He didn't want to be drunk. Didn't the stupid woman realise the only reason he drank so much was to kill the pain? What did it take to get this across to her? Words were not enough. He drew back his right arm and smacked her hard across the cheek. Victoria's head snapped to one side and he followed up with a punch on her left shoulder.

"Simon!" she screamed, "Stop it!" She put a hand protectively over her ribs.

He seemed barely to be focussing on her now and he took another swig of vodka before hitting her again on the face, splitting a lip. She tried to defend herself, putting her arms up to cover her face and backing away across the landing, but he swung the heavy vodka bottle against them. She screamed in agony and stepped back further. He came after her with yet another punch to her chest and this time she lost her footing at the top of the stairs.

She tried to save herself as she fell, but her head made contact with the treads and she tumbled down to where Louise and Mark, unable to contain their fearful curiosity, were standing in the hallway. As she lay still, the sudden silence was broken by a hammering at the door.

"Hello! What's happening in there? Open the door!" a man yelled through the letterbox.

Louise turned and opened it. Simon, at the top of the stairs waving the vodka bottle and staring at his wife, suddenly looked at the children. He opened his mouth to tell them not to touch the door, but the words would not come out and within seconds, their next-door neighbour, Darren Box, was staring at the scene before them.

"For God's sake!" he exclaimed, striding to Victoria's body. Blood was seeping out from under her head. He checked her throat for a pulse, looked up to see Simon staring down at him.

"The police have been called," said Box. "I think we need the ambulance as well."

At last Simon spoke. "You leave her alone. Clear off out of here, we're all right. Just mind your own business."

Box stared at him, as he unhooked a mobile phone from his belt. "You call this "all right'? Your wife unconscious, in a pool of blood, obviously beaten up as well. You think that's "all right'? Well, all you have to do is convince the police and you can get on with your private life."

Simon's brows came together again and he started down the stairs as Box dialled .

"Ambulance, please," he said, as the call was answered. As Simon stepped over his wife and advanced towards him, Box stood up. He was no weakling. Caring for a flock of sheep as he did, involving much hard labour, he was as strong and heavy as Simon, and not intimidated.

"Take one more step towards me," he said angrily, "and I'll put you down."

It was a long time since anyone had threatened Simon so convincingly and he stopped. It was not many minutes later that a siren broke the stillness outside and a police car drew up outside. Meanwhile, Box hastily gave directions over the phone to the ambulance service and explained the nature of the emergency, then stood aside as two officers entered the hallway. The first, a woman, glanced quickly at the men and the children who had been silent during the events of the last few minutes. Then, as she crouched beside Victoria, she turned to Box. "Who are you?"

"I'm Darren Box. I live next door and it was my wife who called you. That's Victoria, and that's Simon Stalland, her husband," he explained, pointing.

"Can you take the children into the living room, sir. I need to talk to Mr Stalland, so I'd be glad if you would look after the children for a little while, please," she said.

Simon was blinking slowly, trying to make sense of what was going on. He could not remember how Victoria had fallen. The pain had mostly gone away and he was in a curious state of detachment. She seemed somehow to have no connection with him. He was beginning to see himself as an innocent bystander, caught up in a nightmare of violence.

As Box took Louise and Mark into the living room, a second police officer entered the hallway, a tall and broad-shouldered man, who had to duck as he stepped inside.

"She's alive," the first officer reported. "I think there's an ambulance on its way. Can you check? And then perhaps you'd like to talk to Mr Stalland here – " she indicated Simon "– about what happened."

"Right," said her colleague and got on the radio. The ambulance confirmed, he turned to Simon. "Shall we go through into the kitchen, sir," he said, taking Simon's arm in a light grip. "And perhaps we should put the bottle down somewhere."

Simon started to move, then suddenly pulled away. "No! Get out of my house. I don't want you here."

"Now then, sir, we've got to ask a few questions." The officer grabbed his arm, more firmly this time, but Simon again pulled away. Within a second, he found he was in an armlock from which he couldn't escape.

"Into the kitchen, sir," said the officer.

He applied a little judicious pressure, which hurt Simon's shoulder but propelled him in the required direction. In the kitchen, the policeman released the armlock and took the bottle out of Simon's grasp. Simon was staring at it as if he hadn't seen it before. They sat at right-angles to each other at the corner of the table. While the officer asked him some routine questions, Simon began to worry about Victoria. She seemed to be injured. Where were their children, he suddenly thought, the memory of where he had last seen them only fleeting in his mind. Something odd had happened to his hearing.

The voice of the man sitting beside him had faded into the distance and he was having trouble understanding the words. Worse, when he tried to tell the man this, either he wasn't shouting loudly enough, or the bloke was deaf, because he didn't seem to understand the answers.

Outside, the beat of the air ambulance's rotors ricocheted off the surrounding hills and brought children and their parents out of all the houses in the little hamlet. It settled just over the road from the Stalland's house and a paramedic and doctor disembarked. The doorway into the kitchen from the hall opened and the female police officer who'd been fussing over Victoria came in with Darren Box at her side. The large officer beside Simon asked her about the children.

"Mrs Box came round and has taken them back next door."

Simon was trying to remember why Victoria had been laying on the floor. The pain in his head was threatening to make a comeback and he figured he needed another couple of belts of vodka. He eyed the bottle, which the large constable sitting near him had put on the draining board.

The woman started speaking. "I'm PC Speight. I don't know if my colleague has introduced himself, but he's PC Ackroyd. We're from Skipton Police Station."

Simon gazed at her uncomprehendingly. He was nearly better, just needed another mouthful or two of vodka. He made to stand up, but in a flash, the deceptively slothful-looking PC Ackroyd had his wrist and elbow in painful contraposition, forcing him to remain seated.

Speight turned to Darren Box. "How did you come to be involved, Mr Box?"

"My wife and I have known for some time that things have not been running smoothly here. A couple of days ago, she came round and found Victoria upset and hurt." He stared at Simon. "Apparently he broke some of her ribs, and then, just as they were healing, broke them again. There might be more, but I don't know."

Speight turned to Simon. "Is that right, Mr Stalland? Did you break your wife's ribs?"

Simon shook his head and laughed incredulously. "Me? Hurt Victoria? No."

Speight pursed her lips. "Well, I'll have to talk to Mrs Box and find out why she's saying such things." She turned back to Darren. "What caused you to come round tonight?"

Before he could reply, Simon interrupted, his expression contrite. "Aye, well, maybe I did, sort of, 'it 'er. It were an accident."

Speight raised her hand at Darren to have him wait, and gave her attention to Simon. "And what about tonight?"

"We... 'ad an argument."

"Over what?"

He swallowed and stared at the table-top. "I don't rightly remember. Y'see I've got an 'eadache. I just wanted to sleep, and she kept shouting at me."

Speight glanced briefly at Ackroyd, who was failing to disguise his disgust, before pressing on. "What was she shouting about?"

Simon crossed his arms and rocked against them. "I don't know. Somethin' to do wi' t' kids."

"Have you hurt either of your children?"

He looked up at her. "Hurt the kids? No! No! I never would!"

She studied his face for a moment and seemed satisfied he was telling the truth.

"How did your wife end up at the foot of the stairs, unconscious, with bruises and head injuries?"

Simon stared at her. Bruises? Head injury? How? "W-what's happened?"

"No, sir. The way we do it, I ask the questions and you tell me the truth. How did she get to the bottom of the stairs? I take it she started at the top – she wasn't injured going up, so it was the nature of her descent?"

Simon had a recollection of Victoria on the landing, and he could remember the feeling as he'd hit her. He stared at his right hand, holding it in front of him as if it was unfamiliar.

"Sir?"

He looked up at her and tried to focus. "She must have fallen," he said vaguely.

"What would make her do that, Mr Stalland?"

Simon shook his head. He was beginning to recall that he had shoved her, but the recollection swam in and out of his mind, and he couldn't be sure.

"I don't know," he said.

"Well, let's see: was she drunk? Oh, no. You're the one who's drunk. So, would she have thrown herself down the stairs?"

He shook his head again. He wished she'd go away and stop asking him these questions. "No."

"So, was there anybody up there with her who might have pushed her downstairs?" She peered into his eyes from under her finely-drawn brows.

"No. Only me," he said.

"Then a reasonable person might be forced to conclude that you did the shoving, eh, Mr Stalland?"

Simon leaned on his hands, feeling tears beginning to spill down his cheeks. He nodded. "Yes," he whispered.

Speight leaned towards him. "Did you cause the bruises on her body as well, Mr Stalland?" she asked.

Simon was beginning to sob quietly. He nodded again. "I must 'ave. I did," he said.

Speight made a subtle indication with her head to warn Ackroyd to be ready. "Mr Stalland: I'm arresting you on suspicion of assault causing grievous bodily harm. You do not have to say anything, but it may harm your defence if you fail to mention when questioned anything you later rely on in court. Anything you do say may be taken down and used in evidence. Do you understand?"

Simon stared at her. Suddenly, along with a return of pain to his forehead, came the clear recollection of punching Victoria, shoving her, and watching her fall down the stairs. He gasped and very slowly nodded his head. He shut his eyes and squeezed them tightly until the tears ran down his cheeks. Neither constable was impressed by the appearance of remorse.

"Go with PC Ackroyd, then, Mr Stalland."

"I'm going to have to put handcuffs on you for the journey, sir," said the burly constable.

Simon said nothing, merely holding out his arms, the wrists touching.

With a smart double click, the cuffs were applied and locked in place. He was led out of the kitchen, through the hall. Victoria had been taken by the ambulance people but as they went outside, he could see her, strapped onto a stretcher, being loaded into the helicopter. Speight turned to Darren Box.

"Sorry to have to stop you earlier, Mr Box. Now, what brought you round here tonight?"

"We heard what must have been Victoria falling down the stairs. There had been raised voices before that, and after the other night, when Jo found Victoria extremely distressed, we didn't want to take any chances. It's as well we didn't wait."

Speight smiled. "That's a fact. Can you drop into the police station in Skipton tomorrow and give us a statement?"

"It'll be my pleasure."

"What shall I do about the children? Do I need to get social services in tonight?" asked Speight.

He shook his head. "No. We'll look after them. They play with our kids, and go to the same schools. It's no problem. They'll be happy with us. We're registered foster-parents anyway. They've known us all their lives."

Speight nodded, satisfied. "Right. Thank you – and thanks to Mrs Box as well. We'll get off and let Mr Stalland enjoy a night in the police cells at Skipton. I feel sure he'll have to get used to them."

She left him to lock up and went to the car just as the helicopter lifted off. Simon, in the back and still handcuffed, was aware of the small crowd of onlookers and felt ashamed. He watched as the helicopter clattered into the distance, leaving behind the scent of burnt kerosene in the still, sharp air. He saw Jo Box watching from her doorway, her disgust plain to see. The car began to move. He sat quietly while Speight drove the few miles to Skipton. Despite still being in what passed for rush hour in the little market town, there was not much traffic about and very soon they were in the car park at the back of the police station.

This was not the welcoming façade the police authority had worked hard to create at the front of the building on the street, but the business end, where police officers came and went and brought their prisoners. A door fitted with a security lock opened to admit them to the custody area, where Simon joined a queue of other people waiting to be processed by a harassed-looking sergeant standing behind a raised desk at the far end of the room.

The waiting area was long, stretching before him. Along the left side, leading up to the sergeant's desk, was a wide corridor, whilst opening on to it, on the right, was a series of cages, lined on three sides with metal benches, where prisoners were seated until it was their turn to see the Custody Sergeant.

Simon was led into one of the cages by PC Ackroyd, while Speight went up to the sergeant to begin the paperwork. Ackroyd removed the handcuffs and Simon rubbed his wrists. He found himself sitting opposite a man wearing an anorak smeared with vomit and reeking of drink, and a girl who looked barely sixteen, with a white face and dead-looking eyes outlined in black. She was bare-legged and wore a short skirt and a top which

103

looked more like an item of lingerie than outerwear and concealed very little. She gazed at him insolently and keeping her eyes on his, very slowly and deliberately re-crossed her legs. His glance, attracted by the movement, became riveted on the thong which became visible in the process and barely covered her. Next to him, PC Ackroyd leaned forward.

"You'll be catching your death of cold, Christine, if you don't put a few more clothes on."

"Better for business though as I am," she replied, her gaze travelling back to Simon. "He's interested – aren't you, mate?" she asked Simon.

He twisted away from her, not daring to answer, for the truth was that she had caused a stir in his loins. She offered something he craved – uncomplicated sex. He couldn't remember how long it had been since he had made love to his wife and somehow such a thing seemed to have so many conditions attached, things which got in the way of simple and pure gratification.

He looked back at her and saw that she was smiling sardonically at him. Maybe, when he got out of this place... Behind the elevated desk at the end of the room the sergeant called her name and she jumped to her feet right in front of Simon. The movement caused her skirt to lift momentarily and caused him to stare at her white thighs. He detected the sour smell of her sex. With a chuckle, she turned away from him and went up to the desk. Simon stared after her.

The drunk bestirred himself – Christine wasn't the only one to have noticed Simon's interest. "I shouldn't have anything to do with her, mate," said the drunk, leaning so close Simon could smell the alcohol on his breath, "She's got spots on her arse and 'as had more pricks than a second-hand dartboard."

Simon glanced at the drunk but didn't say anything. Ackroyd watched him: his smile was feral.

It took three hours to process him, but eventually Simon was taken into a small soundproof room to be interviewed formally by Speight and Ackroyd. He declined the offer of a solicitor. Ackroyd set up the Neal interview recorder with a fresh disc, and started it.

Simon watched him, but addressed Speight. "Where's my wife? What's happened to her?"

"She was taken to Leeds General Infirmary. We'll be talking about what happened to her in a few minutes," she said, "but when she left the house I can tell you she had broken bones and a mass of bruising."

He buried his head in his hands. "Oh, God!"

"Come on, let's get this interview started." It was important to get his comments and reactions on the disc as anything not recorded could more easily be challenged in court.

When the formalities had been gone through, she took him through every step and every detail, asking for his explanation of why things had happened, questions many of which he was unable to answer.

Simon's head had cleared but his memory of events was still incomplete. One thing which was becoming obvious to him was that it seemed he had put Victoria in hospital. After the interview, he was taken back to the Custody Sergeant and charged. More bits of paper were created.

"I think bail should be refused, Sarge," said Speight.

"Oh? Why?"

She explained her concern that if Simon were released, there would be nothing to stop him going back home, getting drunk, losing his temper again, this time with only the children to take it out on. The sergeant considered this, then agreed.

"Protection of witnesses," he muttered as he ticked a box on the bail record. He looked up at Simon. "You'll stay here tonight and appear in court tomorrow."

Simon was led along another corridor and put in a cell containing a small table and chair, both fixed firmly to the floor, a narrow bunk and a metal toilet. A harsh light shone from a flush ceiling fitting, illuminating every corner. The walls were covered in a dappled paint pattern, supposed to make graffiti impossible, but determined former occupants had managed to leave evidence of their presence anyway.

In one corner, above the bunk and in a hard-to-reach spot, there was a suspicious streak of something brown down the corner of the walls. Simon didn't want to get close enough to find out what it was. The cell door clanged shut behind him and he was left alone.

He'd never realised how much noise there was in the cell block of a central police station. Drunks were singing raucously and a couple of young women were having an argument at the top of their voices about who had been trespassing on who's pitch. In another cell, a man appeared to be praying, his voice rising and falling, but the hope of redemption never expelling the note of desperation in his cadences.

One of the older female prisoners kept screaming for attention, demanding to be allowed to sleep somewhere quiet. Simon settled down expecting a long wakeful night, his headache now a pulse in the background.

In the event, exhaustion caught up with him and he drifted off, to be woken at six o'clock the following morning at the beginning of the long processes of ablutions, breakfast and preparation for   court.

CHAPTER 9

Craig had been dreaming of happy childhood days when he and his parents had gone on their annual trip to Saltburn or Filey. As he reached towards consciousness, the knowledge that they were no longer around, there would be no more family Christmases, no more of that love which only parents can give, crept back in his mind.

He opened one eye and found he was being studied by Jemma, who smiled at him. She at least made the loneliness bearable, if only temporarily. He reached for her and held her tightly as she nestled in his arms. Jemma's hands started to work their mischief on him, pulling and teasing, until he could pretend to ignore it no longer. While he used his tongue and fingers on her, she reached out to the bedside cabinet and found a condom, which she tore open with her teeth.

They were interrupted by a hammering on the back door. They stared at each other for a moment before Craig sighed and rolled to the edge of the bed. Jemma giggled as he struggled to get his underpants and jeans on. He glanced at her as he opened the bedroom door, watching for a moment as she stretched out luxuriously, making use of as much of the double bed as possible. Craig wondered what the fuss was about. He wrenched open the kitchen door and was surprised to find Kelly on the step, looking annoyed.

"Come in," he said, stepping back into the kitchen. "What's the matter?"

He saw her gaze take in Jemma's bag on the table and the remains of his erection, filling out his jeans. She looked up at him, the anger gone, replaced by a knowing smirk.

"Simon's not here. I thought you'd want to know." She moistened her lips with the tip of her tongue. "Hope I didn't interrupt anything," she added, glancing at the ceiling.

"Oh. Uh, thanks, Kelly. Can you and Susie manage for a while?"

"Oh, sure."

"If you need anything, just ask."

She opened the door, glancing at his crotch again. "I think we'll cope."

He watched as she walked across the yard to the stables, suddenly aware that Jemma was standing at his shoulder.

"Jailbait," she said.

He chuckled and shut the door, turning and enfolding her in his arms again. She'd slipped a T-shirt and leggings on and he guessed she must have felt the effect her body had on him because she backed away, grinning. "I'd better finish getting dressed."

"I'll get us some breakfast," he said, "but first, I need to give Simon a ring."

By the time she returned, clutching her toilet bag, he'd discovered that neither Simon nor Victoria was answering their phone, and arranged with Simon's father to keep an eye on the stables and make sure the girls were okay. Neither man could think of an explanation for Simon's absence. Craig said he would drive over to his house, reasoning that Victoria at least should not be far away as he didn't think she had a job.

An hour later, he found himself in Jo Box's kitchen. She had emerged from her house when she heard him knocking on Simon's door, and invited him in for a cup of tea. She'd given him an edited version of recent events in the Stalland household, which confirmed for him that the problems he'd suspected existed between Simon and Victoria were real, and much worse than he could have imagined. It was clear Jo disapproved strongly of Simon, and Craig figured that if what she'd told him was true, the disapproval was fully deserved. Hitting a woman was not on, in any circumstances, in his book.

At half-past ten, he found himself standing in the precinct of the Magistrates' Court. After learning from the Ushers that Simon had been granted conditional bail by the court, he waited outside the exit from the cells until Simon was released. He was looking haggard, dark stubble shadowing his jowls, but his eyes were bright beneath his bushy brows. He raised an eyebrow in query.

"What's tha doin' here?" he asked. "Come to gloat, hast tha?"

"I came to find you when you didn't turn up for work. Your neighbour said you'd been arrested. The police said you were here. What's brought all this on?" He waved a hand at the court building behind them.

Simon scanned the area, avoiding Craig's eyes. "I don't remember," he mumbled. "That Jo Box ought to keep her neb out of other people's business."

"The Ushers said you were charged with GBH. You don't remember?"

A flash of annoyance crossed Simon's face. "I said not, di'n't I?"

"Your neighbour said you knocked Victoria down stairs. It's a big thing not to remember."

Simon suddenly moved fast, catching Craig's shirt just below his chin, and thrusting his face up until they were nearly touching, nose to nose.

"Keep thy nose out o' my business, or it'll be you they're picking up in t' 'elicopter."

Craig pushed him away. "So some of it you remember."

"Keep out o' my business," Simon repeated.

"I've come to take you home."

"Aye, well! I can't *go* home."

"Why?"

"Because I'm out on bail, and I'm banned from talking to t' wife or kids. 'mustn't contact them directly or indirectly', t'beak said."

They walked in silence for a while. Craig felt he had some responsibility towards Simon and was wondering whether he'd have to offer to accommodate him at Holt Carr. "Where are you going to live?"

"I gev 'em me dad's address. Who's looking after the 'orses?"

"He is, with Kelly and Susie."

"Let's go then, and I can send my dad home." They climbed into Craig's Land-Rover and set off for Holt Carr.

Simon's father was with Kelly and Susie, enjoying mugs of tea after the early chores. He scowled at Simon.

"I never thought to see a son of mine in court," he said. "We're not a family as beats our wives. Or we weren't."

Simon hung his head. "Tha knaws, then?"

William Stalland's displeasure was palpable. He clenched his jaw.

"Aye. They rang to ask if I'd house thee when they were thinking of granting you bail. I suppose if I'd said no, tha'd be in Armley or Durham by now." He licked his lips. "Mebbe I should've. Teach thee a lesson I never thought you'd need. Your mother'll be turnin' in her grave, such shame as tha's brought on this family."

He took a step towards the door. "Anyway, tha'd better come home."

"When I'm finished here."

William Stalland turned abruptly and left. Simon watched his retreating back.

Craig turned to the girls who had been listening in silence to Simon and his father. "You both okay?" he asked. They nodded, both staring at Simon with curiosity.

"Right. I'll go." He turned to Simon. "I'll see what I can find out about Victoria. I expect you'd like to know."

Simon nodded. "Aye. Thanks – and thanks for coming to court. I – I'm sorry about them things as I said."

*

110

With Craig gone, Simon turned to the girls. "Any more tea in the pot?"

"I'll get you some," said Kelly, moving past Susie and reaching up to the cupboard for a mug. Simon took the opportunity to appreciate the way her breasts thrust against her polo shirt and felt a sudden throb of lust. He found Kelly attractive in a basic, earthy, visceral sort of way. The young prostitute in the Custody Office, Christine, had made him realise that he was attracted to teenagers, and Kelly put out all the right signals which told him she might well be available if he chose.

He sat in the old armchair and sneaked a few covert glances at her. If anything, she looked curvier than usual. Maybe, he thought, she was wearing one of those very uplifting bras. Or maybe she was just built like that. Her jodhpurs clung to her, too, concealing nothing of her shape. Simon figured Kelly for about the same age as Christine. She passed him the mug of tea. She was clearly still thinking about what he'd done. The look in her eyes was hard but she was civil enough that he figured she wasn't ready yet to set him aside. As her gaze raked down from his face, he made no effort to conceal the evidence of his arousal, and watched as her eyes fixed on it. The hard look was replaced by a glimmer of amusement.

Susie interrupted the little scene. "Can we take a couple of the horses out for a hack?"

Simon dragged his gaze away from the voluptuous Kelly. "If your jobs are up to date."

"They are," she said.

He watched them go. The girls saddled up the horses and led them out into the yard. Simon stood in the stables doorway and watched as they tightened the girths. Kelly looked over as she posed, one foot in the stirrup, the other still on the ground.

"Give me a leg up, Simon," she said.

He grinned at her. There was something between them, he felt sure: he was attracted to her, and she knew it. Best of all, she didn't mind. She removed her foot from the stirrup as he leant forward to cup it and made sure his head brushed the side of her leg as he leaned forward. In return, he used one hand to steady her, allowing it to slip up the inside of her thigh before she swung her leg over the saddle. She grinned down at him, and he smiled back. Yes, he thought, definitely something between them.

He watched the two girls walk their horses out of the yard and returned to the tack room. Left alone with his thoughts, he eyed the fridge, but denied himself.

*

At the Dig, Jemma was wrapping finds in protective packaging ready for them to be taken to the county museum. More burials had been found and the human remains from them were stacking up in boxes awaiting her attention. Dave Pountney pulled aside the flap of the marquee and came in, grinning.

Jemma looked at him askance. "What have you been up to, Dave? 'Cat' and 'cream' are two words which come to mind." She grinned. "That's feline-type cat."

Cat smiled and looked at Dave, who was obviously bursting with news. "Prepare for fame and fortune, ladies," he said.

"Oh yeah?"

"Yeah!" He sighed dramatically. "After today, I just know you two are going to be overwhelmed with offers."

"Offers, Dave?" asked Cat with a hint of scepticism in her voice.

"Yes, no doubt of both a professional and personal nature."

Jemma and Cat exchanged glances.

"Professional *and* personal? What have you been up to?"

For a moment, he looked shocked, then his face broke into a smile again. "You're going to be on TV," he said conspiratorially.

112

"Huh?"

"*Calendar,* the local TV news, have heard about the wonderful things we're unearthing and they're sending a camera crew along to film us."

The women exchanged glances again.

Cat rolled her eyes. "Fame at last. I knew it would come to me sooner or later, even if it's only on local television. I just wish it could have been later."

Dave laughed while picking up his trowel and an old paintbrush he used for dusting away grains of soil. "I'll see you later." He left them alone.

Jemma giggled. "I wonder who they'll send to interview us? Hope it's that Jason Toller. He's such a dish."

"I thought you were spoken for?" Cat said, and immediately worried that she sounded waspish to her own ears.

Jemma glanced at her. "For now." Her gaze turned inward and she grinned. "But if Jason Toller were to come sniffing around, I would have to work hard at controlling my tart gene."

Cat laughed. "I can remember being your age. Fun isn't it?"

"I'm glad you see it as such."

Outside the tent, they heard a car engine labouring up the track. Believing it to be Mike and Diarmuid returning, they got on with their work and consequently Cat was startled when the flap covering the entrance to the marquee was pulled aside and Alan Crossley entered.

"Alan!" she exclaimed, surprised to see him.

"None other," he said. He glanced around. "You seem a bit thin on the ground. I thought there were more of you?"

Dave Pountney re-entered the marquee and came to a halt at the sight of their visitor.

Cat said, "Two of the guys have gone to York to drop off some finds at the museum. But our Site Director's right behind you."

Alan turned and Cat introduced them.

"I was busy," said Dave. "Want to have a look?"

113

He took Alan outside. Jemma turned her mouth down. "You don't suppose he's here in place of Jason, do you?"

Cat shrugged. "I don't know for certain, but I do know he's got a job on that Channel 4 archæology programme."

Jemma cocked her head to one side. "How do you know that?"

Cat felt her colour rise. "We – we were living together until I came here... on the day I turned down his proposal of marriage.

Jemma bit her lip. "He asked you – ? Sorry, I didn't mean to sound astonished."

"Thank you," said Cat. "I shall just assume you aren't shocked that anyone could think of marrying me. I'm not that ancient." A smile hesitated on her lips. "If I bothered to look for it, I expect *I* still have a tart gene in working order. Just forgot where I left it."

Jemma grinned. "I could – and probably should – let you have mine, on a kind of timeshare basis."

"Oh, thanks, but I expect you need it more than I should. At my time of life, you know." Both of them chuckled.

Jemma finished what she'd been doing and picked up her trowel and brush. "I'd better go and do some work. Leave you to it," she said, and left the tent.

Cat worked on, slowly and methodically, wondering whether Alan was in fact going to present the item for *Calendar*. A few minutes later, he reappeared in the marquee and she was able to ask him.

"Yes. You can't keep a good telly-presenter down, apparently. Will you mind?"

She shook her head. "No. Why should I? Find anything interesting for the TV cameras on the other job?" she asked.

"A chariot burial is all," he said.

Cat stopped what she was doing, her eyes opening wide in disbelief. "You're joking?"

114

He shook his head, bursting with news. "No. It's only the second one to be found in North Yorkshire," he said.

"Oh, how wonderful! I saw the other one, up near Catterick. Was this as well-preserved?"

"We think so. It was so complicated, they couldn't finish it within their schedule, but the county have put a scratch team in to continue uncovering it. We've already had some really magnificent finds: bronze sword-hilts set with precious stones, some pottery almost undamaged, the wheel hubs. Personal items like pins. We hadn't got under the chariot, so we haven't confirmed there's a burial, but it would be mighty strange if there weren't, given all that we *have* found. What's been happening here?"

"Nothing as exciting. We have a small Viking burial ground up here, with fairly good bone preservation. Look."

Cat led him to a box containing a skull which bore few signs of deterioration apart from a jagged hole in its occiput.

"This one died from a head wound." She pointed to the damaged part at the back of the cranium. "See the sharp edges. I'd say it was incurred at the time of death or within a short time before. There's no sign of healing." She led him to another box. This, too, contained a skull, but it was different. "You see how the cranial vault on this one is enlarged and the face elongated?"

Alan nodded. "Let me guess: hydrocephalus?"

"Yes. It wasn't uncommon."

He was looking around the marquee. "Are you actually sleeping in this tent?"

"Yes. Come and look: our sleeping quarters are at the back." She led the way to the screened-off sleeping quarters and held the sheeting aside so he could see.

"Nearly all the comforts of home," she said.

"Think I prefer hotels. It's amazing how easily one can slide from poverty-struck academic to well-paid telly-person, able to afford all the comforts of home." He slipped an arm round her waist. "Except one. I don't suppose you'll change your mind now I'm almost rich and famous?"

She turned within his grasp. "If you think your financial standing was ever a factor in my declining your proposal, then you didn't know me as well as I thought you did."

His arm fell to his side. "You and Jemma sleep here?"

"When she's here. We get on well together."

"'When she's here'? Are there times when she isn't?" he asked.

Cat turned away from him. "She's formed an attachment for our landowner," she said.

Alan's eyebrows arched. "Is that a problem?" he asked. "Who is the landowner?"

"His name is Craig Jordon. I knew him... once."

"Oh-ho! In the biblical sense, or were you just good friends?"

She glanced at his face. "In the sense of friends."

He studied her expression. She turned away, cowed by his gaze.

"I think I should meet him."

"Why?"

"We're going to be filming on his land. I think he has a right to know."

She nodded. Of course. She was being foolish. Anyway, there was no reason to keep them apart.

"I'll come and introduce you," she said.

He nodded.

Ten minutes later, in the kitchen at Holt Carr, Alan explained his business, while Cat debated whether she should return to the site and leave the men to talk. When Alan went outside to make a phone call, Craig lifted a whisky bottle out of a large old dresser.

"Get you a drink?" he asked.

"Not for me, thanks," she said, sitting at the table. He found a glass and splashed some of the golden spirit into it.

"Don't often drink before the sun's over the yard-arm, but I occasionally find myself thinking about my parents. I missed the funeral, you know. They took so long to find me in Canada."

She watched him drain the glass and refill it. "I'm really sorry about what happened to them," she said.

Craig waved away her concern. "No reason for you to remember." He drained the glass again and poured another. It looked as if Craig was in the mood to get drunk. She didn't like it, but she could understand it, though she hoped it wasn't a regular pastime.

Alan returned to the warmth, looking pleased with himself. "That's sorted out then. The crew will be here tomorrow. Hope that will be okay with both of you." He smiled. "Fancy dining out tonight? On the television company." Cat shook her head. "I'm not really kitted out for civilised eating."

"Cat, however you're dressed, you'll scintillate," Alan replied.

"Or even later," she said, remembering the old joke.

He laughed, turning to Craig. "I build it up, and she comes back with the punch-line."

Craig had watched this exchange and at its finish, drained his glass once again. "You know each other." It was not a question.

"Knew," said Cat. "We're no longer together."

He turned slowly back to Alan. "I'll decline your offer of food, if you don't mind."

Alan shrugged. "Right. Well, I'll be off. See you tomorrow."

"Wait! I'm coming back to the site," Cat said, following him to the door. "See you later," she said to Craig.

"Bye, Cat. Bye, Alan," Craig said, settling into one of the kitchen armchairs as the door closed behind his visitors. He drained his glass again and refilled it. The level in the bottle was going down fast.

CHAPTER 10

Kelly and Susie returned from their ride, rosy-cheeked and smiling. Simon watched them enter the yard through the open door of the tack room and strolled out to meet them. Somewhere in his mind was the question of how far Kelly was prepared to let him go. Leaving Susie to dismount unaided, he stood beside Kelly's horse, and when she swung her leg over its back, caught her in his arms and let her slide down him to the ground. She grinned even more broadly, knowing perfectly well what he was doing and enjoying it.

Letting her go, he said, "I was just waiting for thee to get back before checking the hay and water. It won't take long, then I can run thee home in the pickup if you like."

After they had completed all the jobs, Simon loaded the girls' bikes into the back of the pickup before they all climbed aboard and he set off down the valley. Kelly had taken the centre seat, leaving Susie to sit nearest the door. Simon dropped her off first, and as they drove away from her house, turned to Kelly.

"Where do you fancy going now, Kelly?" he asked.

"Aren't you going to take me home?" she asked innocently.

"Well, yes, but I thought we might go along the valley a bit and do a bit of bird watching."

Kelly understood the code and grinned. "What sort of birds?"

"I dunno. Do you reckon there's any tits up here?"

Kelly chortled. "I wouldn't be surprised."

"They might take a bit of finding," he said.

"Not that much, I reckon," she said, a blush tinting her cheeks. He backed the pickup through a gateway into a field at the edge of a wood. There was a farm track which skirted the trees and he didn't have to go far along it before they were hidden from the road. Kelly flipped open the glove compartment.

"What are you looking for, Kel?" Simon asked.

"Binoculars," she replied, "ain't they what you use for bird watching?"

He stretched an arm along the back of her seat. "Depends how big the bird is, and how close she's sitting."

She turned her head to stare at him. He brought his arm down and round her shoulders, pulling her gently towards him. She focussed on his lips.

"Are you sure we should, Simon?"

"Why not! I'm sure you've been in this situation before, Kel, I know I have."

"Got a thing for young girls, have you, Simon?"

"Got a thing for you, Kelly. And as Victoria's left me and taken the kids, I reckon as I'm a free agent."

She grinned again, but didn't reply. This time when he pressed his lips on hers, she didn't object. His hand insinuated itself underneath her sweater and began exploring her body. His fingers slipped under her bra and he moved them around her breasts, flicking the nipples and feeling them harden. He felt a pleasant tension in his groin and using his other hand, took hers and placed it on it.

*

She began to wonder about the wisdom of what she was doing. It was very exciting: already, his questing fingers were making her insides twist and clench, and she wriggled in her seat, pressing her thighs together. She knew that if she didn't stop Simon now, they would probably have sex. That'd be something to tell the other girls at school, and having a lover twenty years older than her would be quite a coup.

For a moment she wondered about her ability to control Simon, but figured he'd be no problem.

119

There had been that girl on EastEnders whose philosophy had been 'treat 'em mean to keep 'em keen', which seemed to work effectively. Judging by what lay beneath her hand, he was plenty keen enough. Perhaps, though, she thought, not this time. She pulled away from him and brushed his hand out from under her jumper.

"Simon, you've got to stop now," she said.

"Why?"

"Because I say so. Maybe some other time, but not now."

She hoped that a deferment of her deflowering would make him even keener. Anyway, she didn't want her first time to be across the seat of a pickup truck: she had her standards.

"Will you take me home now, please," she said, adjusting the fit of her bra and pulling her sweater down. She could see he was not happy, but to her secret delight, he did as she asked, dropping her and her bicycle off outside her home, before driving back to his father's house.

*

Simon dozed off after dinner, and his father had left him sleeping in an easy chair when he'd gone to bed. Suddenly, there was a loud knock at the front door and he sprang up, brushing the sleep from his eyes. He glanced at the clock on the wall and wondered who could be calling so late: it was after midnight. He got to his feet and went into the hallway, pulling open the front door. PC Ackroyd stood outside, looking stern.

"What do you want?" asked Simon.

"Just checking you're complying with the conditions of your bail, Mr Stalland." He glanced past Simon, who turned and saw his father on the stairs. "Sorry to disturb you, sir. You'd be Mr Stalland Senior, I guess?"

"Aye." He looked at his son. "Don't forget to lock t' door when you've done. You don't know who's wandering about out there these days," he added with a pointed glance at Ackroyd.

"That's very good advice, sir," said the policeman, unfazed. "We should be spending more of our time chasing the villains instead of harassing people who've yet to be found guilty in a court of law."

William Stalland nodded and headed back upstairs.

"I blame the politicians, myself," Ackroyd muttered in his direction. He focussed on Simon. "Right. Well, I'll be off. See you later, maybe."

"Are you going to do this a lot? Disturb innocent folks' sleep?" asked Simon.

A glimmer of a smile crossed Ackroyd's lips. "I have to make sure you're meeting the conditions of your bail, Mr Stalland." He turned away.

"Are you coming back tonight?"

Ackroyd turned back. "Look at it from my point of view, Mr Stalland. I'd be a right bloody idiot if I told you that."

He turned again and walked to his car. Simon stared at him as he considered the implications. He could be woken in the middle of the night. Judging from Ackroyd's expression, he almost certainly would be.

Damn the man, thought Simon as he closed the door. He dragged himself upstairs where he sat on the edge of his old bed, still feeling very sorry for himself. After a few minutes of that, he got up, stripped off and climbed into the shower. Afterwards, he shaved away two days' growth of stubble and, feeling better than he had, slipped under the large quilt. It occurred to him that he didn't know where his family was and needed to make some enquiries. Despite knowing there was nothing he could do at this time, it was still after three before he fell into a fitful sleep.

*

At Holt Carr early next morning, Craig woke up, still in the kitchen armchair. His mouth felt furry and his head ached. He shuffled over to the kitchen sink and filled a glass with cold water, downed it in one and got a refill which he drank more slowly. He glanced around in the gloom. Someone had turned out the lights: he guessed that Jemma might have been there to shower and switched the lights out as she left. It was cold, as the central heating hadn't started. The Aga was nevertheless warm and keeping the temperature in the kitchen above that in the rest of the house. Craig decided to shower and change and made his way upstairs.

The bathroom was clean and tidy, but the scent of Jemma was still in the air and his nostrils opened as he drew it in. His eyes closed briefly with the evocative odour. He pulled himself together and stripped off, showering and shaving, before going through into his bedroom to find fresh clothes. He turned on one set of wall-lights so he could see what he was doing and was surprised to find Jemma curled up and asleep in his bed. For a moment, he contemplated slipping in beside her, but something stopped him. As he finished dressing, he became aware that she was watching him. "Morning."

"Well, the sleeper awakes! Enjoy your nightcap, Craig?"

He smiled. "At least when I have too much to drink I only fall asleep. Could be worse."

"That's true – but you're no good to me when you're asleep."

"Am I good for you when I'm awake?" he asked, teasing.

She grinned. "What do you think?"

"I think you're drop-dead gorgeous, most of the time."

She smiled up at the ceiling. "One day I'll get old and wrinkly." He sat on the bed to pull a pair of socks on. "We all get to that stage – and I'll be there before you are."

"Do you think we should be thinking that far ahead?" she asked.

"I'm not: it was you who raised the 'old and wrinkly' thing. I thought you and I were strictly short-term."

She nodded. "We can be shorter, if you met another woman who was, you know, like, The One. The long-term One."

He stretched out an arm onto an unoccupied part of the bed and leaned towards her, inclining his head in query.

"Did you want out of our sleeping arrangements?" he asked.

"Do you?"

"No," he replied, though as soon as he spoke he remembered Cat. But there was nothing left of their old relationship, and he now realised he might have hurt her feelings when he decided on a clean break. If he could have his time over again, he wouldn't have done that but it was too late now for regrets. He realised Jemma was watching him. She turned away.

*

"Victoria Scanlon. Goodness me, it's been a long time."

"Sukey! You're still here!"

"On and off. Agency work. Glad to see you're still around – though not, it seems, in the best of shape." Susan Key took in the range of Victoria's injuries, and flipped through the charts beside the bed. "You're married to the man you met here?"

Victoria nodded. "Simon. We have two children, Louise and Mark."

"A hospital romance!" she said, "Now that's a novelty."

Victoria smiled, her teeth gritted against the pain.

Sukey hesitated, then looked again at her friend's face. "If you're up to it, let's go and grab a coffee. There's a nice place on the ground floor."

Victoria shook her head. "Sorry, but I don't have any money."

"Hasn't Simon made sure you're all right?"

Victoria dropped her gaze. "He... he hasn't been here." She looked up and found her friend staring at her.

"How is he expecting you to get home?"

123

"I suppose he expects I'll be taken in an ambulance."

"So he's just left you here without any money?"

Victoria pressed her lips together and nodded, feeling ashamed but too exhausted to defend her husband.

"Wait here a minute," said her friend, who went over to the Nurses' Station before returning with a wheelchair. "Come on. We're going for a coffee. It'll give them a chance to change the sheets as well. And you need a break from this place."

Susan Key and Victoria had been best friends when they'd been training together as nurses. Since Victoria's marriage, when she gave up work and moved far up Wharfedale, they had not been in touch. But meeting her again brought nothing but happy memories for her and she felt much better by the time they emerged from the lift into the large concourse on the ground floor of the infirmary containing, in one corner, an open-plan cafeteria. The two women sat at a table for two away to the side where they could talk without being overheard. It was Sukey's choice.

"Now the last time I saw you," she began, "you were going out with Simon."

"Yes. Obviously, it wasn't something I wanted to talk about: I had this idea that the hospital wouldn't be pleased if they learned I was having an affair with a patient."

"Probably put you in line for a lecture on professional ethics," murmured Sukey, holding her coffee with both hands.

"It got worse: I was pregnant when I left nursing."

Sukey raised an eyebrow. "But he did the decent thing?"

"Yes. We've been happily married – until recently. We had Mark a couple of years after Louise, but over the past few years, I don't know what's happened. Simon has changed. He gets really bad headaches and drinks vodka until he passes out."

"Hasn't he been to see a doctor?"

"A couple of years ago. It's difficult persuading him to go. The doctor said he was suffering from migraines and told him he could buy tablets for them over the counter at the chemist's."

"And do they do the trick?"

"No. I've seen Simon taking stuff meant for horses – he works with horses – to kill the pain."

"That's dangerous!" said Sukey. "So how come you're in this condition?" She nodded at the bruises and bandages.

Victoria didn't answer. Her eyes filled with tears and she shook her head, dashing at them with her good hand.

Sukey rested her fingers lightly on her arm and leaned closer. "Why hasn't your husband been to see you? What's happened, Victoria?"

A sob caught in Victoria's throat. She shook her head again, her lips pressed together.

Sukey rested her fingers on Victoria's uninjured arm. "The last time I met a woman with bruising like yours," she said quietly, almost into Victoria's ear, "she had been regularly beaten up by her husband over a period of years."

Victoria sobbed again, and moved her arm, but Sukey would not be put off.

"The amazing thing was, she was still loyal to him. Now loyalty is a wonderful and necessary thing, between husbands and wives, but it has to work both ways. And there has to be a limit. What this woman's husband had done to her was pure and simple bullying. He'd starved her of cash, freedom and respect. She didn't even respect herself – obviously: if she had, she wouldn't have put up with his behaviour for five minutes."

Victoria had stopped crying and was staring at her dully.

"The trouble was," Sukey went on, 'she thought she was on her own. She had children to look after – the youngest was only two, and from what she told me later, when she'd made up her mind to

125

talk, she'd been practically raped when the child was conceived."

"You said she thought she was on her own as if it wasn't true," Victoria interrupted.

"It wasn't – it isn't – true. There are people these women can talk to, places they can go with their children and be safe."

"What people? I don't have that many friends."

"People like me, Victoria. When I'm not doing the day job, I counsel victims of domestic violence. And I can get you and the children into a refuge for a few days or weeks until we can find a more permanent solution."

"You mean, leave Simon?" How would she manage?

"I expect you're worrying about all the consequences of leaving your husband," said Sukey. "Let me say this: they are not as terrible as the consequences of your *not* leaving him."

"But Simon might – "

"I really think we should worry about you. He's a man, he can take care of himself. The instinct of self-preservation is very powerful, you know. You should tap into your own. We can sort out the children – they'll probably be relieved at not having to live in the same house as Simon. I take it they're aware of what he's been doing?"

Victoria nodded. The memory of that moment in front of the television when she'd realised the children knew what was going on, and how worried she had been that knowing their father was hurting their mother would traumatize them.

She looked down at her broken arm and figured she probably looked like hell. She couldn't let the children see her like this. She wondered where they were, if Simon was looking after them properly. Suddenly, she needed to know. Without a mobile phone or the means to use the payphone beside her bed, she'd been unable to contact them.

"I need to talk to them," she said. She rubbed her face with her free hand. One good thing, the enforced rest in the hospital had finally allowed her ribs to mend and the pain in her side had correspondingly lessened. "I wonder if I went to the bank, they'd let me have some money."

"Don't worry about it," said Sukey. "There's a fund I can tap into on your behalf, so you'll have a few pounds to meet your immediate requirements." She pulled her mobile phone from the pocket of her uniform. "Here. Use this if you want to make some calls."

Victoria accepted the offer gratefully, and rang her home. There was no reply. "I'll try his place of work. Hope I can remember the number properly." She dialled Holt Carr. Craig answered.

As she listened to his explanation of what had happened since she'd been brought into hospital, her mouth fell open and she stared past her friend. Finally, she hung up and passed the instrument back.

"Simon's been arrested and charged with assault," she said, her tone of voice disclosing her incredulity. "The children are being looked after by Jo Box." She glanced at Sukey. "She's my next-door neighbour. Nearest thing I have to a friend." She squeezed her eyes shut to hold back a sudden burst of self-pity. Sukey came round the table and, being careful where she placed her hands, hugged her gently.

"I feel," she sobbed, "as if my life has fallen apart. All I wanted was a nice husband and a couple of children. I never wanted to be rich as long as we had food and shelter and the occasional holiday. But look at me now..."

Sukey held her, murmuring comfortable words, until Victoria had cried herself out. "Will you let me help until you're back on your feet?" she asked.

Victoria, feeling as if she was at the bottom of a well of depression, nodded.

"That's my old friend," said Sukey, tears streaming down her own cheeks while other customers were looking away, embarrassed. "We'll sort everything out in no time."

*

127

In the stables the girls were grooming brood mares. Kelly was chattering cheerfully to Susie, ignoring Simon at first when she saw him listening. She got on to her favourite subject.

"I was in a chatroom last night, Suse." She knew full well that Susie's parents wouldn't let her have a computer in her bedroom. There was only the one they kept in the living room and it was loaded with 'parental controls'. Kelly had heard about such things, which she scorned as 'censorship', and felt herself superior to her classmate since there were no such restrictions on the PC she could use at home – and it was sited in the small bedroom where she could surf the 'net without someone looking over her shoulder all the time. She'd found chatrooms and social networking websites, where she tended to interact with members she suspected were older – in their late teens or twenties – as all the ones around her own age were so boring. Empty bottles make most noise, her mother said, and there was truth in it. The older ones seemed a bit more interested in her, and she liked that.

Simon sidled closer. "What's a chatroom?" he asked.

Kelly affected to have only just noticed him. "Oh, hello Simon. It's a place on the internet where you can kind of meet people."

"What? You mean people come here to meet you?"

Kelly laughed. "No. You meet them in cyberspace."

"Cyberspace?"

Kelly shook her head in mock sorrow. "It's, like, virtual, not real. You don't normally meet anyone in a chatroom, you just send each other messages."

"Oh," said Simon, "I obviously have a lot to learn about the internet."

"Yeah, well, possibly," said Kelly, anxious to stress her superior knowledge. "S'pose you don't know about search engines, either?"

Simon shook his head. "No."

"I'll have to take you in hand, and boost your education a bit," she said, lifting an eyebrow to indicate she was speaking in code again.

Simon raised his own eyebrow to signal understanding. "You will. Sometime when the boss is out, we can go and use his laptop and you can show me how it's done."

"Yeah, okay." Kelly paused for a moment, then resumed stroking the horse's flanks with sweeps of her brush. "Pity, really..." she added, wondering if Simon would pick up the gauntlet.

"What is?" he asked.

"Well, if I had one of those mobile phones that take pictures, I could show you how to send photos to other people on the worldwide web."

"That's what you need is it?" he asked.

"Yeah. More than anything," she added, "I'd be very grateful to anyone who gives me one for Christmas – a phone I mean," she giggled.

"Oh," said Simon, nodding as he understood. "Well, you'll have to see. Santa only gives presents to girls who've been good."

She looked round coyly. "Haven't I been good, Simon? Wasn't I good the other night?" Let Susie make what she would of that remark!

"You were, Kel, you were," he said, turning and strolling back into the tack room.

CHAPTER 11

The telephone rang in the hall at Holt Carr. Craig stuck his head out of the bathroom and listened to be sure before emerging and running downstairs two at a time still dragging his dressing gown over his nakedness.

"Craig Jordon," he said, breathing hard.

"Hi, Craig." It was the voice of Gerry Ancrom, delayed a few seconds by the satellites bouncing the call over from Whitehorse.

"Gerry! How are you?"

"Fine, fine. How's everything with you?"

"Not bad. Difficult to judge what'll happen to dad's horse business. I've had to get somebody in to look after it."

"How are you coping yourself?"

"I'm okay, thanks, Gerry. There's a few things to tie up – the folks mortgaged the house to pay for a new indoor exercise ring, and I am going to have to find a way of repaying that because I don't want the bank taking Holt Carr."

"Gee, how're you gonna do that?"

"Still working on the answer to that. Maybe if I could sell the arena? My parents must have had plans for developing the business, because it really isn't necessary for what we do at present."

"Hope you manage to sort it out. I guess you'll be waiting on probate as well?"

"That could take a year or more. But the solicitors are on to it."

"Good. Look, I won't keep you hanging around – it's about one o'clock in the morning here, and I want my bed – but there's something I thought you might want to know."

"What's that?"

"The company wants to set up a specialist team doing what you've been doing so well."

130

"Sounds interesting. How will it affect me?"

"We'd really like you to run it. There's a big raise for you if you take the job. You know what Boards of Directors are like – come up with an idea one minute and want it done the next. They want the prospecting team up and running A-sap. I know you've only had three weeks so far, but how do you feel about it?" Craig chewed his lip. Into his mind came the déjà vu-type realisation that this offer would be taking him away from Cat – this time for ever, without a doubt. Why, he asked himself, was *she* his first thought?

"Can you give me a few days to think about it, Gerry?" he asked. "There's other people I need to talk to about this."

The line crackled. "No problem, Craig. Look: I'll keep the wolves at bay for another three weeks if necessary, but the sooner you can get back the better. We definitely want to be up and running straight after Christmas, so I need you back here before then."

"Thanks, Gerry. That'll be fine. I'll get back to you. It sounds really good."

"It'll sound even better if I drop you a hint about the pay." Gerry mentioned a figure which set Craig's previous salary in the shade. "Of course, you also qualify for the benefits that go with management."

Craig knew roughly what they would be, and the package was mouth-wateringly tempting. The offer, if he accepted it, would be a major step up the career ladder, putting him on a level with Gerry in the company, and ensuring his future prosperity. It was equivalent to the big step up from shop-floor to senior manager.

Afterwards, in the kitchen, he made coffee and tried to figure out what to do. What he really needed was to sort out in his head why Cat kept appearing in his thoughts. True: she was still a gorgeous woman, and her intelligence and personality simple added to her appeal. Undeniably true: he had treated her very badly. He now

131

accepted that his decision to make a clean break with her, for what had seemed like the best of reasons at the time, was wrong. Also true: she was still the woman he fancied most as a partner for life.

This last factor burst upon him burst upon him without warning. Close on its heels was the realisation that he'd really blown his chances, not helped when she'd arrived at Holt Carr to find him in a relationship with Jemma. He closed his eyes. That was that, then! Shot in the foot. *The Engineer hoist with his own petard,* as Shakespeare put it, more colourfully. Something like that, anyway. He collapsed heavily into the nearest armchair, his mind in turmoil.

On the one hand, Jemma, he knew, was strictly short-term. When the dig finished, she would be gone. Her agenda was very like his own had been at her age: qualifications and career meant everything. Friends of the opposite sex were essentially recreational, and very secondary. He had always understood this.

On the other hand, there was Cat. He wondered if he was just obsessing about her, because once there had been something between them, and now she was near he felt as if he had a proprietorial interest in her. It was rubbish, of course; just the leftover primitive male desire to own things which had led to women being regarded for centuries as chattels.

They weren't seeing each other – they'd scarcely spoken since she'd come to work at Holt Carr. He knew she'd used the shower while he'd been out, because he recognised the scents he associated with her, in the shower. And when she had turned up while he was at home, those same scents combined with her physical presence had hit his senses like a hammer-blow and made him suddenly ache with loss of things past.

Cat represented a very uncertain future. Even more pressing was the matter of the mortgage. Holt Carr had been in his family since it was built, back in the 19th century. There was absolutely no way he could allow it to be taken away from him. Back home in Whitehorse, he had a portfolio of investments, bought with the proceeds of his gold-panning, but he'd need to get back there before he could sell any of them, and he wasn't sure he wanted to do that, anyway, if other means could be found of paying off the bank. He'd had a letter from them the previous day.

He got out of the armchair and sat at the kitchen table, dragging the letter towards him. He propped his head in his hands and rested both elbows on the table while he read it again: it was polite but with an aggressive undertone, pointing out how much his father had borrowed to build the new indoor exercise arena and asking when it might expect repayment of the loan, which was overdue.

He figured the best course of action was to try to reschedule the debt, to give him some more time. He should, he realised, put the building on the market as soon as possible, or find someone who would invest a large sum in it and use it for what it would do best: breaking-in horses. He took a deep breath and went into the hallway to phone for an appointment to talk about it. They would be happy to see him as soon as he could get down there. He put on his waxed jacket and comfortable boots and went out to the Land-Rover.

*

Kelly was covertly watching Simon as he gently brushed the flanks of a foal just a few hours old. Its mother had been moved into the adjacent stall, and was leaning her sleek black head over the dividing wall to watch. Something in the way his strong hands moved the stiff brush over the foal's flanks briefly held her attention. Outside, a door slammed, and Simon moved so he could glance through the open doorway across the yard. He turned and saw Kelly watching him.

"Yon Craig's gone out," he told her, jerking his thumb towards the house. "Wouldst like to show me t'internet? Them chat rooms an' things. It's a good moment, if you're not too busy."

"Ooh, I dunno," she replied, looking up at him, wide-eyed and pushing her chest out under his nose.

His eyes were drawn reflexively to her breasts. He dragged his gaze up to meet her eyes, which were full of amusement. Kelly glanced round to see that Susie was changing the bedding in one of the stalls.

"Just going down to the house with Simon," she informed her. Walking ahead of Simon across the yard, she emphasised the natural swing of her hips. The way he watched her, almost drooling, she thought, amused her greatly. He nodded agreement, but before moving off in the direction of Holt Carr, he took a moment to admire Kelly's swaying hips as she walked back into the stable block.

At the house, he led the way to the living room. "The computer's through here," he said.

The laptop was on a small table in the corner of the room and a dining chair was set conveniently in front of it. Kelly sat down and switched the machine on. Simon stood behind her, looking at the screen over her shoulders. She couldn't see what he was looking at, but she could guess. As she waited for the machine to warm up, she smiled innocently at him.

"It's warm in here," she announced pulling her sweater over her head and revealing a black camisole top with bootlace straps Simon's eyes were riveted on the jut of her breasts, visible from his vantage point, almost to their pink tips. He rested his hands on her shoulders and massaged the back of her neck in a way she found pleasant. She wriggled.

"Ooh, Simon, that's nice," she said. She figured he'd gradually explore other parts of her and her nipples began to crinkle in anticipation. It was a very pleasant feeling and left her breathless. The internet appeared on the screen before them. Kelly quickly brought up the Google website.

"Look, Simon, this is a search engine."

"Oh, aye. What do you do there?"

"Search for things," she said, smiling indulgently at his apparent ignorance. "Ooh!" she added, as his fingers flicked and rubbed. She wriggled.

"Like what?"

"Well, suppose I want to search for information about Skipton, I type 'Skipton' into the box here and click on Search. And, within seconds, there's nearly two million references in the UK section alone." Simon left a trail of kisses down her neck, across her shoulders, and was heading for the slope of her breasts when she stopped him.

"You're a bit keen, aren't you?" she said.

"You're such a beautiful girl, Kelly," he replied gruffly. She nestled her cheek against his head: she was enjoying the effect of alternating reward with discouragement. "Eh, what else can you search for?"

"Well, anything. When you see something you want to look at in more detail, just click on it and you go to their website."

"What I see and want to look at in more detail isn't on the computer," he said, resuming his exploration of her breasts.

She giggled again, brushing ineffectually at his face. "Pay attention, Simon. Do you want to see some of the other things on the internet?"

"Like?" asked Simon, whose hands were beginning to slip down Kelly's arms.

Any moment now, she thought, and trembled with anticipation.

"Well, I can tell—" she squirmed again as his fingers found a sensitive spot "—you like girls," said Kelly, grinning. "Look what happens when you go here..."

She typed in the address of a website she'd looked up at home. It offered a large selection of photographs of young girls ranging from indecent to obscene in nature. There was a link to a 'tour' offering 'free samples', which Kelly followed. As Simon watched, his hands began to move onto the firm slope of her breasts. Kelly brushed them away.

"Simon! That's naughty," she said, mock-stern.

For a moment his hands retreated to her shoulders but in a few seconds, as he watched the procession of photographs on the computer monitor, they slipped back, this time down the firm slope of her breasts under the camisole.

"Simon, you're not supposed to do that," she protested, but didn't stop him.

He felt her nipples stiffen, and enjoyed the luxurious feel of her warm, firm breasts.

Kelly clenched her thighs together as the nervous beats from her breasts arrowed into her groin.

"Simon! Stop it," she breathed.

She could feel herself becoming very aroused. He took no notice and the delicious sensations drenched her. She made sure the computer screen gave Simon a lot of material to look at while he fondled her. At the same time, he brushed her neck with his lips and made her whole body tremble.

"Simon!" she gasped, "we can't do it here, now."

"There's no-one about. You're enjoying it aren't you?"

"It's making me feel uncomfortable."

She brushed his hands away again, becoming aware of the scent of his arousal. This time, when his hands returned, one pushed up under the camisole and took possession of an entire breast while the other slid down her belly towards her groin. She grabbed it with both hands, giggling.

"Simon! That's rude. You can't want to go down there."

He buried his lips in her hair and muttered, "Oh yes I can."

"Well, we're not doing it here."

She had to stop because suddenly heat was flooding her belly and for a moment she couldn't speak. With hands that shook, she shut down the computer and twisted round to face Simon.

"Maybe later, if you're good."

"When?" he demanded.

"After Susie's gone home," said Kelly.

"I'll hold you to that," he said, his voice thick with desire. He tugged the camisole under her breasts and as they stuck out proudly, crouched to lick and suck on both of them in turn.

Kelly put her hands behind his head and stroked him before patting him lightly on the shoulders.

"I think we should be getting back," she said,

He looked up into her eyes. His were bright and burning with desire, hers big pools of interest. She was gratified to see a thin sheen of sweat on his face and further delighted when she glanced down and saw the effect she'd had within his tight-fitting trousers.

She leaned forward and kissed him. "You'll have to learn to be gentle with me, Simon," she said, "and do as I say. Then maybe I'll let you do what you want for a while. Is that a deal?"

"Of course it is. I hope I've earned my reward today?"

"Could be," she said looking away and smiling enigmatically.

"Thanks for the lesson," he said, "I'll look forward to the next."

She grinned, regaining her composure. "So will I," she said, sliding one hand up his thigh as she spoke.

She reached for her sweater and pulled it on, afterwards checking her hair was still tightly held in its ponytail.

"Best I get back to Susie, or she'll wonder what we're up to," she said.

"Aye," said Simon, making sure the chair was put back exactly where they'd found it. He rested a proprietorial hand on her shoulder as they walked back through the house.

She shook it off as they went outside into the yard. Susie was near the door to the stables, leaning on a broom and watching them. Kelly was feeling the buzz from knowing the effect she had on Simon.

She didn't demur when Susie called to her. "Come on, Kel, there's still two stalls to clean out. I've done my share."

"Okay."

She saw Susie's expression resolve into suspicion, and almost giggled. Let her think what she liked, Kelly was moving up the scale by which she compared herself with her contemporaries, while Susie, only a couple of months younger, still looked and acted like a child. She heard Simon, in the tack room, pop the tab on a can of beer.

*

Craig got back from the bank in the late afternoon. The meeting had been polite, to the point of being restrained, but the unctuous loans manager had made it abundantly plain that in granting him an extension of the loan for a few weeks until the end of the year, they were conferring a favour on him due almost entirely to the bank's generosity and the fact that his parents had kept all their savings in it. The trouble was that nobody could access them, until his parents' estates had been wound up. The bank had been able to confirm what he had suspected; that his parents had planned on expanding the business into horse-breaking and training, but they'd been killed before that aspect of the business got off the ground.

There were two messages on the answering machine, both from owners of brood mares requesting information about his plans for the business. The future, he had to admit, when looked at in the cold light of day, was bleak.

While he was pouring himself a coffee in the kitchen, the telephone rang. Expecting another doubting owner, Craig took his mug through into the hallway. He was glad the caller couldn't see the grim expression on his face as he picked up the phone. He was pleased to find that the person on the other end was Victoria.

She sounded strained. "Craig? How's Simon?"

"Hi, Victoria. He seems... much the same. How are you?"

"Oh, we're coping," she sighed. "It's not the same as being at home."

"No. Still, it's probably only until his case comes up in court."

"They – the people here – have been talking. I never knew there were so many women being assaulted by their partners. Here, they call it abuse, because it isn't always physical. They've made me see that Simon was abusing me in other ways as well – keeping me short of money, blaming me for things which weren't really my fault."

Craig was surprised but not dismissive. "It sounds as though they've helped you to see what's been going on and where it might lead."

"Yes. I think whatever the outcome of the trial, I'll have to leave Simon, for the children's sake as well as my own."

"How are they coping?"

"At the moment, it's all a bit of a game, an adventure. But sharing a house with five other families is a bit restrictive, and I'm sure the novelty will wear off soon."

"What about their schooling?"

"The authorities have been very helpful so far. They've been admitted to a school local to us, temporarily. It seems that the school is used to taking in children from the refuge and they actually have measures in place to make sure they can't be got-at by unauthorised people – like Simon, for instance." She hesitated a moment. "If you're ever in Skipton, perhaps we could meet and have a coffee together? Frankly, I'd like to be able to talk to someone I can trust, who knows what's going on."

"Sure. Tomorrow morning?" he suggested.

She agreed at once, and they fixed a time and place to meet.

*

Victoria hung up. Why had she done that? she wondered. The truth, she admitted to herself, was that she was fed up with unremitting female company, much of it with depressing stories to tell, similar to her own. She'd learned that she was one of the least-suffering, having only had a couple of years of Simon's really barbarous treatment, and she'd been physically struck no more times than she had fingers. Some of the women had suffered over thirty physical assaults before telling anyone.

Several, like her, were waiting for their partners to appear in court; some still refused to bear witness either out of fear of reprisals or because they still believed it was possible to repair their relationships. Victoria had been tempted towards that view, but Sukey had given her a stern talking-to. Once they start physically and mentally abusing their partners, she'd said, the statistics show that men rarely stop of their own volition.

But Victoria remembered that Simon had only started to change about three years previously. Most of the women in the refuge had been in abusive relationships since they married, and a large proportion of them had been brought up in homes where their mothers were regularly abused by their fathers. What made Victoria take a stronger line was the thought that her mother would never have let her father behave like these other men without doing something to stop him. Not that her father had ever been abusive, as best she remembered him. He had died of a heart-attack when she'd been eight, and her mother had passed away six years ago from breast cancer.

Victoria's temperament was not an unhappy one by nature, and the thought of seeing a 'friendly face', as she thought of Craig, was enough to send her to bed in a more-than-usually-content state of mind.

*

At the stables, Susie got her bike out and switched on the lights. "I'm off, Kel," she said.

Kelly was pretending to be busy. "See you tomorrow, Suse," she said.

She listened to the noise of the bicycle moving away across the yard and went into the tack room to await Simon, who had driven into Skipton. She sat herself in the propped-up armchair, leaned across to open the fridge, and pulled the vodka bottle out. She unscrewed the cap and drank a couple of mouthfuls. It tasted odd: it didn't occur to her that the bottle might contain something more than vodka. She was considering taking another swig from the bottle when she heard the sound of Simon's return. Hastily she replaced the bottle and sprawled across the chair, one leg over one of the arms, and waited for him to come in. He appeared in the doorway and swept his gaze across her careless attitude.

"Hello, Kelly, anyone else about?"

"I don't think so. Susie's gone home."

"Oh," he said, nodding. "I've brought you a little something for Christmas."

He came into the room and closed the door behind him, dropping the latch. Kelly's eyes widened as he produced a box from behind his back. When she read the lid, she clapped her hands with delight.

"Oh, Simon, a mobile phone!"

She stood up and impulsively put her arms round his neck to kiss him. He watched as she removed the telephone from its packaging, plugged in the battery charger and switched it on. The tiny colour screen glowed, and she aimed it at him. The flash which followed as she took the picture hurt his eyes and made him blink but she didn't seem to notice. She took a few more photographs of the tack room while she learned how to use the machine, then, seeming to remember that Simon was still there, she put the phone carefully on a work surface next to its box, and reached up to kiss him again.

141

This time she ground her crotch against him. Simon took the opportunity to slip his hands beneath her sweater. She embraced him and ran her hands up and down his back, feeling his desire growing against her. He took hold of her sweater and pulled it over her head. Whether intentionally or not, her camisole came off with it, and left her standing topless before him. She felt her body responding to his admiring gaze. He knuckled his forehead, and she wondered if he was experiencing one of his headaches.

"You want a drink?" he asked, reaching across to the fridge door and opening it.

"Yeah," she breathed.

"There's a glass on the drainer."

She fetched it and held it out. He half-filled it.

"Down the hatch," he said and drank from the bottle, while Kelly tipped the fiery liquid down her throat at the same time. She held out the glass again and he put rather more in this time. Again they drank together. When he held the bottle up in a silent offer to give her more, she shook her head.

"I'd better not."

In fact the strong liquor with its hidden dose of analgesic had gone quite quickly to her head. God! This was better than her friends at school! None of them had an admirer like Simon. They'd be insanely jealous, she thought, if they knew. *When* they knew. She had worked out just how to drop a few casual hints that would tell them without anything so crassly obvious as a straightforward statement.

She wondered sometimes if Simon was too old, but it was very flattering that he should be interested. And she'd put him off enough times. He frightened her just a little: she could sense a sort of anger in him, just below the surface, though he'd never been really nasty with her. He'd beaten up his wife, she knew, but she was probably a cow and deserved it. She figured there was no way he'd treat her the same. Anyway, she was confident in her control of him, and the thought of it made her stomach flutter.

She felt a sudden ball of heat expand in her belly. She put the glass down on top of the fridge and ran her hands down the curves of her hips. It caught his attention. She kicked off her shoes then slowly unfastened the waistband of her jodhpurs and rolled them down. She was gratified when she saw the intent look on Simon's face and noticed the presence again of a thin film of sweat. Pushing the tight pants off her feet, she stood in front of him in just her pale pink cotton knickers, her arms crossed over her breasts.

Simon bent forward to kiss them, moving her arms away, then knelt in front of her as he slowly peeled her panties down. He trailed kisses down her belly into the light brown patch of curling hair which covered her mound. While he was thus occupied, she put her hands behind his head and ruffled his hair. When he straightened up, she unfastened the belt of his trousers and pulled the zip down with some difficulty. As she burrowed within, Simon slid one finger under her crotch. Kelly drew in a deep breath as he touched her most intimate parts. Muscles in her belly went into little spasms as his finger worked into her.

His trousers slid down and she pulled his underpants to release his erection. It was the first one she'd seen and it looked huge. With it, she detected the musky aroma of his sex, and it made her knees want to buckle.

Suddenly, without warning, he picked her up and laid her on the hard concrete floor with just her discarded clothes for padding. She moved her legs apart as he knelt between them and a moment later she felt him force his penis into her. Simon's breath pounded in her ear and as he pushed past her virginity he grunted. She whimpered with the pain, then felt him as he jammed himself deep inside her belly. He lifted his head and stared into her eyes for a moment. She screwed them shut as his hot breath hit her face. Expecting nothing but pleasure, she felt nothing but pain and the sensation of being stuffed. His buttocks worked rhythmically, and the cold of the floor passed through her clothes into her back. She heard him grunt three times, the last being a long noise of relief as he thrust hard against her and pulsed until he was drained. For a moment, he collapsed on her chest, almost suffocating her, before he pulled away from her and stood up, looking down at the mess in her crotch.

Kelly snivelled. "Simon! You hurt me!"

"You'll get over it," he said. "You wanted a bit of rough, didn't you? Something you could tell your girlfriends?"

"I wanted you, Simon, but not like that. It was like... animals," she sobbed.

"Get dressed. You'll catch cold. Next time'll be better. You were a virgin, weren't you?"

In her distress, she still blushed. "Yes," she admitted.

"You should have mentioned it and I'd have gone steadier. Too late now. As I say, next time it'll feel a lot better."

She snuffled, climbing painfully to her feet and finding her knickers.

"There won't be a next time," she said sullenly.

Simon reached over and caught her pony tail. He jerked her head so that she was looking into his eyes.

"Oh yes there will. That telephone cost a hundred and thirty quid, and even at twenty pound a pop, like they charge down in Leeds, that's a good five more pops you owe me. You're good with horses, Kelly: now you're good at something else. I'll see you in the morning."

"You could have got me pregnant," she accused.

He fastened his trousers and glanced up at her. "That were careless, then. Tha'd better get one o' them mornin'-after pills if you're that worried."

He turned and left her, tear-stained, to finish dressing. She felt sorry for herself. Simon had turned out to be a real bastard. But it was

144

woman's lot to put up with the brutishness of men – well, some men, anyway. All the magazines she read at least hinted at it, if they didn't say so out right. Maybe it was just what happened to men after they'd had their way with a girl? Which meant he'd come round later and be wanting more. Despite her current wretchedness, the memory of the lust in his eyes and the way he'd driven himself into her in an onslaught of passion caused her body to feel alive and desired again. Next time, she decided, she'd control him better.

*

Simon walked out of the yard and across the moor to his father's home, grinning. He felt quite proud of the way he'd led the girl on, letting her think she was making the running. Now he'd got into her pants, he'd show her who was boss. Meantime, he needed to get a move on as there was a good chance of another late night call from PC Ackroyd checking on his whereabouts.

CHAPTER 12

A blustery winter wind rattled the canvas walls of the archæological team's marquee on the exposed moor above Holt Carr. The men had taken more boxes of finds to York, but inside the tent, Cat was still entering data into her laptop while Jemma was carefully wrapping and packing more finds ready for transfer to the county museum. They were working on adjacent tables.

"You were a bit quiet last night," said Jemma. "Something on your mind?"

Cat shrugged. She'd been wrestling with her feelings about Craig but she could hardly discuss them with Jemma.

"Not particularly. I thought you would have gone down to the house?"

Jemma stopped working and stared at the table-top unseeingly. "Hmm. I would have... but the last time I was there... " She stopped, looked up at Cat and waved away the subject. "It's nothing. Probably. Anyway, I won't be going to the house again tonight."

"Oh," said Cat, surprised by the sudden change of subject. "Is Craig being some sort of problem?"

Jemma shrugged. "Not really. It's probably just me. The age difference... Canada... you know. He probably thought nothing of it. Maybe he was being, uh, gallant, in his own way." She grinned.

"Gallant? How?" asked Cat, aware she was being nosey. Jemma was blushing.

"He fell asleep in the kitchen. He'd had a lot of scotch. I had a shower and then... got into his bed. In the morning – it must have been quite early – he found me. I expected him to get in bed, but he didn't. He got dressed instead, and seemed... well, I'd have said embarrassed, except there was

146

nothing to be embarrassed about. It – it wasn't the first time."

Cat nodded sympathetically. This must have taken place after she'd been down to the house herself. He'd been drinking then. She had the thought that Craig wasn't the sort of man who often got drunk.

"Maybe he was suffering from Brand's Droop," she said, grinning.

Jemma stared at her for a moment before smiling as well. "Of course! It's not something I'd have expected about Craig, but I guess it can happen to any man after a few glasses of booze."

Cat wasn't so sure. Although she'd suggested the idea, she couldn't imagine Craig ever being so drunk he couldn't perform in bed. And he'd apparently been asleep for some time, so the effects would have worn off to a degree. Still, Jemma seemed happier to think she now knew the reason he'd stayed out of her bed.

Cat wasn't about to share her doubts with the younger woman. They worked in silence for a few minutes.

Jemma said, "Did you know Simon goes into the house when Craig's away? And not to have a shower. I suppose I should be glad of that."

Cat glanced up. "Why does he do that?"

Jemma shrugged. "I don't know. Just being nosey, perhaps?"

"Have you mentioned it to Craig?"

"No. He told us we could use the facilities down there any time. He's probably told Simon and the stable girl the same."

"Which girl?" asked Cat, curious because she hadn't seen Simon with a girl, hadn't suspected that with his domestic problems he'd be getting involved with someone else.

"She works in the stables. Very... generous figure," Jemma said, twisting her lips to indicate that she wasn't lost in total admiration. "Junoesque."

147

Cat tapped away at her keyboard and responded without looking up. "Lot of overweight girls about these days: too much fatty food, not enough exercise."

"Oh, she's not fat. I suppose if I'm honest she's got a really good figure – the sort men like, anyway: voluptuous – big boobs, bit of a bum, and everything visible through tight sweaters and jodhpurs. I'd hate her already if she was my age." She grinned and sticky-taped some bubble-wrap round a piece of pottery.

Cat glanced up and smiled. "I shouldn't think you're worried about competition. She's not Craig's type."

"The thing is, are you?" blurted Jemma, stopping her work and watching Cat.

Cat sat back from the computer, feeling colour rushing to her cheeks. "I don't know why you ask me that. I told you that Craig and I had a bit of a thing going about twelve years ago, but not since." Jemma seemed about to speak when Cat muttered, "We had our chance and blew it."

Jemma sighed. "I'll take that as a yes, then!"

Cat shook her head. "No, no! We've moved on. He's certainly moved on. We've had no contact all the time he's been away, so of course, he's got a life I know nothing about, and that doesn't include me."

"But you wish it did, don't you!"

"No! I... " Cat stopped, biting her lip.

"Oh, come on, Cat!" exclaimed Gemma, "you still fancy him – and quite a lot – don't you?"

Cat turned away. She felt her cheeks flushing. It was the question she'd avoided putting to herself ever since Craig had returned. The memory of him, stepping outside the terminal building at the airport, the instant recognition... the ache in her heart whenever Jemma had gone down to the house. Words were unnecessary, it seemed. Jemma came round the table and slipped a comforting arm round her shoulders.

"I told you that Craig and I are quite temporary, didn't I? I meant it. If I can make any sense out of the pair of you, you both seem to fancy each other still, but both believe the other has put the past behind them. You're both standing on the edge of a cliff and waiting for the other to jump."

Cat looked at her askance. "I'm not sure I like your metaphor."

"Put it any way you like. If he asked you out, you'd go. And if *you* asked *him* out, *he'd* go." She removed her arm and went back to where she was working. "I'm going to hurt him very slightly— "

"What?"

"Only his pride. Because I'm going to stop sleeping with him, and only use the shower during the times he's out, when the rest of us usually go."

"Could get a bit crowded in there. It's only big enough for two," joked Cat.

Jemma grinned but refused to be deflected. "Your mission, if you choose to accept it, Cat, is to pick up the pieces and make him a very happy fellow – before you both self-destruct."

Cat shook her head. "I can't. You're forgetting, he's going to go back to Canada as soon as he's sorted things out here."

"No I'm not. Your point is?"

"Well, obviously: I work and live here, he works and lives there."

"If you've loved each other for twelve years, despite his lack of contact – and yours, too, incidentally – I reckon you'll find a way of sorting that one out. You're intelligent people; it should be something you're both capable of."

Cat felt very close to the edge of the precipice Jemma had mentioned, and very exposed. She wondered whether she would be able to bring off her 'impossible mission', or if she'd founder in the attempt and screw up the rest of her life.

Jemma grinned. "Cheer up. You know it's what you want."

Cat stood up and paced away from the table. "I don't know whether I can pull it off. It isn't as easy – especially when you're as old as I am."

"Cat! Don't talk as if you were knocking on the door of middle age: you're only about ten years older than me."

Cat focussed on the piece of skull in her hand and smiled. "But that's the definition of middle-aged: someone ten years older than yourself."

Jemma laughed. "You know what I mean. We are both still young women in our prime. The world is our lobster."

Cat chuckled. "It's easy for you: you only have to snap your fingers to have the men come running."

Jemma scoffed. "You think? I wish!"

Cat grinned. "All right. Have it your way – I'm not going to say it again. I remember being twenty-two, you know. And you get out of practice."

"Better sharpen your hooks, then."

"I forgot to pack my suspender belt and short skirt. Somehow never occurred to me that I'd need them."

Jemma tilted her head slightly to one side. "I reckon you won't need them. You're not exactly unattractive, you know."

Cat wished she felt as confident of her attractiveness as Jemma was.

*

"Hello, Victoria," Craig said.

The bruising round her eyes had faded to light discolouration and the plaster cast on her arm had been replaced with a light bandage. It was still rather a shock to see her.

"Thanks for coming, Craig. I hope you don't mind," she said as he set down a mug of coffee in front of each of them. There were half a dozen other customers, well-spaced among the tables, and none nearby. The street market was busy outside the plate-glass window.

"Not at all," he said gently as she hesitated. "I know we don't know each other very well, but you seemed like the sort of person I could talk to." She paused again. "Besides, you've known Simon quite well for a long time – "

"We were at school together," Craig said.

"I know." She took a sip of her coffee.

"If you were wondering," he said, "I can't explain why he's done... what he's done... to you."

"Oh. I thought there might have been something in his past... you know."

"The only time I knew him to be violent was when he attacked me and Cat."

"He said that was because you'd taken Cat away from him. He was jealous and drunk, and not in a fit state to fight someone as... as fit as you," she said, her gaze fixed on his chest.

"I suppose that's right," Craig admitted. "He was drunk. I didn't know he still had a thing for Cat." He looked up, catching her eyes. "When she and I started going out, she'd already dumped him, you know."

Victoria looked at him askance. "No, I didn't know that. He said they were still an item and that you took her away from him. That was why he was angry."

"If you want, I can ask Cat to tell you herself."

Victoria took a long look at him. "You'd better tell me the rest, because I'm beginning to think maybe he didn't tell me everything. If you don't mind?"

He took a sip of the hot drink. "There's not a lot to tell. Cat and I were heading back to Hall – you know, our Hall of Residence at the uni. We'd been out for a cheap meal – pub grub and a pint of Yorkshire's best – in the city, away from the Union Bar." He shrugged. "Simon suddenly appeared, swinging this hammer, nearly hitting us, so I knocked him down. He hit his head on the kerb – I hadn't intended that: I was just stopping him from belting us, or me, really – and knocked himself out. We got an ambulance and he was taken to the LGI where I gather he met you."

Victoria sipped her coffee and regarded him over the rim of the mug. "And that's the truth, is it?"

"Yes. Isn't that what Simon said?"

"He didn't mention the hammer."

"He was doing an apprenticeship with a farrier at the time. It was one of those long-handled hammers they use when they're shaping red-hot metal on the anvil."

"Pretty lethal then?"

"Very. That's why I had to react quite, uh, strongly."

"So you *reacted* in self-defence?"

"Yes."

She took another long, thoughtful sip of her coffee. "But Simon was never prosecuted?"

"No. Up to that point, we'd been friends. Well, friendly rivals. I wasn't going to give evidence against him. After all, in the end, he didn't hurt us, and had a long stay in hospital. Punishment enough, I say." He took another mouthful of coffee. "How did you meet? I mean, I know it was at Leeds General Infirmary."

She smiled reminiscently. "I was a nursing student. I'd started at Jimmy's – you know, St James's – but then I got sent to the Infirmary." She looked up at him under raised eyebrows. "I was terribly young and naïve," she added. "Home was up here in the Dales and I was away from my parents for the first time in my life." She sipped again, looking down into the mug. "I was very green. They told us not to form attachments to the patients, but I felt sorry for Simon, and he was, well, attentive and I thought he was good looking." She looked at Craig. "Of course, he told me a slightly expurgated version of the fight, in which you were clearly the aggressor and he was the victim." She looked out of the window at the shoppers. "I fell in love with him, and stupidly didn't make sure he used a condom when we made love. Two weeks later, I missed my period and it was too late to worry." She faced Craig again. "I

152

was delighted and, to be honest, a bit surprised when he suggested we get married. My parents would have gone mad if they'd found out I was pregnant. They weren't too pleased when it became obvious we'd, uh, anticipated the marriage, but by then, I think they were just glad, like I was, that Simon had done the right thing, as they saw it."

"And you were both very happy until he started mistreating you? When was that?" Craig asked.

"A couple of years ago. He began to suffer from migraines." She looked up. "He went to the doctor's but he told him he could buy migraine tablets over the counter. Since then, the headaches seem to have worsened and the tablets don't seem to have much effect."

She moved her hands so she could lift the coffee to her lips. Craig saw the pain in her eyes. She looked as if she was not sleeping very well. "Simon's response has been to drink lots of vodka until he passes out. But sometimes, when he's drunk, he gets into such rages – and that's when he hits me."

"Perhaps he should have gone back to the doctor? Maybe if he'd been prescribed more powerful pain-killers...?"

Victoria looked down at her cooling coffee. "Maybe. I'd wondered whether counselling would help – you know, marriage guidance."

"It might, but I still think he needs to see a doctor."

She hesitated before looking up. "Do you think you could suggest it to him for me?"

"If you want me to, I will," said Craig. He leaned forward slightly. "I maybe shouldn't say this, but you're amazing, you know, still prepared to hold out an olive branch despite what he did."

She looked down at her coffee. "I'm no more amazing, as you put it, than any other woman who takes her marriage vows seriously. 'For better, for worse, in sickness and in health' means just what it says."

He finished his drink. "How are the children holding up?" he asked, knowing that the welfare of Louise and Mark would be her biggest concern.

She smiled. "They've surprised me. I didn't realise how much they'd seen, but they knew Simon had punched me a couple of times and they've been very supportive. I try to tell them that their father is not well and isn't really responsible for what he'd doing and so far, they've stopped short of outright condemnation. I'm glad about that, because I really do think he's ill." She stopped for a moment and drained her cup. "Ugh, that was cold. Would you like another one?"

Craig nodded and she went to the counter, returning shortly with two cups and two plates bearing slices of fruit cake.

"I suddenly felt hungry," she said.

"Thanks, haven't had a slice of cake since my mother's, last Christmas," said Craig, thinking that he would never enjoy any of his mother's baking again.

"How're things with you?" she asked.

He pursed his lips. "Nasty letter from the bank. I've been to see them and I guess the bottom line is if I don't repay a loan my parents took out, they'll foreclose."

Victoria put her hand on his arm. "The loan was secured on the property?"

"Yes. I don't know what possessed them, unless they had some way of repaying it that isn't obvious to me."

"No sign of a buried biscuit tin containing a fortune?" she joked lightly.

He grinned. "No."

"So how will you raise the money?"

"Frankly, I don't know." He pursed his lips wryly. "The horse breeding business, I'm learning, is quite involved and I don't have enough knowledge to be in it. Simon does, of course, but I don't know what will be happening to him next week when his case comes up. I know I can't keep relying on his father to step in at a moment's notice, like he has been." Craig shook his head. "I'm going to have to give it some serious thought."

"We both have some thinking to do, Craig," said Victoria. She stood up. "I'd better go now."

He pushed back his chair. "Don't forget, if you want to chat..."

"I won't. Thanks for listening." For a moment, she looked as if she was thinking of kissing him, but obviously decided against it, and then she was gone. He finished his cake and coffee then followed her outside.

*

Simon was in the tack room suffering a throbbing headache that was affecting his vision and even the strength in his left side. He clutched his bottle of Equipalazone-laced vodka from which he took large gulps before dozing off to sleep. Thirty minutes later, Kelly strolled in, swinging her new camera phone from its wrist strap.

"Hi, Simon. Can I have a drop of that?"

Simon woke up. The headache had moderated to a steady throb which he could handle. He smiled at Kelly and gazed at her nubile form from the comfort of a barbiturate and alcoholic haze and felt his interest stir. He held out the bottle which had lain against his chest while he slept and smiled.

"Sure you can, Kelly. Girl as good looking as you is hard to refuse."

She swigged from the bottle then ran her hand along his thigh from the knee.

"Keep thinking that, Simon, and you'll go far," she grinned.

"I thought I'd already gone all the way," he joked.

Her hand trailed across the tightness of his crotch. "Yeah, but who says once is enough?"

He reached his own hand out and ran it up the back of her leg. "Not me, girl. You want to do it again?"

She shrugged, staring at him hard. "Maybe. But not here. It's uncomfortable."

"Mebbe we'll have to take our chances down at t' house then. I can't go home and I can't take you to my dad's place." He sat up. "Did you want to try it on the chair, here?"

"No, I've got to go home. Anyway, you bloody-well hurt me, Simon Stalland! You've got to learn how to be nice to a girl – *this* girl. You promise me, you'll be more gentle, and maybe – just maybe – I'll let you do it again."

Simon gripped her buttocks, letting his fingers slide under her crotch. "Aye, I promise thee. Dost want t'chair now?"

"No. And take your hand away!"

"Well, at least you can give me a kiss, can't you?" he asked.

She hesitated a moment before leaning forward, giving him the opportunity to cup a breast with his other hand as she did. She kissed him briefly then stepped away.

"That'll have to last you. I'm going."

She collected her bicycle from where it stood in an empty stall. A minute or two later, Simon was alone with his thoughts.

*

After returning from Skipton, Craig took a case of beer he'd bought up to the marquee where the archæologists were having another barbecue. He had expected Jemma to come to his side when they were all sitting round the grill and was slightly surprised when she remained where she was, beside Cat. A few compact discs were produced and played on one of the laptops, and Mike kept food coming from the barbecue.

With Christmas only weeks away, there was an atmosphere of rush, trying to do as much as possible before the holiday. Dave had spent a lot of time trying to persuade those holding the purse-strings that the dig should resume in the New Year, but so far his arguments had fallen on deaf ears.

"Please remember," he said, "that the television cameras will be here tomorrow, and that Alan

156

Crossley, who's going to be the one asking the questions, is an archaeologist and likely to know the answers, so don't try and blind him with science. He's not here to reveal his own brilliance to the viewers, but ours. And so that you are all at your tip-top best, peak of condition, et cetera, et cetera, can I suggest you go easy on the booze and get to bed this side of midnight."

There were a few theatrical groans, but they didn't last long as Mike announced the lamb kebabs were ready and the rest of the group formed a queue to be served. Craig was behind Jemma.

He leaned down to her ear. "Are you coming down to the house tonight?"

She turned to him and shook her head slightly. "No, thanks. I'll be down for a shower tomorrow, though, if that's all right."

"Of course," he replied. By the time he'd stripped the lamb, peppers and tomatoes off their skewer into a pouch of pitta bread, she'd taken his place, leaving him with the one next to Cat. He sat down, frowning.

*

Jemma saw Cat glance at him, then at her own bland expression. The two women grinned at each other. It had caused her a slight pang when she'd decided that Craig and Cat needed to be able to sort out their past and, possibly, their future, and she was just in the way. She turned and engaged Dave Pountney in conversation for the rest of the evening.

She'd never really talked to him about anything much beyond work, and discovered that he could be quite funny and knew a lot about many things. Out of the corner of her eye, she saw Craig stand up, glancing at his watch, and decided to put the second part of her plan into operation. Excusing herself from Dave, she moved until she was at Cat's shoulder.

"Cat, I don't know if I should mention it, but," she wrinkled her nose theatrically, "you need a

157

shower." Her voice was pitched just loudly enough so that Cat would be sure Craig heard.

Cat stared at her flushing with embarrassment. "Thanks very much!" Then the import of Jemma's innocent expression sank in.

"Oh," she continued, and turned to Craig, whose expression confirmed her suspicion that he *had* heard.. "Would you mind awfully? My friend here seems to think I smell." He stared at her and shrugged. "Of course, Cat, you're welcome to take a shower at the house. I was thinking of going anyway, mindful of Dave's edict. Perhaps I could walk down the path with you?"

"Just wait until I get my things."

Cat went into the curtained-off sleeping area at the rear of the marquee.

Jemma smiled at him. "You got your shower-guest after all."

He frowned. "Yes – but I don't know why you think Cat needs a shower. She seems just fine to me."

Jemma shook her head briefly, grinning. "Really? I was thinking it would take the efforts of both of you to soap her up and dry her off, and it's a good job the shower cubicle is big enough for two." She tapped his chest lightly. "Well, I'm for my bed. Night, Craig." She turned abruptly and went after Cat.

*

Cat wondered what she was supposed to do now. Jemma had been very devious, providing her with an opportunity to go home with Craig. As soon as she'd realised the girl was setting them up, she'd felt her heart beat a little faster, but no matter her physiological response, there was absolutely no way she was sleeping with him tonight. Perhaps, though, they could talk. She rolled clean underwear, shampoo and shower gel in her towel as Jemma came through the curtain, grinning.

Cat glanced at her. "I suppose you think that was subtle?" she asked, without heat.

Jemma adopted a look of injured innocence. "But of course. I don't think Craig noticed I passed the baton – in a manner of speaking. Do you?"

"I suppose not." She raised an eyebrow. "Really! I can manage without help, you know."

"I understand. I do. It's up to you. Pick up the baton, if you want it. I've done my bit; I'm just a bystander now." Jemma changed quickly into her pyjamas as she spoke. "Or you can go out there and tell him you've changed your mind about the shower."

Cat pouted. "And have him think I'm a smelly cow?" She sighed. "No, I'll just have to go."

Jemma smiled. "You've no choice, really," she said with mock sympathy.

"Oh, stop it! I never realised how manipulative you can be."

Jemma pulled her sleeping bag up until just her head was left showing. "Only when necessary. Switch the light off as you go."

"I might be back in half an hour," said Cat as she opened the flap to leave the sleeping compartment.

Jemma scoffed quietly, so the men wouldn't hear. "I saw which set of underwear you rolled up in your towel. You're not planning to be back before morning."

She rolled over. Cat stared at the back of her head inscrutably for a moment, then went to join Craig, who was waiting near the entrance to the marquee.

CHAPTER 13

The bathroom was full of steam. A little hotter, Cat thought, and it would have passed for a sauna. She finished towelling herself dry and pulled the shower cap off her head. As she slipped into her clean underwear, she found herself wondering for a moment just why she had brought this particular set with her. The panties weren't very brief, covering her quite modestly, but made of pure silk. The bra, also silk, was a triumph of subtle design, comfortable to wear, revealing but decent. In fact, she acknowledged, as she studied her reflection in the full-length mirror behind the bathroom door, the overall effect was sexy but tasteful.

The lingerie was comfortable to wear, and the wearer would not be uncomfortable to be seen in it – and nothing else. Not that she had any intention of letting Craig see her in just her underwear, whatever Jemma might think. With her jeans and top back on, she pulled a brush through her hair, seeking to achieve order out of the chaos of her curls.

Finally, she slipped her feet into her shoes and packed her shower gel and towel into the bag she'd brought them in, turned off the light and went downstairs. In the kitchen, Craig had brewed coffee. The aroma filled the room and made her nostrils twitch. She inhaled, appreciating the richness of the blend. Craig was beside the worktop on which stood two mugs.

"I figured you'd like a coffee before you went back."

"Thanks," she said, sitting in one of the old armchairs, enjoying the way the leather was warmed by the heat radiating from the nearby Aga. It wasn't much of a decision – to stay and drink a decently-brewed coffee with Craig. He eased his length into the chair opposite, holding his mug and resting it on the arm.

"I didn't used to like coffee," he said.

"I remember."

"The Canadians taught me to like it, and showed me a good way of making it."

She lifted her mug to her lips and nodded. "I can tell." She sipped the hot liquid. He sipped from his own mug. "You used to be a very picky eater."

"Still am. Perhaps not as much as I used to be. When I'm out doing fieldwork like this, you have to accept – more or less – the food you're given. Otherwise it causes resentment."

"Do you all take turns to cook, up at the dig?"

"Mike does most of it. Fortunately, he's quite good."

They both sipped. "Alan seemed like a nice guy," he said.

She wondered what was coming. "He was."

"So, why'd you break up? I think you said you were no longer together. Was that until recently?"

"What's this? The third degree on my private life?"

She sensed him draw back. "Sorry. I just wondered. None of my business I know."

Just remember that, she thought. Was he making polite conversation, or was it important to him for some reason? She decided to throw him a tit-bit of the information he'd requested, narrowing her eyes as she watched for his reaction.

"Alan had been living with me for six months. He asked me to marry him, and moved out when I decided I didn't want to, at least at this time."

"Oh," he said.

She drank the last of her coffee while she waited in vain for him to amplify that response. Suddenly, she saw the hint of a smile break out on his lips. It surprised her for a moment, and she had to stop herself responding in kind. He reached for her empty mug.

161

"Want another? There's just enough left in the pot."

She felt she should leave but was curious to know what was coming next. She sensed that Craig had taken the first uncertain steps on some kind of mental journey. She accepted the offer of coffee when she realised she wanted to find out where he was going on it. She watched him standing beside the kitchen unit where the coffee maker stood. He still had a good figure – perhaps not surprising considering he was probably at his physical peak. She reflected wryly that she was at almost the latest recommended age for having a first child, and the best candidate for father had just gone out of her life. Not quite the best, she amended, her eyes fixed on Craig's backside while his gluteus muscles tensed and relaxed as he moved.

He turned towards her and brought two fresh mugs of coffee.

"What are you going to do with this place?" she asked. "I suppose you're going to leave again as soon as you can?"

He nursed his mug with both hands after settling in his chair. "I think I must sell the business. But I can't part with Holt Carr, not permanently. I could let it while I'm away. I really can't see any alternative."

"When are you going?"

He told her about the promotion he'd been offered. "But they want me back as soon as possible."

She was aware of a chill creeping through her. "How soon is that?"

"Within three weeks. Soon as I can sort things out here." He sipped his drink and glanced up at her. "I don't suppose you'd consider coming with me?"

She stared at him. "Absolutely not!" The words were no sooner said than she wished she could unsay them.

"Any particular reason?" he asked.

Because you don't love me, she thought. "I'm settled here. Career, home, so on," she said.

He smiled wanly and nodded. "No change there then."

"No, no change at all," she echoed, standing. She put her mug on the table and picked up her bag. "I'm going now. Thanks for the shower and the coffee."

She had almost reached the door when he called her back.

"Cat!"

She turned. "Yes?"

He'd stood up and put his own mug beside hers, letting his arms fall to his sides. His shoulders rose and fell.

"I'm really sorry, Cat."

A lump developed in her throat preventing a reply. She nodded quickly, and slipped outside before he could see the tears gathering in her eyes.

*

Simon spent much of the next morning where he could keep an eye on Kelly. He was becoming obsessed with her. She was a little temptress, and he was very much of a mind to be tempted. He took opportunities to touch her, as she did him, and he had no doubt that having been in her knickers once, he would be again.

Around lunchtime, he decided to send Susie out on one of the hacks, to exercise a pair of mares on leading reins.

As Kelly watched her leave the yard, Simon came up behind her and put a hand on her shoulder. She turned and looked up at him, leaning against his body.

"Time to polish one of the saddles," he told her.

"Huh?" She frowned.

He grinned with cunning. "I'll show thee."

He guided her ahead of him into the tack room, turning her towards him and slipping his hands under her top until he could hold her breasts. She wrapped her arms round him and grabbed the cheeks of his backside, pulling him

163

close until she could sit his aroused penis between her breasts. As he worked her top off, she unfastened the belt of his trousers. As she shoved his underpants down, following his jeans into a wrinkled pool on the floor, the engorged tip of his penis sprang close to her mouth.

"Coo, Simon, is that all for me? All *because* of me?" she asked coyly.

He was trying to take her jodhpurs off, but they were a very tight fit. "Aye, lass. Let's just get these off and I'll show thee."

His gaze was fixed on her breasts, not shifting even when she hooked her thumbs into the waistband of her jods and rolled her hips to help slip them down. She bent to tug them off completely, and he took the opportunity to slide his fingers inside her knickers.

"This doesn't seem to have much to do with saddles, Simon," she said.

He leaned down to suckle at each breast before replying. He straightened up and grinned. Suddenly he picked her up bodily, feeling her legs automatically wrap around him, her arms going round his neck. He stepped away from their discarded clothes and deposited her on the worktop between a pair of saddles, which were stored on stout wooden supports which stood out from the long wall of the tack room.

"Na' then," he said, "tha steadies thy sen by hooking your arms over the saddles either side. He pulled her knickers off and pushed her back, so she was open to him.

"Simon, don't you think we should use a rubber?" she said.

He looked at her slightly askance. "I don't have any. Never use 'em."

"All the same, you don't want to get me pregnant do you!"

"Don't worry about it, Kelly," he said, sliding into her before she could stop him.

"You'll... have... to... pull... out..." she said, in time with his thrusts.

"Oh, aye," he said, feeling his moment of release approaching.

"... or... you'll... get... me... pregnant... "

The thought made him feel powerful, virile. He grunted, thrusting hard into her and gripped her bottom so she could not back away as he spurted inside her. Her eyes rolled up in their sockets and he found that she was holding on to him. She moaned softly until he finished, then slowly relaxed against him. She took a couple of deep breaths then looked up into his face.

"You bastard, Simon. You came in me!" she said reproachfully.

He held her so she couldn't get away. "Aye, I did," he breathed. "Tha's just so sexy, Kelly. I couldn't 'elp it."

"I won't be so bloody sexy if I get a fat belly. Look," she continued, pushing against him with her feet and hands, "get off. I need to go to the toilet."

He moved away from her, grinning. "Art sure? We could go again and not worry," he said, picking up her knickers and wiping himself on them.

"What!"

"We could fuck again and not worry. If you're pregnant, another fuck won't make any difference."

"If by some miracle I'm not, another fuck might just succeed."

"Eh, tha's reet. Come 'ere!" he grinned, reaching for her.

She swept his arm aside. "Fuck off!" she said, wriggling off the worktop, avoiding his hand, and picking up her discarded clothes. "I may be some time," she told him as she locked herself in the toilet.

Simon dressed himself and got his adulterated vodka from the fridge. He swallowed several mouthfuls, feeling the spirit spread its warmth through his system. He was for once without the headache which almost continually nagged him, and he was feeling good about himself.

Outside, the sound of vehicle engines passing on their way up to the dig site aroused his curiosity and he went to the yard door to see what was happening. A big Renault van bearing the logo of a TV satellite uplink company and fitted with a dish antenna, currently folded flat on its roof, and a cherry-picker, followed a four-by-four up the track.

Beyond it, coming over the skyline, Susie was returning across the moor with the horses.

*

Cat was kneeling in a shallow trench, helping Jemma uncover a thousand-year-old burial when the television company arrived. Alan Crossley climbed out of the four-by-four with another man, whilst the satellite van swung off the track to find more level ground, stopping and extending stabilisers to prevent it rocking. The two women watched as the dish on its roof erected itself and swung round to point at the communications satellite it was going to use. Alan waved and came towards them. The other man, his bald patch incongruous against a grey-haired pony-tail, followed, clutching a clipboard.

Dave Pountney, who was working another trench with Diarmuid and Mike, stood up and shook hands with Alan and the other man, who was introduced as the Producer. Jemma and Cat sat back on their haunches and eased their lumbar muscles. Both women watched as someone mounted a camera on the cherry-picker, cables were run out, and a man wearing headphones waved a large furry microphone on a stick near Dave. It seemed no time at all before the cherry-picker rose into the air, a young woman behind the camera, and the Producer stepped towards the van, presumably to get out of shot. Alan had Dave lead him around the site, showing him where structures had been uncovered and artefacts found. The women realised that they would be visiting their trench soon, and as if by mutual agreement, busied themselves with their work.

166

"And here's an old friend of mine," said Alan, suddenly standing almost next to where Cat knelt in the trench.

She looked up and saw he'd turned towards the distant camera, which was slowly swooping in their direction.

"Dr Cat Mitchell of Mid-Yorks University." He squatted next to her. The furry microphone appeared at the edge of her vision. Cat sighed and stopped work.

"Tell us, what is your job here, Cat," said Alan.

"I catalogue and examine bones."

Alan was nodding as if expecting more. When she kept silent, he spoke again. "You're a highly respected forensic archæologist specialising in osteology, I believe," he said.

She shrugged. "Yes."

"I believe you have a complete skeleton in the marquee? Can we see it?"

She glanced at Dave, who was grinning happily, obviously expecting her to comply. She stood up and turned towards the marquee.

"Cut!" The Producer was striding towards them, the cherry-picker sinking to the ground. Someone pulled a stout tripod out of the van while the operator released the camera from its mounting on the cherry-picker. Someone else appeared carrying a lamp attached to a large battery hanging from their shoulder.

"We'll need some cutaways of the bones in the trench," shouted the Producer at the camera operator, "and then relocate to the marquee." He came up to Cat, smiling professionally. "Right, love, you're doing fine. Just remember exactly where you're standing, then move out of the way so Clarissa can get a few shots of the bones in the trench – where are they, by the way?"

Cat pointed.

"Oh, ta, love." He turned to the girl with the camera. "Here you are, love, can you get a few shots of this lot." Dave cleared his throat. "Preferably from outside the trench, please." The

Producer frowned, and turned back to Clarissa. "Keep outside the trench, dear." He glanced at his watch. "Come on now, people, we haven't got all day, there are deadlines to meet!"

Cat and Jemma stepped out of the trench.

The Producer looked round and waved his hands in a negative gesture at Jemma.

"No, no, love. You stay in the trench. Let Clarissa film you doing whatever it is you do with the bones." He switched on a smile. "Does no harm to the viewing figures to get a pretty girl in shot – and doing such clever things, too."

Cat and Jemma glanced at each other and both bit their lips.

Jemma turned an innocent expression on the Producer. "Ooh, you'd better tell me what you want me to do," she said. "Perhaps you'd better show me."

Dave was frowning at her in puzzlement. Jemma had spoken in a little-girl voice not at all like her own. "Erm, if you can avoid treading on the bones..." he said, showing the man where to walk avoiding damage to the skeleton.

The Producer moved next to Jemma and squatted beside her. "Now then, what have we got here?" he asked, avuncularly.

Jemma pointed with the tip of a trowel at a shoulder blade. "There: I think that's a hip bone," she said. Cat was astonished. Jemma knew perfectly well just about all the names of bones in the human skeleton, and what they looked like. She was about to correct her when Jemma caught her eye.

The Producer was apparently smarter than anyone thought. He shook his head. "No, I think not. That's a scapula." He pointed at a broken piece of pelvis. "I think *that's* part of a hip bone, as you call it."

Jemma gazed worshipfully into his eyes. "What do you call it?" she asked breathily.

He coughed. "Erm, a pelvis."

She blinked at him. He slipped an arm round her.

"Gosh," she said, "you must be very clever, knowing about bones and cameras, and everything."

Cat saw him blush and glanced at the others. Everyone, it seemed from their expressions, was now aware that the Producer was being gently ridiculed. Clarissa, Cat noticed, was casually and without seeming to, recording the moment on videotape. She wondered if it would see the light of day at the television company's Christmas party.

The Producer, unaware, continued. "Oh, archæology is an interest of mine. Been on one or two digs. How many have you been on?"

Jemma giggled. "Can't remember. Have this trouble with numbers, you know. Sometimes I forget my bra size and have to measure my boobs all over again."

The Producer's gaze travelled across her tight sweater, lingering on the view it gave of the curve of her breasts.

"I expect plenty of people are prepared to help."

Mike, who was watching them from the far side of the trench, spoke. "Absolutely. Fortunately, Diarmuid and I are usually around when she wants her, uh, boobs measured. Dave can't, of course, because he's married."

The Producer, whose mouth had fallen open while Mike was speaking, suddenly realised what was happening and stood up.

"Ah, uh, anyway, Miss, thank you for all of that," he said, clambering out of the trench, narrowly missing an arm bone. "Come on, people. Like I said, we haven't got all day." He glared at Clarissa. "Need to get some shots in the trench," he added.

She smiled and patted the camera. "In the can, Frank. Hope you like them."

He did a sort of double-take before striding over to the marquee. "Right! We'll move in here. Shot through the entrance – Alan and Dr Mitchell coming over."

Jemma climbed out of the trench.

Frank shouted, and waved his arms. "No, girl!" He turned to one of the dogsbodies. "Stop her – the blonde." He turned back to Jemma. "No, dear, you have to stay in the trench, where you were. It's continuity, d'you see," he called.

Jemma touched her fingers to her lips. "Ooh, sorry. I must be having a blonde moment."

"Yes, well, just stay there. Julian will put you in position."

The dogsbody moved to obey, but Jemma neatly sidestepped him and returned to kneel beside the skeleton.

Cat had been having difficulty concealing her mirth.

Alan took her elbow and fairly roughly led her back into the trench.

"Now when he shouts 'Action!', you get up just like you did and we'll walk together towards the marquee." He leaned close to her ear. "And please don't take the piss out of him. It's unbecoming and he can't help it."

"Yes Alan. No Alan."

He grinned at her through gritted teeth. "And don't take the piss out of me, either. I have to make a living."

"Action!"

"It must be so much fun, working with people like Frank. So different from academia, where one is conscious of so much concentrated brain-power."

She stood up and turned towards the marquee, taking Alan's offered hand to steady her as she climbed out of the trench.

"We don't talk about brain-power in front of Frank either," he said out of the corner of his mouth.

Cat tried to keep the grin off her face. She glanced at the far side of the site and saw Craig watching them. In an unplanned, perverse moment, she reached up and kissed Alan on the cheek, with some idea that it might make Craig jealous and prompt him into doing something about it. When she looked back, he was striding back down the track towards Holt Carr. Unable to see the expression on his face, she was unable to judge whether her rather childish act had had the desired effect.

CHAPTER 14

December announced its arrival with a cold wind sweeping down over the moor from the east, keeping people indoors but the temperature was not low enough for ice to be a worry.

Simon was crossing the yard towards the stables when Kelly arrived on her bicycle. She dismounted beside him and walked by his side to the door. The horses kept the temperature up slightly, but the tack room was chilly and unwelcoming. Kelly hugged herself for warmth. Simon noticed and hugged her himself.

"I'll soon get thy temperature up, lass," he said.

Kelly's teeth were chattering. "G-good!" she muttered. She adjusted the fit of her bra.

"You all right?" he asked.

"Boobs are feeling a bit tender."

Simon switched the fan heater on. "Do you want a hot drink?" he asked.

"Yeah. That'd be g-good," she said, shivering.

Under cover of making some drinking chocolate, Simon felt in his pocket for another sachet of the immensely powerful Equipalazone he used to control his headaches and sprinkled some in both their cups. He expected his to reduce his headache and other symptoms, and Kelly's to relax her a bit. Kelly sat in the armchair, still in her coat, and Simon brought their drinks across, standing behind her so he could massage her shoulders and neck again. She sipped the drink and wrinkled her nose.

"Tastes a bit funny, this does, Simon," she remarked.

"Aye. It's the water round here," he explained.

She seemed to accept that and writhed as his thumbs found a sensitive spot. "Ooph!" she gasped, "Aren't you going to drink your chocolate?"

172

"I'm sipping it. I don't want to stop this, but I will if you tell me to," he said.

"Simon, I'm drinking."

"Hurry up. I've something to show thee." Kelly's eyebrows arched. "Oh, yes? Would this be anything I've seen before, or something new?" she asked coyly. Simon slipped his hands under her coat and cupped her breasts. He felt her nipples stiffen almost at once.

"Hh-ahh," she breathed. "Simon, just be careful, my breasts are feeling sore."

He came round the chair to face her. "Then I'll just have to kiss 'em better," he said, pulling her top out of the way and dipping his head to suit his words. He stood up and unzipped his jeans. "Get thy jods off, Kel."

"I'm drinking my chocolate," she said with a pout.

"I can't wait any longer, Kelly. You're just too irresistible."

She put her mug down on the table and tapped his cheek. "You're so naughty, Simon! What if Susie turns up?"

"I don't think this'll take long," he told her, unzipping her jodhpurs and rolling them down her legs.

She still had her boots on and he couldn't wait to remove them. He picked her up, turned her over until she was kneeling on the cushion and forced himself into her from behind. She squealed with pleasure, making huffing noises as they worked together to achieve satisfaction. After they finished, she rolled over to face him. He was wiping himself on her knickers again.

"Wish you wouldn't do that," she whined.

He grinned. "Summat to remember me by."

"You didn't use a rubber again!"

"Aye. Well, I forgot. Not used to it, see; and tha knows I can't resist you long enough to put one on."

She shrugged. "Oh well. There's a couple of girls at school both pregnant."

173

"These things 'appen," said Simon, sounding faintly philosophical as he reached for the rest of his drinking chocolate. Kelly's eyes, he noticed, were beginning to glaze over. He moved so he was standing near her head.

'Reckon you can clean me off, Kel?"

She looked up at him, her eyes blinking as if she was having trouble staying focussed, and quietly began to use her tongue on him. After a few minutes, he was hard again, she had stopped licking and seemed to have passed out. Simon looked at her speculatively for a moment, then pulled off her boots. When she didn't wake, he removed her jodhpurs, and finally he slipped inside her again, rutting to another satisfying conclusion. Afterwards, he slowly dressed her and left her sleeping in the chair.

*

Later in the morning, Craig told Simon to expect a prospective buyer of the horse breeding business. Around half-past ten, a Range Rover pulled into the yard. A man, tall, with a moustache and wearing a flat cap in a fine check climbed down from the driving seat, while the passenger door opened and a woman in jodhpurs and riding boots stepped out. Craig approached them, having seen them arrive through the kitchen window.

"Mr Jordon? Major Clarkson from Appleby." His voice had an unmistakable military ring to it. They shook hands.

"We have one of your mares don't we?" said Craig.

"Highland Storm," said his passenger, holding out her own hand. "Susan Clarkson. I look after our horses." She sounded almost as military as her husband.

"Not here today to talk horses, Susan," said Clarkson.

"No," said Craig, "but perhaps you'd like to have a look at the stables and the exercise yard anyway?"

174

"Seen 'em before, y'know – when we brought HS over."

"We'll have another look, dear!" said his wife.

The major didn't argue. Craig led the way towards the stables. Inside, Simon was cleaning out one of the stalls. Mrs Clarkson found her mare and stroked her rounded flanks.

"Not long now, old girl," she muttered. Clarkson and Simon were staring at each other. She looked from one to the other. "Pleased to see that HS is in good condition, Mr Stalland," she said.

Simon turned to her. "Aye," he said, before turning away and getting on with his work. Clarkson nodded towards the door at the end of the building. "Tack room?"

"That's right," said Craig. "You want to see?"

Simon turned towards him and shook his head. "It's a bit... messy in there. Wouldn't go in if I was you."

Craig stared at him. Simon returned the gaze steadfastly, giving the slightest shake of his head. "Perhaps later..." said Craig, turning back to the Clarksons, "when it's been cleaned up?" He looked at Simon again.

"Aye. I'll get on wi' it."

"Perhaps you'd like to see the exercise yard?" said Craig.

"Very well," said the Major, turning and leading the way outside. Craig quickly opened the door of the tack room and peered inside. Kelly was still asleep in the chair. He closed the door again, aimed a puzzled glance at Simon, and hurried after his visitors. After looking round the indoor exercise yard, the Clarksons decided to leave, telling Craig they'd be in touch. There were, they said, inquiries they had to make. They did not want to employ Simon, but needed someone else with similar skills.

Craig watched them drive away. Before he could go back into the stables to discover what had happened to Kelly, he heard the sound of a tractor coming over the moor. It was William Stalland. He pulled up near the yard entrance and came across to Craig's side. "

"Ey up, lad. That were *Major* Clarkson and 'is missus, wa'n't it?"

"Yup," replied Craig.

Stalland nodded silently. "Looking at buying the place, were they?"

"Yeah."

Stalland said, "Are you intending to sell everything? Holt Carr, the stables, the exercise yard?"

"I don't want to sell the house. The rest, yes."

"And the land rights?"

"Yes."

"Hmm." Craig waited. "Can't say as I'd like the Clarksons as neighbours."

"Why?"

Stalland blew out his cheeks. "They're not, like, real country folk, tha knows."

"Come from the City, eh?"

"Aye, mebbe. 'E's not actually a Major, either."

"Really?"

Stalland glanced at him wryly. "Not unless he's in the Salvation Army."

"Oh. But is he good for the money?"

"I don't know about *him*, but *she's* got pots of the stuff. I think she keeps her fingers firmly on the purse strings."

"I see. They said the horses were *her* interest. I suppose it would make sense then – she's considering indulging herself with this place."

"Aye. Mebbe." Stalland chewed his cheek reflectively. "What sort of sum would you be expecting?" Craig glanced at him, and decided from the man's expression that he might just be considering buying the business himself. He decided to proceed cautiously, figuring that Stalland would offer less than whatever sum he named, so he pitched higher.

Stalland sucked his teeth. "Have you had it valued? That seems a bit optimistic to me."

"What wouldn't be optimistic, in your view?"

176

More tooth sucking. "Well, mebbe three quarters of that."

Ten minutes of haggling later, they had agreed a price.

"Are you thinking of continuing the business?" asked Craig.

"Well, I don't know. There's other kinds of businesses that use horses. Pony-trekking for one. And there's always general livery," he added, referring to the stabling and care of horses for private owners lacking their own facilities.

Craig thought about this. "Pony trekking holidays... you'd need somewhere to accommodate your trekkers, wouldn't you?"

"Aye. That's why I'd be a bit disappointed that Holt Carr isn't included in the deal."

"I wouldn't sell Holt Carr," said Craig, "but I'd let it to you, on a two year lease with an option to renew. That'd give me some income."

"Think we have a deal, then?" asked Stalland. Craig held out his hand. "We have a deal." They shook on it. "It'll take me a couple of days to raise the cash."

"I'll instruct my solicitors."

*

It was growing dark as Susie returned from her last outing of the day, exercising the animals in her care. Kelly had woken at last from her drugged sleep and was keeping Simon at arm's length. He was privately amused and did not try to renew their intimacy. Between the three of them, they completed the final tasks of the day, and the girls went home. Simon went into the tack room.

Shutting the door behind him, he took his vodka from the fridge. He opened a pack of sandwiches and ate them, washed down by the strong liquor. His hands shook, his headache was back, as bad as it had ever been, and he felt as if he was screaming inside, but his natural caution kept him as quiet as possible. Finally, he set off across the yard onto the moor, and spent another night at his father's house.

Kelly pushed the bedclothes off her and glanced at her bedside clock. It was past eight. She would be late at Holt Carr. The weight of her duvet was hurting – both breasts were tender, even more than they had been the previous day. She felt very lazy, very lumpish, and didn't want to get up, but the discomfort – due no doubt, she thought, to over-enthusiastic attention from Simon – persuaded her that she needed to put some moisturiser on them. She rolled into a sitting position and took a few steps over to her dressing table where she scrabbled among various tubes and pots until she found what she was looking for. She opened the lid of a jar and raked around in the bottom of it for enough cream, without success.

Bugger, she thought. Still, mum would have some. Noises drifting upstairs and the smell of fried bacon told Kelly everyone else was already up. Suddenly her stomach spasmed. Normally, she liked the smell of bacon, but suddenly, it made her feel sick. She ran into the bathroom and moments later vomited into the toilet. She continued retching even after there was nothing left to bring up. Her mother came into the bathroom.

"Kelly! What's up? You feeling ill?"

Kelly looked round. What a bloody silly question! she thought. As suddenly as the episode had started, it ended.

"I'm fine."

She filled a glass with water from the basin tap and drank it. She realised her mother was staring at her.

"Is this the first time you've been sick in the morning?" she asked.

"Yes. I told you, I'm fine. Just something I ate." She didn't like the suspicion in her mother's face. "All right? Just something I ate," she repeated.

"Are your breasts sore?"

Kelly realised she had been nursing her breasts without realising it. She dropped her arms. "Might be. Can I have some of your moisturiser? I've run out."

"Kelly! Are you pregnant?" her mother asked.

Kelly shrugged. "Dunno."

Her mother uttered a little scream, and stifled it with her hands. "You stupid girl! You shouldn't be having sex at your age."

"It just, kind of, happened."

"And didn't the boy have enough gumption to use a condom? I thought you all got sex education at school these days." Mary Frobisher couldn't keep the shock out of her voice.

"We do."

"How many weeks?"

"What?" Kelly was getting bored with this display of mundane parental concern.

"How long have you been having sex?" growled Mary.

"About a month. I don't know. I lose track."

Her mother groaned again. "How many boys?"

"Just one! You think I'm some sort of slapper, mother?"

Mary stared at her without answering. She took a deep breath and seemed to come to a decision about something. "You'd better get dressed and come and have your breakfast."

Kelly pouted. "I don't feel hungry."

"You will later. Get dressed and have breakfast."

"Moisturiser?"

Mary nodded. "Come with me."

Ten minutes later, Kelly sat at the table. Rejecting the fry-up, she forced herself to eat a slice of buttered toast, and found it made her feel better. She had another. Her mother went into autopilot mode. Kelly had seen it before, when there was something of moment occupying her mind.

Mary went upstairs and reappeared with the laundry basket. In front of the washing machine, she began to empty its contents into two piles, one of "whites' and one of "coloureds'.

179

Kelly heard her new mobile phone's ringtone and went outside to talk.

*

While Mary was loading the whites into the washing machine, she found three pairs of knickers in a filthy state, looking to her as if they'd been used as a duster. As Mary shook them to dislodge any surface dirt, she became aware that the gussets were spotted with blood and something else. She leaned against the kitchen wall, fighting back the urge to cry. Through the door, she heard Kelly's stage whisper.

"It's true. He got a terrific hard-on just looking at my tits..."

Mary respected her daughter's privacy as a rule, but sometimes a mother had to know what was going on. Kelly's next words, she decided, absolved her from the guilt of eavesdropping.

"What did you *think* we did? You want me to draw you a diagram?" Kelly giggled. "Besides, you know what..." She listened a moment. "Three or four. God, he can be so rough. He couldn't wait the first time – I got him really wound up, you know, like he was going to go off anyway... No, we didn't have time for that, he simply did it."

She paused again to listen.

Mary's blood was running cold, her gaze fixed on the dusty and bloody panties she was carrying. She picked them up and shoved them in the washing machine with the other garments, trusting to the 'biological' aspect of the washing powder to clean away the stains. When Kelly came back indoors, looking flushed, she stopped her and told her to sit down.

"Kelly, you have to tell me who the father is. Does he know?"

"None of your business," said Kelly with a touch of truculence.

"It is, dear. My business, I mean. You're only fifteen. Who've you been with?"

180

"Who do you think? My boyfriend." As she spoke, she was absently massaging one tender breast.

It drew her mother's gaze. "Just who is this boyfriend? You didn't tell me you had a boyfriend."

"Just a man I met."

"A man? You mean someone older; someone not at school with you?" Her blood ran cold. "Is it one of your teachers?"

Kelly laughed, but it was a forced one and her mother noticed. "School isn't the only place I go, mother."

"Only there or up at Holt Carr. Not many other places."

Kelly shrugged again.

"What's his name?" asked her mother.

Kelly thought for a moment. "Craig," she said. It seemed like a safe choice.

"Craig, eh? He's the son who came back from Canada isn't he?"

"Yes, that's right," said Kelly, feeling on safer ground.

"And how old is Craig?"

"I don't know. Maybe thirty. Maybe twenty-something. The age thing isn't important to us."

"Sometimes it's more important than others," said Mary.

Kelly shrugged again. "Just don't make a fuss. It happens. It's not important."

"Not important? Kelly, you're only fifteen: you have your whole life ahead of you. Oh, for God's sake! Is Craig the father?"

Kelly looked away. "I'm not saying."

"Don't be stupid. We have to know."

"Huh! I don't see as it's any of your business," she said haughtily.

Her mother's eyes opened wide. "So it *is* Craig? You weren't... forced were you?" She held the knuckles of one hand to her lips as if defending herself from the possibility.

"No. It was just sex. He fancies me and I fancy him, so we got it together."

181

"Oh my God!" Kelly's mother held her head in her hands.

Kelly watched her impassively.

Suddenly her mother looked up. "We must tell your father."

Kelly was outraged. "Why? It's not his business. It's not yours if it comes to that."

"Kelly, he's your father – he has a right to know."

"I'm not telling anybody anything."

Her mother frowned at her as she stood to leave the room. "I wouldn't be too sure of that, my girl. It's against the law for a man to have sex with a fifteen-year-old. Does this Craig know how young you are?"

"I don't know. He always treats me like an adult – which is more than you and dad do!"

"Are you still seeing him?"

"No. I told you: it was just a fling. He said he loved me."

Her mother's lip curled. "Oh, you stupid girl! Men will say anything to sleep with a woman – especially one who hasn't the sense to insist he wears a bloody condom!"

"I told him to!"

"Oh, well, that's all right then! You told him to! And did he? No. And did you stop him? No. Kelly, where were your wits, girl?"

Mary saw tears begin to fill her daughter's eyes, and reached for her. It was too much all at once. She hugged her, feeling tears flooding down her cheeks. Stupid, stupid girl, she thought, but above all her disappointment and anger, her overriding feeling was of sorrow. Still, she told herself, time enough for sentimentality later. She had to be practical and drive some sense of responsibility into Kelly's head.

*

By lunchtime, Cat was almost up to date with her work. After several days of nonstop tasks, she felt she deserved some time off. Jemma obviously felt the same, despite not being quite as on top of her workload as Cat: since deciding she had no further interest in Craig, she'd spent more time around the site, and on more than one occasion, Cat had seen her chatting comfortably with Dave. She was working in his trench, excavating the remains of a midden which had developed as the Viking inhabitants had exploited a gap between two slabs of sandstone to dispose of their rubbish, while he sat on the edge watching.

Mike and Diarmuid worked two other trenches, leaving Cat to herself. She decided she would take the opportunity to visit Holt Carr House and use the bathroom. While the others were busy, she could take some time over a leisurely soak in the bathtub. Craig was out somewhere in the Land Rover, and she hadn't seen Simon moving around in the yard at all. She gathered her things and walked down the track. The bicycle of one of the girls was leaning against the stable wall, so she guessed somebody was around, taking care of the animals. She let herself into the house and listened.

Apart from the ticking clock, the place was silent. She went upstairs and filled the bath. Fifteen minutes later, up to her neck in warm, foamy water, she found herself drifting off to sleep. She slipped a bookmark in the book she was reading – a far-fetched romance about a feisty and incredibly attractive young woman and a powerful and insensitive, though well-intentioned, alpha-male – put it on the chair near the bath, and allowed her eyes to close.

She woke with a start when the bathroom door burst open. There was a clatter as the bolt fitting hit the floor. She stared at the man in the doorway. He took a step towards her.

"Craig!" she cried. He stopped.

"Sorry Cat. I was worried. Came in, found the bathroom locked, got no reply when I called. Thought you might be in difficulties."

She glanced at herself and saw she was still covered in bubbles, only her head and knees breaking through them.

"H-how did you know it was me?" she asked.

"Actually, I didn't. I don't choose who to worry about drowning. I'm very fair minded. It's an equal-opportunity life-saving policy."

She saw his eyes land on her novel, with its turgid title and the cover photograph of a handsome man and pretty woman in a clinch. Oh, god! she thought. When he looked at her again, were his eyes a shade darker than they had been? She shivered, and not entirely because the water had cooled while she'd slept.

"Well?" she asked.

"What?"

"You've discovered I don't need saving and I would like to get out of the bath."

"Oh, sorry. I, uh, needed the loo, anyway." His eyes, she noticed, were scanning the length of the bathtub. She hoped the bubbles were effectively masking her.

"You'll have to wait," she said.

He chewed his lip. "You'll have to be quick."

"Try using some self-control!"

He began to wriggle. It reminded her of small boys at school who wanted the bathroom but were too shy to ask. She feared an accident.

"Oh! For god's sake, get on with it then," she snapped. She closed her eyes.

"Thanks, Cat," he muttered, moving past her to the lavatory pan, thankfully positioned where she couldn't see it. She slid down the bath until her head was submerged and held her breath, counting seconds. After nearly reaching two hundred, she felt a tap on her knee and quickly surfaced. Rubbing soap out of her eyes, she opened them to find Craig squatting beside the tub, grinning at her.

"Thanks, Cat. I needed that," he said.

"Fine. Now get out," she told him.

His grin broadened and he stood up. She watched him move to the doorway and turn round.

"I'll replace the bolt later," he said.

"Good."

He began to turn away but glanced back at her. "You know about Archimedes and displacement, don't you?"

"Of course," she replied, wondering what he was on about. Her mind associated the name with the water-lift called Archimedes' Screw, and the philosopher's having the first recorded Eureka moment in the bath. She frowned at Craig, feeling certain she was missing something. "What about it? – Him?"

"I'm trying to work out if it was deliberate or not," Craig said.

"If *what* was deliberate?"

"In order to submerge your head, you had to slide down the bath, which meant more of your legs came out of the water."

"Uh, ye-e-s?" She wondered what was coming.

"When your legs came out, less water was displaced so the level in the bath went down." He was grinning infuriatingly.

"And?" Light dawned.

She groaned as she realised what he was telling her and reflexively covered her breasts, now safely once again below the thinning layer of bubbles. Thinning? Christ! She needed to get him out of the way. She would have to try another brand of bubble-bath, one whose bubbles lasted a bit longer!

"Right, Craig! You've had your fun. Now please go so I can get dressed."

His grin, as he closed the door behind him, was annoyingly smug.

She sat up and pulled the plug. Standing in front of the full length mirror a couple of minutes later, she stopped towelling herself and looked at her reflection. Her breasts were firm and nothing to be ashamed of, she decided. She shrugged. What

185

the hell, he'd seen them before, even if it was a long time ago.

CHAPTER 15

Kelly was kept away from school and Holt Carr on the following Monday by her mother.

"But I *wanna* go to school," she insisted.

"You've got a few appointments to keep," said Mary Frobisher, dragging her outside and into her small runabout. Tom had left for work an hour earlier in the old Rover saloon.

"What appointments?"

Mary didn't reply until she had reversed out of the drive and was heading for Skipton.

"The first one is with the chemist. The second one I have in mind rather depends on the outcome of the first, but somehow, I think we'll be keeping it."

Kelly had spent another uncomfortable twenty minutes in the toilet that morning. It was becoming a regular event. At their first port of call, Mary bought a pregnancy test kit.

"Do you have a toilet we can use?" she asked the startled pharmacist. He nodded and pointed the way. Mary gave Kelly the kit. "Go and use this now."

Kelly's first inclination was to tell her mother where to stick the thing, but a moment's reflection decided her that it would probably make no difference to what seemed obvious. She took the offered item into the cubicle, emerging a couple of minutes later staring at the little indicator window. The test instrument was one of the new ones which didn't rely on blue lines or any other colour: this one simply answered the question *Pregnant?* embossed on the plastic handle with a *Yes* or a *No* on the thumbnail-sized screen. Mother and daughter watched as the word *Yes* appeared.

Kelly shrugged.

"Come out to the car," Mary said. She put the tester back in its box and dropped it into her handbag. For a few moments, they sat in silence in the car. Mary rested her elbows on the steering wheel and held her head in her hands for a few moments before sitting back and looking at her daughter.

"So now we're certain," she said. She sounded resigned.

"So what?" said Kelly in what was meant as a truculent manner, but the soft tone used by her mother was so unexpected her prepared response was undermined and emerged from her lips without the required force. It didn't sound convincing. She tried again in a more conciliatory tone. "It was fairly obvious. So what now?"

"Well...What's done is done. You'll have to decide what you're going to do about it."

Kelly turned to her mother. "What? You want me to have an abortion?"

"I said *you* will have to decide what you're going to do about it. I didn't say anything about abortion. It's just one option. If you want, you can go through with it and either keep the baby or put it up for adoption. You don't have to decide now."

Kelly stared through the windscreen, unseeing. For all her mother's words being delivered in a calm voice, she still suspected that she was very angry. With one part of her mind, she wondered what the big deal was: lots of her friends at school boasted about doing sex, and gained much kudos from it. She wouldn't be averse to the same sort of appreciation herself. But another part of her, deep in her psyche, told her that she had done wrong. It wasn't a part of her mind she normally listened to.

Her mother suddenly sat up, pulled a mobile phone from her pocket and dialled Tom's mobile. "You'd better come to Skipton," she told him. "And please come now."

She told him to meet at a coffee shop in the Market Place and closed the connection.

She turned to her daughter. "Let's go. I need caffeine."

They left the car and walked the few hundred yards to the coffee bar. Mary bought herself a coffee, and a mineral water for Kelly. They sat facing each other across a tall wrought-iron table in the window on elaborate wrought-iron bar stools covered in a rich red velveteen.

Kelly affected an uncaring attitude. "You might as well get it over with, and just tell me how terrible you think I am, how the world will end now, and how I've "ruined my chances' of getting married, et cetera, et cetera," she said.

Although her tone was deriding, part of her needed to be told she'd done wrong.

Mary was not so obliging. "I daresay that's what you're expecting," she said, "but there's no use crying over spilt milk."

Kelly eyed her suspiciously. The attack she expected was not coming straight at her, so she would have to be alert for outflanking moves.

"I dunno what you're fussing for," she said.

"Having a baby is a life-changing event, Kelly. You've all your life ahead of you. Everything you do from now on is going to be different from how it would have been if you hadn't got pregnant. You can't ignore a baby. You won't be able to go to university, or travel abroad, go and live in Leeds, or do *anything* without first having to consider how your baby is to be cared for."

"You can care for it if you like it so much!"

"Well, your father and I always looked forward to having a grandchild, and it looks as if we'll be having one sooner than we would have wished. But the lovely thing about grandchildren is that they're not your own: when you get worn out or fed up, or they won't go to sleep, you pass them back to the expert in their care: their mother."

"I'm no bleeding expert!" Kelly exclaimed. "What do I know about babies?"

"Mind your language, Kel," said Mary more calmly than she felt, "You knew enough to start

189

one. The learning curve begins now. How do you think any mother copes? She learns. There'll be help: there'll be other young mums, and you'll be able to swap stories and techniques. You'll be able to try them, keep the ones that work and discard the others. There'll be professionals, mother and baby groups, whatever. Bringing up a baby is a privilege, and it will take over your life."

Kelly stared at her mother. "Ellen Briggs and Tracey Linklater are both pregnant and their mums are going to bring up their babies. Why can't you be like them?"

"The first reason is because I'm *not* like them and I couldn't be like them. I've done my stint of child-rearing, and look where it's got me." She gazed at her daughter for a beat to let the matter sink home. "Secondly, I take leave to doubt that Ellen and Tracey's mums will be so keen after the babies have arrived. It's a tie, looking after a baby. When your mates want to go into town, or down the pub, or whatever, you can't go unless you can afford a babysitter. Very restrictive, and most of us will only put ourselves through it for our own child."

"It'll be your grandchild—"

"—but *your* child, not mine. I don't know how the housing register works," said Mary, suddenly looking through the window into space. "We might have to wait until you're eighteen before you can get on it. But with a two year-old child, you should get fairly close to the top of the list."

She appeared almost to be talking to herself.

Kelly's mouth dropped open. "You're going to throw me out?" she asked.

Her mother brought her gaze back. "No, dear, but obviously, you'll want somewhere to live as soon as possible. It'll have to be social housing, because neither your dad nor I can afford to help you buy a place. You're not old enough to take on a mortgage, and in any case, you can't get one of those unless you're at work."

"Why should I move out?"

"Well, I suppose you might want this Craig to drop by occasionally. I mean, I presume you'll be asking for maintenance from him for yourself and the child. And I don't want him in my house. Not some man who gets fifteen year olds pregnant. Actually, I don't want you entertaining any boyfriends under my roof from now on. I don't suppose this will matter once you've had the baby – if that's what you decide – because you'll be too tired for sex, and by the time you feel more like it, you'll be old enough to make your own way in life."

Kelly looked to be in a state of shock. "You can't do this: I'm your daughter!"

"And I love you dearly, Kelly," said her mother, tears welling up and spilling down her cheeks.

"You don't! You wouldn't do this otherwise."

Her mother looked down at her cooling coffee, still untouched. "I have to think what is the best thing I can do for you." She looked up. "Is it to mollycoddle you, treat you like the child you once were? Or should I make you stand on your own two feet and become self-reliant, even if, in the process, you have to forego the rest of your childhood? I think mollycoddling would be an expression of sentimentality, whereas the other thing is what I should do if I love you. And if you think that is an easy option, think again!"

"It seems the dead selfish option to me."

"If you want to talk about being selfish, I'm not the one who got pregnant without a thought for the consequences. Don't you think I'd rather things had stayed as they were? But that isn't an option now, and I have to make decisions which I'd never imagined I'd have to and never wanted to."

Kelly's eyes grew moist. "Mum," she said softly, "I need to know what to do."

Mary looked at her sadly and sighed. "We all need to know that, Kelly," she said.

"Yes. But should I keep the baby or have an abortion?"

"Like I said earlier, that's a decision you have to make. It's an adult decision and a great deal depends on it, so you have to weigh the consequences before you take it."

Kelly twisted her cup round in the saucer. Mary finished her coffee. A few minutes later, Tom Frobisher arrived to find his wife and daughter both tearful and unhappy.

Mary looked up. "You might as well grab yourself a coffee. There's something you need to know. I need a refill," she added.

"Kelly?" asked her father.

She shook her head and took another sip of her mineral water. He purchased coffees for himself and his wife and joined them at the table. Outside the window, the normal life of Skipton went on: shoppers, delivery vans, a driver in animated discussion with a traffic warden. Inside the coffee shop, Tom looked from wife to daughter and waited.

Mary looked up. "Kelly's pregnant," she said.

He stared at her, then at Kelly, his eyebrows arching in surprise.

"Pregnant!" he echoed, loud enough to be heard at other tables.

Mary shushed him. "Don't make a fuss here," she told him.

"Pregnant?" he repeated, only slightly quieter. He stared at Kelly, his eyebrows raised in enquiry and disbelief. She returned his gaze. "Pregnant?" he asked again.

She nodded.

"We've been discussing the choices *she* has to make," said Mary.

It was obvious from the suddenly strained expression on Tom Frobisher's face that some of those 'choices' were occurring to him.

"One thing that is going to have to be done is to get the baby's father to pay maintenance," said Mary, "and I think the sooner we go visit this Craig and tell him he's got a few more responsibilities the better."

She turned to Kelly who was refusing to meet her gaze.

"Well? This Craig you told me about, he is the father? You're sure?" Kelly avoided her mother's gaze, looking down at her half-empty cup on the table-top.

"I'm not getting him into trouble," she said sullenly. She looked up. "So I'm not saying anything more! And I'll deny saying it was him."

"You'll need his money," said Mary, "bringing up a child isn't cheap."

"If I have it adopted, or... the other thing," she said, "I won't need his money."

"That's true, but we need to know who it is anyway."

"Why?"

"Because he's done wrong. Men shouldn't be having sex with girls under sixteen."

"What are you talking about? Happens all the time," Kelly replied spiritedly.

"Not perhaps as much as you'd think," said her mum. "I'm not sure you're telling me the truth." She scrutinised her daughter's face shrewdly. "I'm not sure Craig is the father – you came up with his name rather too quickly."

Kelly's mouth turned down and she scowled at her mother.

"Well," Mary continued, "if you won't tell us, maybe you'll tell the police."

"The police? You're not going to tell them are you?" Kelly was aghast.

"What do you think? Get your things. There's no time like the present."

Her mother's uncompromising tone left Kelly speechless. Tom was surprised by his wife's determination, but he'd always supported her and he wasn't about to argue with her now in front of Kelly.

Mary led the way along the pavement and glanced sideways at Tom. He kept looking at his daughter and blinking, as if he couldn't believe what he'd heard.

"How did it happen?" he muttered.

193

"How do you think!" replied his wife tartly. They reached the police station and followed her inside. A civilian Front Desk Officer greeted them. "Can I help you?"

"My daughter is pregnant and only fifteen. I think that's a crime isn't it? So I want to report it."

The FDO stared at her for just a moment, then dragged his incident pad over. "Right," he said, "can I just have your names, please."

Mary Frobisher supplied them. Meanwhile Kelly had realised what was happening and was backing towards the door. Her mother turned and grabbed her. "You're staying here till we've sorted this out."

"But Mum! It's not a problem. And in any case, I'm not saying anything," she said.

"It *is* a problem and you're going to explain who the father is."

"No!" cried Kelly, trying to free herself from her mother's grip.

"We'll see!" She turned back to the desk.

The FDO had been telephoning someone and now he turned to her. "Someone is coming right down. Take a seat for a minute, please."

He pointed at a row of uncomfortable-looking iron benches screwed to the floor against the opposite wall. Scarcely had they sat down than a door opened and PC Stephanie Speight was beckoning them through into the corridor. She led them into an interview room and sat them all down.

"Could you tell me from the beginning why you're here?" she asked Mary, after she'd introduced herself.

Kelly fidgeted while her mother explained events. Tom looked surprised when it became clear that his wife had had her suspicions for several days without telling him.

"So you think the father is this Craig?" asked PC Speight. She turned to Kelly. "Is that right? The father is called Craig?"

Kelly adopted a mulish expression. "I'm not saying that."

Speight looked at her mildly. "Would you mind telling me who the father is?"

"No."

Speight considered Kelly in silence for a moment, then turned to her parents. "I wonder if you'd mind if I talked to Kelly alone for a few minutes?"

Mary caught Tom's eye and jerked her head towards the door. They stood up and left the room. Speight turned her attention back to Kelly.

"Let me explain, Kelly," she said, "The position is that if a man has sex with a girl under sixteen, then it's a criminal offence whether or not she consents. Now, I take it, for the record, that you didn't object?"

Kelly thought for a moment, then nodded.

"Right. Unfortunately for him, that doesn't count because in law, you can't consent until you reach sixteen. That's why it's called the age of consent. Now what do you call it when a man has sex with a girl who doesn't consent? Eh?"

Kelly's lip trembled. "Rape," she whispered.

"That's right. Now because you're fifteen and you didn't actually object to what the man did, we don't treat it like we would rape. It's a serious offence still, but not quite as serious as rape. Do you understand?"

Kelly nodded again. "What will happen to him?"

"Well, a lot depends on whether he knew you were only fifteen. Did he think you were older?"

Kelly shrugged. "I don't know. He never asked, and I never told him."

"Well then, that could constitute a defence."

"And what does that mean?"

"If he went to court and could show that he believed you were sixteen or over, then he would probably get off."

"So why are we making all this fuss?" asked Kelly.

"I think your mum wants to clear the air. I reckon she cares about you, and she won't have wanted you to become pregnant yet – I expect like

195

lots of mums, she'd have an idea in her mind that one day she'd love to have grandchildren, but when that happens, I guess she'd prefer you to be happily married. Mums are like that – I know mine is."

"Have you got any children?" asked Kelly, momentarily diverted.

PC Speight grinned and shook her head. "No. But then, I haven't married anyone yet and in our family, that comes first."

Kelly smiled a little, and let go some breath she seemed to have been holding for a while.

"So, to clear the air for your mum, will you tell me who the father of your baby is? Does he know yet, by the way?"

"No."

"Ah. Early days, is it? How long have you been having sex?"

"About a month... Six weeks," said Kelly.

"Is this your first sexual relationship?"

Kelly nodded.

"And have you only had one sexual partner?"

"Yes." She looked up defiantly. "I'm not a slapper, you know."

"I'm not judging you. I *do* know that passion can drive common sense out of the window." Speight leaned back from the table. "Where were you when it happened?"

"At wor— Oh!" exclaimed Kelly.

Speight put her hand on the girl's. "Don't worry about it. These things have to be said sometime. Better sooner than later. Where do you work?"

Kelly pulled her hand away and tucked it under the table at which they sat. "At a place called Holt Carr. Down the dale a bit."

"I think I've heard of it," said Speight. In fact something stirred in her mind about Holt Carr. The recollection of a road accident several weeks ago. "Who's running it now? I seem to recall the owners were killed," she asked.

"The house is Craig Jordon's. But he doesn't know anything about the business."

"That's right, I remember now. Mr and Mrs Jordon. Nasty car accident in fog – a milk tanker jack-knifed more or less in front of them. They didn't have a chance. Very sad. So who runs the business?"

"Simon. He's really good with the horses."

"And is that what you do? Help with the horses?"

"Yes. Me and Susie. She's a girl from school."

"A friend of yours?"

Kelly shrugged. "Yeah."

"Is it just you that Simon fancies?"

Kelly scoffed. "Well, it isn't Su— Oh."

Speight rested her elbows on the table and her chin on her hands. She kept her voice even. "So Simon is your lover?"

Kelly would have denied it, but she could feel the colour rise in her face and knew it gave her away. She nodded. "Will he be all right?" she asked in a small voice.

"I told you the position. We'll have to go and talk to him, and maybe arrest him. But first, I want you tell your mum and dad what you've told me while I'll get us all a cup of tea – unless you'd like a cold drink? We have some tinnies somewhere."

Kelly shook her head.

"I'll be back in about ten minutes. Let's get your parents back in."

"I don't want them to know," said Kelly.

Speight paused on her way to the door. "Any particular reason?"

Kelly wrung her hands. "Because I don't want my dad going after him. He seems all placid, but I think he could go and beat up Simon."

"Right then. It's a deal. We'll keep that information to ourselves for now – it'll probably come out later, but by then I expect everyone will have calmed down."

Kelly nodded, still unsure but wanting to believe.

"At the minute, I should think your mum and dad are desperately trying to come to terms with becoming grandparents sooner than they expected." Speight grinned.

Kelly's mouth twitched a little, before she went back to studying the table top.

Speight went out of the room, closing the door behind her. Kelly's parents were standing a little way down the corridor.

"Sorry to keep you waiting," she said. "Would you like to go back in there. I'm organising a cup of tea and getting a statement typed up."

"Has she told you who the father is?"

"Yes. Just at this time, she's asked me not to tell you – she's afraid you might lay him out," she grinned at Kelly's father.

"I'd like to!" he said.

"Well, don't do it during my shift," said Speight. "We'll be going to see him this afternoon," she added on a more serious note. "There's a chance he's not guilty, if it turns out he didn't realise how young she was. It's a defence if he reasonably believed Kelly was sixteen or older. But leave it with us and we'll investigate. I'd advise that just at this moment you avoid recriminations, and just project a bit of sympathy. It will help my job if she doesn't get all anti – I remember how often I did when I was fifteen!"

Kelly's mother nodded her agreement and both parents went to join their daughter.

An hour later, with a signed statement in the file and PC Ackroyd at her side, Speight drove out to Holt Carr.

*

The morning had started badly for Simon. He awoke in his childhood bed to discover that once again his left side was not functioning. His head was beginning to hurt, and the remorseless pain was driving him mad. He struggled to sit upright on the edge of the bed, feeling a mixture of frustration and panic. His life was being lived increasingly in the present as recollections of the

198

past faded. He still knew who he was, where he was, and how to do things, but his life with Victoria and the children hardly ever impinged upon his consciousness now.

His arm and leg began to tingle as feeling once again returned. He felt in the cupboard for the vodka he'd bought as soon as he could. He'd added a sachet of Equipalazone, having found that it helped to put him to sleep and deaden the pain in his head. As he downed some, the silent cry filled his mind: whatever is happening to me? He dressed and went down into the kitchen to fix himself some breakfast. His father was putting dirty laundry into the washing machine. Simon glanced at the kitchen clock. As he sat down, William Stalland took the chair opposite him and shook his head.

"Tha looks a reet mess, Simon," he said. "What hast tha done to end up like this?"

"I have headaches, Dad. I don't know what to do to make them go away."

"Di'n't thy doctor sort thee out?"

"He said I have migraines. Suggested I buy migraine tablets at the chemist's. They don't touch it."

William was silent as Simon chewed through some bacon and eggs. "Is that all it is? Headaches? I mean, it du'n't seem like much to make thee knock Victoria downstairs."

"Is that what I did?"

William frowned. "Thou doesn't remember? Tha nearly killed her."

Simon bit his lip and lost his taste for the food. "Nay, surely not?"

"What dost tha think *Grievous Bodily Harm* means? Tha knows tha's looking at Crown Court and prison for that, doesn't tha?"

Simon rested his head in his hands and nodded. "Aye."

William shook his head, but said no more. After walking the short distance to Holt Carr, Simon went into the tack room to have another slug of vodka before joining Susie cleaning out the stables. She was alone, changing the horses' bedding.

"No sign of Kelly?" he asked.

"Her mother rang. She's not coming to work."

"Did she say why?"

"No. And I've got to get off to school, so I'll be off, now you've got here."

Simon nodded. A few minutes later, Susie had disappeared down the track to the main road on her bicycle and he picked up the pitchfork she'd been using and started work. By lunchtime, the bulk of the work was done and Simon had a doorstep-thick ham sandwich slathered with mustard for lunch, washed down with more vodka. His hand shook slightly as he did, and some spilled and ran down his chin. He put the bottle down and allowed his eyelids to droop. He had been asleep for a few minutes when suddenly the door from the stables opened. He raised an eyebrow in lazy curiosity to see Craig standing in front of him.

"Simon," he said, "somebody to see you."

He stepped to one side behind Simon's chair to allow the large form of Police Constable Ackroyd, to enter the room, followed by Stephanie Speight. She stood to one side of him.

"Mr Stalland?" she asked.

"Yes." He was wide awake now. She turned to Craig. "Thank you, Mr Jordon. We'd like a word with Mr Stalland in private, if you don't mind."

He nodded and left the room, closing the door.

Speight turned back to Simon. "Do you know Kelly Frobisher?"

"Yes, she works here." His eyebrows arched in surprise.

"Have you had sexual intercourse with her?" Simon gazed at her for a moment as if deciding what to reply. "Yes. Only once or twice. Why? What's she saying?"

"Simon Stalland, I'm arresting you on suspicion of having had unlawful sexual intercourse with a child under sixteen," she said.

For a moment it didn't make sense. Surely Kelly was older than that? Was it possible? His headache began to pound, this time from stress.

"Stand up, please," said Speight. As he stood, Ackroyd moved in behind him and cuffed him, while Speight formally cautioned him.

Simon didn't know what to say, his head was feeling muzzy but he didn't know whether it was the drink or something else that was causing it. His eyes rolled wildly while the police officers escorted him out to their car. His last view before they shut him in the back seat was of Craig watching impassively as he was driven away. About half way to Skipton, the mustard on his ham reacted with the vodka and he threw up without warning in the back of the car. Ackroyd wound down his window to let the stench out and looked mighty huffily at Speight who was driving carefully over the snow-packed road.

"I knew we should have brought the van," he grumbled. Speight flashed a grin at him. "You're right, Roger, we should. Tell you what, as soon as I've got matey booked in, I'll come and help you clean the back seat up."

"You're the driver: I should be the one booking matey in while you clean up."

"Just because I'm a woman doesn't mean I am the cleaner."

"You know the rules," Ackroyd muttered.

"Now don't get sexist with me."

"Sexist!" Ackroyd almost exploded. "Sexist? You're using the threat of sexism to get out of cleaning the car, when the rules plainly state that the condition of the vehicle is the responsibility of the driver."

The argument continued in a low key, jocular way. Simon tried not to listen to them, keeping his eyes shut and wishing the whole nightmare would somehow go away. At the police station they helped Simon out of the car and Speight led him indoors through the security entrance to the Custody Office. They went through the same procedures

Simon had been through just a few days before, and finally he was put in a cell until the effects of the vodka had worn off. Speight, as she had promised, went back into the yard to help Ackroyd clean the interior of the vehicle.

*

Susie had returned to Holt Carr after school, and found Craig in the stables, on the phone to William Stalland to find out what needed doing.

"Oh, Susie's just arrived," he said, "hang on a moment, please." He turned to the girl. "Susie, Kelly's not here, and Simon has been taken away by the police. Can you show me what needs doing to make sure the horses are okay for the night?"

"Sure," she smiled shyly.

Craig told Stalland and rang off. "Where do we begin?"

Later, when they'd finished, Craig invited her into the kitchen of Holt Carr for a well-earned cup of tea.

"I don't know if Kelly will be back in the morning," he told her. "Perhaps I need to find another girl if she's going to be unreliable. In the meantime, there's just you and me. Mr Stalland has agreed to help, but he can't be here all the time."

"I'll do what I can, Craig, but I have to go to school." He smiled at her. "I know. I'll manage during the day, but I need your help whenever you can spare the time. You know I don't know what I'm doing when it comes to horses."

"Can I say something?" she asked.

"Of course."

"I wonder why you don't ride, after spending all those years in Canada. I thought they had a lot of horses out there."

He grinned. "Most Canadians I know drive cars, like the rest of us. It's not the Wild West anymore." He clasped his hands. "But the real reason I don't like going near horses is because I fell off one once and broke my leg. I guess you should get back on a horse as soon as possible, but it took a while for the fracture to heal, and when I was finally fit enough, I never wanted, or needed, to get back on a horse. I suppose I'm scared of coming off and breaking another bone."

Susie nodded sagely. "Why don't you try now? I mean you have your own hacks."

"I suppose I could."

"I'll saddle one up for you tomorrow evening, if you like."

He thought about it. "I suppose it would do no harm – as long as I don't fall off again."

"You have to fall off three times before you can call yourself a rider," she told him gravely.

"My aim, then, is never to achieve that particular qualification," he said.

She grinned.

*

Speight and Ackroyd faced Simon Stalland and the duty solicitor across the screwed-down table in an interview room at Skipton Police Station. The recorder was running, and Speight had once again run through the caution. Simon was experiencing the same sort of changed awareness he had noticed last time he had been interviewed here. It was almost as if his spirit had left his body and was floating near the ceiling, no longer involved or concerned with the earthly events going on in the room.

"I'll ask you again, did you know Kelly was not yet sixteen?" said Speight.

Simon looked at her and could not recall what she was talking about. She held his gaze, trying to read his mind through his eyes. Very slowly, he shook his head, more in bafflement that in answer to her question.

"You didn't know?"

He stared at her again. "What?"

"That Kelly is not yet sixteen."

"Isn't she?" He seemed only slightly concerned, and interested even less.

Speight fought to prevent her exasperation showing. Was he going to be claiming diminished responsibility, she wondered.

"When was the first time you and Kelly had sex?" she asked.

"I can't remember," said Simon after thinking about it. "Last week? Last month?"

"Tell me what happened."

Simon gazed at her blankly for a few moments before he began to speak, with many hesitations. He looked down at the table top. "She'd been, you know, like, teasing me for a while. My wife's left home." He glanced up at her. "You know that, I suppose?"

Speight said nothing.

Simon looked back at the table and continued in an almost rambling tone. "Anyway, I wasn't having any sex... Kelly was up for it, as I said. Let me get my hands on her tits a few times."

Speight kept her expression immobile, bland, just watching him. Still looking down at the table, he began to swing his head from side to side. He stopped and looked up suddenly, an evil smile on his face which shocked her, making her sit back from him.

"She knew how to lead a man on," he said, "once she decided teasing wasn't enough any longer, she stripped off."

"Did you help her take her clothes off?"

"Not at first. Not till she got down to her pants. She didn't wear a bra much." He grinned, remembering the warm firm breasts he had held.

"Did she ever tell you she didn't want to have sex?"

Simon thought for a moment, rocking slightly back and forth. "Not that time. Plenty of times before, like, when we were, like, petting and teasing, I'd be keen, but she'd say no, some other time, or later."

"And you stopped? You didn't force her?"

Simon leaned back looking shocked. "Nay! Nay, I didn't make her do owt she didn't want to. Is that was they're saying?"

Speight ignored the question. "Do you know how old Susie is?"

Simon furrowed his brow with the effort of remembering. It had seemed so very unimportant at the time.

"Weren't she... fifteen or, or fourteen p'raps? She still has that little-girl puppy-fat. Reckon she'll be nice-looking when she loses that."

"You like young girls, Simon?"

He shrugged. "I haven't thought much about it before. But now things aren't happening at home, I suppose I'm noticing other women more."

"Young ones?"

He cackled. "They're all right to practice on. I prefer women a bit older, like that Cat. She were allus a stunner, and clever with it."

"Cat? What's her proper name?" Simon screwed up his face while he dredged his memory. "Mitchell. Cat Mitchell. Short for Catriona. Used to hear her mother calling her when we came out of school. Allus used her Sunday name."

"And where does Cat live?" asked Speight, figuring that if she'd been at school with Stalland, she must be around his age. "I don't know," he said, his head still moving like a boxer's. "But at t'minute, she's up at t'archæology site at Holt Carr. A cracker she is," he added, nodding.

"Kelly's in the same class as Susie at school, isn't she?"

Simon screwed up his face again.

"Aye. I think so."

"Do you think that might make them the same age?"

He arched his eyebrows as he considered the question. It seemed a reasonable assumption.

He nodded. "Aye."

Speight sat back, feeling she'd extracted a valuable admission. "What do you know about the age of consent, Simon?" she asked. His eyes took on a glazed fixity while he thought, his head swinging left and right again. At last he muttered something she didn't hear properly.

"Can you say that again, louder, for the tape?"

He looked up into her eyes, a tired and resigned look in his own. "You mean sixteen?"

"Yes, thank you."

"I'd forgotten. You know how it is."

Speight stared at him for a moment. She'd noted the resignation in his eyes as he spoke. "I think that's all I need for now, Simon. Interview terminated." She glanced at her wristwatch and added the time to her formal announcement.

Ackroyd stopped the tape recorder and began the procedure to safeguard the recording. When he had finished, they escorted Simon back to a cell and went to confer with their sergeant.

"Sounds good enough to me," he said, when Speight had explained what had transpired in the interview. "Better get him charged."

"One thing, sarge." He looked up. "He's on court bail for GBH, pending committal to the Crown Court. I think he's due up before the Bench this week."

"Aye, well, charge him and see if Jimmy will agree to a remand in custody on the basis of risk of re-offending."

Jimmy was the sergeant who determined bail applications on behalf of his Inspector.

An hour later, Simon was facing another night in the noisy cell block at Skipton. He huddled under a thin blanket on the thin hard mattress and rested his head on his arms, his arms on his knees. Life was somehow out of his control. Unseen by his gaolers, tears ran down his stubbly cheeks.

CHAPTER 16

Presumably, Craig wasn't interested. Cat thought that after the business in the bathroom, he might have at least taken an opportunity to chat to her. Instead he'd been invisible for several days. She'd heard about the problems with Simon having been arrested and kept in custody until his court appearance today. This had meant that Craig had had to manage the horse business with occasional recourse to William Stalland for advice, and was probably responsible for his staying away from the dig.

Of course, another interpretation might be that he simply didn't want anything to do with her.

It was in this ambivalent frame of mind that she saw him at last, riding one of the hacks somewhat stiffly up the track to the site, leading another horse, saddled. He reached her and stopped.

"Hi, Cat," he said. "Got half an hour? I need to talk to you."

She thought about the work awaiting her attention and figured she could spare the time. Besides, she was curious.

"I guess so," she said.

"Can you ride?" he asked.

"I used to – about twenty years ago."

He grinned and unclipped a hard hat from his belt. He offered it to her.

"Well, I've had about two days of this. Haven't ridden for quite a long time."

She put the hat on and buckled the strap beneath her chin.

"Did you saddle this?" she asked, stroking the flank of the spare animal.

"Yes. Susie has been showing me how. I think I've gotten it right." Cat slid the stirrups down their straps and adjusted their length to what she thought she'd need. At the last minute, she remembered to check the tightness of the girths: she didn't want to come off as a result of the girths slipping sideways, like some character in a Norman Thelwell cartoon. Satisfied, she placed one foot in the stirrup and swung her other leg over the horse's back. Craig passed her the reins. They turned away from the dig site and headed up the moor towards the summit. It surprised her that she remembered how to ride after all that time. Keeping her back straight, she allowed her hips to roll with the movements of the animal and felt comfortable. Later, she expected she would feel the ache in her thighs concomitant with horse-riding.

"Well?" she asked when they reached a part of the track wide enough to ride abreast. "What is it you need to say?"

At that moment, they reached the ridge atop the moor and the vista of the valley beyond opened up before them. The town of Keighley was to the west, and more or less straight ahead was the distant outline of the city of Bradford. Nearer to them, the dale, its fields marked out with dry stone walls and dotted with ancient stone barns, some of obvious mediæval origin, judging by the arrow-slit apertures in their walls. Craig gazed at the scene before turning to her. His expression made her think that bad news was to come.

"Cat... I'm going back to Canada."

"Oh," she said. She was aware of feeling numb. "I don't think that's a surprise."

"I've been offered a promotion. A really good one. Make my fortune, and all that; life never the same again."

She wanted to cry – not tears of sadness but of anger. She fought them back. "And why shouldn't you? You did it before."

"I know. That's why I didn't feel good about it this time."

"Really? You sounded a moment ago as if you were dead keen to go."

208

"I am. But I wanted to know how you feel about it; I wanted to be sure this time I wasn't leaving you when I shouldn't."

She felt a lump rising in her throat and walked her horse in a circle while she forced it down. The bastard! she thought. She'd allowed a little flame to take light and burn in a corner of her heart, believing it possible that she and Craig could rekindle their earlier happy relationship, but with this information, it died away. She faced him again.

"Why should what I think matter to you?" she said, fighting to keep the disappointment out of her voice. Clearly, he had no strong feelings for her: she'd been mistaken if she'd ever thought there was.

He watched her face for a moment. She strove to keep her expression impassive.

"That's what I thought. Okay then," he said, wheeling his animal to face back down the track. "Just wanted to be sure that this time, I didn't hurt you." He began to trot.

She turned her horse and urged it to catch up with him. How dare he suggest it wouldn't hurt! Well, she'd make sure it didn't. As soon as she got back to York, she was going to... well, get out more. Attend a few Christmas parties, check out a few good looking men. She'd soon get over Mr Craig Jordon. She'd done it before, she'd do it again. She'd nearly caught up with him when a thought occurred. She'd never let him know how much pain he'd caused her last time he left, so why should he think this time might be hurtful... unless it wasn't her hurt he was thinking about, but his own? They clattered into the yard at Holt Carr. He dismounted ahead of her and turned to steady her horse while she followed suit. She unfastened her hat and passed it to him, wondering how to elicit confirmation of her theory from him, but before she could he smiled rather wanly.

"I'm off in a couple of days, Cat."

209

She stared at him. "And this time? It'll be for how long?"

"Well, I hope to come back from time to time. Hope you'll still be around."

"Hope I – ?"

"Well, obviously, I expect you and Alan will have patched up your differences. I saw you together when the television crew were here. I guess you're very suited to each other."

She realised her mouth was open and shut it. "You *do* know he asked me to marry him and I turned him down?"

Craig shrugged. "Doesn't mean you don't still love each other."

"Since when were you such an expert on love?"

"Since I realised I'd made a helluva mistake when I left you here twelve years ago. Should have carried you off over my saddle-bow, figuratively speaking."

She shook her head, unable to find words, or at least to express the thought that came into her mind: *why the hell didn't you?*

He was still talking. "Y'know, for a while, after I came back, I thought meeting you again was destiny playing its part, if you believe in all that stuff. I really wondered if we might have got it together, but obviously, I'm just a bit stupid. I keep forgetting there's twelve years of water under both our bridges." He nodded as if agreeing with a thought. "Anyhow. Better go. Got all sorts of stuff to arrange and no time hardly to do it in. Sorry it was such a short ride. Any time you want a horse, just take one of the hacks. I'll tell Susie."

He turned and led both horses into the stables, leaving Cat alone in the middle of the yard as the evening gloom gathered. Surely, this was the moment she should tell him that she'd felt the same about the destiny thing? That she felt that, whatever pain there'd been twelve years ago, she would be prepared for them to try again? But when she considered the last few weeks, she had to admit he'd hardly behaved at all lover-like. At least, not with her.

Of course, when she arrived, he'd been having an affair with Jemma, one that would in all probability still be going on had not the girl decided, quite nobly, to stand aside so Cat could find out how she and Craig really felt about each other. And obviously, the answer was *not enough*. If he'd really wanted her – especially in the light of what he'd just told her – he'd have asked her to go with him, or made his feelings known. Clearly, the fact he hadn't meant he didn't. Slowly, with fat tears rolling down her cheeks, she began to make her way back to the dig site.

*

"Court rise!" The Clerk of the Court got to his feet as he spoke and waited for the Bench of three magistrates to take their seats in courtroom number three. As everyone else sat down, he turned to Simon, in the glass-enclosed dock.

"Remain standing, please. I need to identify you formally. You are Mr Simon Stalland?"

Simon nodded. "Yes'.

The Clerk verified his address and date of birth, then proceeded with the charge. Simon felt the proceedings wash over him. There was a good deal of technical stuff about where the case should be heard, and at one point he was asked how he pleaded. Simon glanced at the duty solicitor, cleared his throat and turned to face the magistrates.

"Not guilty."

"Very well. May he be seated, sir?" the Clerk asked, turning round to face the Bench and address the Chairman.

"Yes, please sit down, Mr Stalland," said the Chairman. "Mr Brand, can we hear an outline of the offence."

A tall thin man in a dark suit and conservative tie, thinning hair and tortoise-shell glasses rose to his feet smiled and ducked his head briefly at the Bench.

"Yes, your Worships. This case involves a fifteen year-old girl, and I should be grateful if you would make a section thirty-nine order prohibiting the media from identifying her."

"So ordered," said the Chairman, glancing across pointedly at the desk where a reporter was making notes. She shrugged, expecting what she heard.

"Thank you, sir," said Mr Brand.

He proceeded to outline the case against Simon, mentioning also that Simon's defence was that he hadn't been aware how young the girl had been.

"He says she looked older than sixteen to him. On the other hand," said Mr Brand, "he made no effort to enquire. He and the girl have had unprotected intercourse on several occasions, as a result of which the girl is now pregnant."

The three magistrates glanced at each other, with much shaking of heads.

"Finally, Your Worships," concluded Brand, "this offence is alleged to have taken place while the accused is on bail to appear before the Crown Court on another matter."

The Bench conversed inaudibly again, briefly, before the Chairman switched his microphone on.

"Mr Stalland, please stand up."

Simon did so.

"Mr Stalland, the bench has decided that in view of the seriousness of this matter, and the fact that you are already bailed to appear at the Crown Court, this case too should be committed to the Crown Court to be heard there. Is there an application for bail?"

Both the prosecutor and duty solicitor expressed opposing views on the subject, but the clinching argument seemed to be the point made by the Crown that Simon represented a substantial risk of committing an offence whilst on bail – again – and interfering with witnesses. He described Kelly as a "vulnerable victim", easily influenced by the defendant.

The magistrates considered the merits of the counter arguments and remanded Simon in custody until the case should be heard by the higher court. The security guards either side of Simon went through the process of handcuffing him for the walk downstairs to the cells below the courts.

Simon's left arm was tingling, and his left leg was threatening to buckle under him as they went down the stairs. They arrived in a reception area, arranged like a cross. Immediately adjacent to the stairway he had come down was an office for the security staff. Beyond it was another stairway leading up to other courts. To the right and left were blocks of cells.

As Simon stood, leaning on the tiled wall, waiting to be processed by the staff, a large prisoner, with the build and appearance of a gorilla, was beginning to object loudly to his incarceration. One or two others were encouraging him, and some pushing and shoving was beginning at the far side of the area.

There were only two security guards apart from the ones either side of Simon, and they seemed in danger of being assaulted. The guard handcuffed to Simon watched helplessly for a few seconds before releasing the cuffs and telling Simon to stay where he was. The four security guards then concentrated on controlling the gorilla.

Outside, two vans had arrived together, which meant that while one got into the yard, the other was stuck in the gateway. As the travelling guard from the first van opened the steel door into the reception area, saw the struggle and went to help, Simon saw his chance and hobbled outside.

Praying his leg would hold him, he ran as fast as he could past the second van out into the street. Using his knowledge of Skipton, he dodged into small alleys and through shops, slowing his pace as he went. His almost permanent headache throbbed, and his breath wheezed in his throat. He hid in an alleyway beside a sandwich shop,

213

listening for a hue and cry, but none was forthcoming. A police car went past the end of the alley but didn't stop.

He hunkered down behind the waste skips and waited. As closing time approached one of the shop assistants threw a bag of old sandwiches into a bin. After the man had gone back inside, Simon grabbed the bag and stuffed it in his pockets. A thought occurred to him, and, making sure his booty was well concealed, he went round to the front of the shop and stole a half-litre bottle of mineral water. His heart beat rapidly, but there were no searchers. Emerging from the shop, he walked to the end of the road and, checking that no-one was watching, scrambled over a wall into a closed cemetery. The back wall of the cemetery gave onto the moors, and Simon clambered over it, sobbing with fear and panting with the effort. He had only one thought, to get away, and he struck out in the general direction of Holt Carr.

*

Inside the stable block, when Craig arrived, Susie was comforting a mare, laid on her bedding, in the throes of delivering a foal.

"I hope you don't mind, Craig, but I rang the vets. She doesn't seem right to me."

Craig glanced at the horse. "No, of course not." He could not see anything obvious causing the mare distress, but she was sweating and her flanks heaved. "Have you mentioned it to Mr Stalland?" he asked, thinking the older man's experience might be helpful.

"I left a message on his answer-phone. I think he's out somewhere."

"Ah, well. Nothing more we can do, just hope the vet gets here soon."

On cue, the sound of a heavy diesel engine heralded the vet's arrival. Close on his heels was a horse box which pulled into the yard outside the stables. While the vet examined the gravid mare, Craig went to see the box's driver, who turned out to be one of the owners, come to remove his mare and foal. He nodded at the vet's truck. "Spot of bother, Mr Jordon?"

"Precautions only, Mr...?"

"Crabtree. Bernard Crabtree. Come to collect Night Runner and her foal, as I said on the phone."

"Do you want to come in?" asked Craig, leading the way into the stable block. Crabtree followed, looking around. For a few minutes, they watched the vet at work.

"Sorry to hear about your parents," Crabtree said.

"It was quite a shock," Craig replied.

"Aye, it would be. You were away, weren't you?"

"Yes, in Canada. The Yukon."

"Wasn't that gold rush country?"

"Yes – in eighteen ninety-eight."

"None left now, then?"

"Not much," said Craig, recalling the number of times on his travels he'd spent an hour or two of an evening panning in likely streams near his camps. Crabtree seemed satisfied with the answer, and untied the leading rein of his mare. She followed him as he led her outside, the foal tagging on behind. Craig helped him load both animals into the box, and guided Crabtree as he reversed it so he could leave the yard. The owner leaned out of the cab to thank him.

"Put your bill in the post, Mr Jordon, and it'll be settled at the end of the month."

"Thanks."

Craig watched as the big vehicle trundled carefully down the track to the road, then turned and went into the stables. The mare which had been the cause for concern was on her feet, licking her new foal. The vet and Susie stood quietly watching the miracle of life.

"Everything looks all right in here," observed Craig.

Susie glanced up at him. The vet spoke without turning his head.

"Susie did the right thing to call me. The foal's legs were trapped and he couldn't get out without a

215

bit of help." He paused, seemed satisfied that he had done all that was necessary and that mother and son were going along just fine, and turned towards the tack room. "I'll just wash up, if you don't mind," he said.

"Help yourself – and thanks," said Craig. He turned to Susie. "And thanks to you, too. I reckon that deserves a bonus in the pay packet." Susie looked pleased. The vet returned from the tack room, rolling down his sleeves.

"Right, I'll be off," he said, collecting his anorak from a peg and picking up his bag.

"Thanks again," Craig called after him. He watched the vet drive away. Meanwhile, Susie had turned to one of the other foals, and was absently brushing its flank. Craig watched her for a moment.

"Is there any tea or coffee in the tack room?" he asked.

"Simon kept some vodka in the fridge. I don't like coffee much. There might be some tea-bags."

"Let's go and have a look. If there aren't the makings of a drink, we'll go down to the house and make one there."

Susie didn't say anything for a few moments, but carried on with the brushing. "I don't know that I want to go down to the house. Kelly and Simon used to go in there when you were out."

"Really?"

"Yeah."

Craig wondered what they might have done, and where they might have done it. He couldn't find tea-bags. "Would you like some tea, or something else? You've earned a break. I'll go and put some in a flask and you can drink it up here, alone, if you prefer it."

He withdrew as far as the doorway. "I am not like Simon though. Please understand that. Not many men are."

She turned to study him. After a moment, she nodded. "I guess you're right. I'll come down to the house with you."

Later, they sat in the kitchen at Holt Carr, sipping tea. Susie was taciturn, but Craig knew this was normal for her.

"Have you been up to the dig?" he asked.

"No."

"Would you like to see what they're doing?"

She shrugged.

"I could take you up there with me if you like."

She thought for a moment. Then shook her head. "No thanks. Mr Stalland'll be coming over later when we bed the horses down for the night."

"There's another box coming up this afternoon. Another customer leaving us."

She looked up. "Sorry, Mr Jordon."

He shook his head. "Not your fault, Susie. The fact is, I don't know anything about the horse breeding business. I've sold it to Mr Stalland. I think he has plans to turn Holt Carr into a pony trekking centre."

"Oh."

"From tomorrow, Mr Stalland will be in charge."

She raised an eyebrow and finished her drink. "Do you think he'll still want me?"

"Well, I don't know for certain, but I do know he can't run his farm and pony trekking centre by himself."

"I suppose he'll have Simon."

Craig chewed his lip. "I suspect Simon may well be out of the reckoning for a while," he said wryly.

"Do you think he'll go to prison?"

"I think there's a good chance of it."

Susie nodded and rinsed her cup under the kitchen tap. "I'm off home now, Craig."

"Thanks for all your help, Susie."

*

From a vantage point on the moor, screened by bracken on three sides, Simon watched as the lights in the yard went out, followed a moment later by the pinpoint of light that was Susie's cycle headlamp, moving off down the track. He peered through the gloom towards the dig site, several hundred yards away. It was similarly dark and quiet. The cold of the December night was beginning to chill him even through his coat.

He set off down the moor side towards the yard. There were no signs of life, apart from some rustling sounds from the stables as the horses shifted and made themselves comfortable. The stable door was locked, but he knew where Craig kept a key, in the kitchen. As he expected, the house was not locked. He opened the kitchen door quietly and went to the sink unit. In its drawer was the spare key. Footsteps on the stairs hastened his retreat, and a moment later, he crept around the walls of the yard until he came to the stable door.

He was about to let himself in when the kitchen light came on and the door of the house opened, casting a beam of light across the dark concrete. Craig had a quick look round then went back inside. Simon had squeezed into a corner between the stables and the dry stone wall around the yard, keeping very still until Craig had gone back inside.

Quickly, he let himself into the stables, locking the door behind him, and went into the tack room where a lamp had been left burning. He remembered from his first day the whereabouts of the old sawn-off shotgun and cartridges. He stuffed the cartridges in his pockets and kept the gun at his side. He stared at the fridge a few moments before giving in to temptation and dragging the adulterated vodka out of it. He unscrewed the cap, lifted the bottle to his lips, and drank until the bottle was empty. Then he settled in the old armchair and went to sleep.

*

Cat had a disturbed night, for reasons she felt unable to share with Jemma, despite her offer of a sympathetic ear. She was up early, and used the portable latrine. She was not going anywhere near Holt Carr whilst Craig remained there.

Slowly the archæologists got ready for work. With breakfast out of the way, Dave and the students went out to the trenches and Cat went to one of the tables in the marquee to start on a fresh box of bones. She knew Craig was leaving for Canada but not when, and the thought kept her feeling miserable all day.

*

Simon woke early, his back aching from the night in the tack room armchair. His headache sprang to life at once and was almost constant now. He listened actively, heard nothing but the occasional noises caused by the horses. He rinsed his face and hands at the sink in the corner of the room and felt in his pocket for another stale sandwich.

He did not know what to do. He had no plan: all his concentration was focussed on evading recapture. To this end, he knew he couldn't stay in the tack room or anywhere else on the property during the day. He checked he had left no signs of occupation. He refilled his water bottle and let himself out, past the horses and the empty stalls, into the yard. He locked the door again, but decided to keep the key in case he needed to use it again. He didn't care if Craig discovered it was gone.

He studied the house but could see no signs of life: well, Craig had never been much of an early riser, thought Simon. No signs of anyone, but you could never tell what the police might be doing. He didn't doubt that that Speight woman and Ackroyd would be searching for him relentlessly, aided by dozens more drafted in from round the county. The thought made him feel jittery, and he set off away from the stables up onto the moors.

His left leg suddenly began to falter, and he nearly fell down. At the same time, he realised that he could hardly see with his left eye. He knelt in a patch of bracken, waiting to recover. His head pounded. Then he heard low voices. He spent time trying to figure out if they were real or just in his head, but the unmistakable sound of a boot scraping on the stony path nearby impelled him to move away from the sound and lay flat out behind a stunted bush. Two early morning hikers appeared over the brow of a rise, talking to each

219

other. Simon took in their appearance – walking boots, shorts, cagoules and back-packs – and breathed a sigh of relief that they obviously weren't police searchers. They walked past him. He waited until they were nearly four hundred metres up the slope before he left his temporary refuge. The rest had done some good: his leg was functioning again.

There was a stretch of the moor path from which he could look down into the valley and see the house where Kelly lived. He felt exposed, because to anyone down there, he would be on the skyline and very noticeable. Quickly, he ran, stumbling, along the path for a couple of hundred metres, then turned, away from the houses below, and struck out across the moor towards the old stone   quarry.

CHAPTER 17

Whilst emptying a wheelbarrow of soil at one end of her trench, Jemma's eye was caught by a discolouration at the other, which she hadn't previously noticed. Leaving the empty barrow, she picked up her trowel and a stiff brush, and went to investigate. Dave Pountney, puffing with the effort of back-filling a trench, stopped working when Jemma began picking delicately at the ground. He watched her for a few moments and, when she didn't leave whatever had interested her, put down his shovel and crossed the site to see what had caught her interest.

"This shape in the ground," she said, when he asked. "It's curved round *here*," she pointed, tracing the line with the tip of her trowel, "then disappears under the turf."

"You thinking of a cooking pot? Funerary urn?"

"I'd like to take the turf back a couple of feet, to establish if it's circular or whether it's... longer and straighter."

"As it would be if it were a burial, you mean? We really haven't the time or the resources."

"If it's a pot, it can stay there," Jemma said, "but if it should be a burial, and there's a complete skeleton in there... well, shouldn't we have a look?"

Dave was not impervious either to the pleading note in her voice, the wide blueness of her eyes, or the force of her argument.

"Okay, let's strip a metre of turf back. I'll give you a hand, and leave the rest of the site to the boys."

Mike and Diarmuid were back-filling their trenches. Dave went to tell them of the development before returning to Jemma's trench.

*

221

Kelly saw the figure on the skyline and recognised Simon at once. He was walking unsteadily and for a moment, she felt antagonism towards him. He looked to be drunk, reminding her that he'd been drinking each time they'd made love. Perhaps, if he hadn't been, he wouldn't have made her pregnant, though deep inside, she acknowledged that it just wasn't in his nature to use contraception. If she'd been older, she could have been on the pill, but her parents would have gone berserk at the idea of her going on it at only fifteen.

Still, she thought, dragging her mind back to more immediate and relevant considerations, Simon had to be told he was going to be a father again. Kelly left her bedroom and listened over the banister to the voices of her parents. Since the episode at Skipton police station, they'd spent a lot of time, not exactly shouting at each other, but deep in earnest conversation to which she was not a party. They were in the lounge, with the door shut, and it was easy for her to slip out of the house and cycle away, up towards the moor.

The road approached the stone quarry, towards which Simon had been heading, from the opposite direction. As she reached it, panting after hard pedalling up the slope, she saw Simon's head above a rise in the ground. She laid her bike in some concealing bracken and made her way to the lip of the quarry, leaning forward so she could see inside it, and clear through to the entrance.

He reached the quarry near a wooden refreshment stall down near the car park. She saw him change direction towards it, keeping out of sight of the owner, and pull a newspaper out of the rack hanging from the side of the building. He tucked it into a pocket of his coat and walked quickly into the quarry. Kelly pulled as far back from the lip as she could whilst keeping him in sight. He climbed up some rocks, covered in various coarse plants, and disappeared from sight.

She realised that there must be a cave whose entrance was hidden by the foliage. Feeling a

222

certain amount of satisfaction that she'd found out where he was hiding, she retrieved her bike and cycled down the path to the hut. Figuring that Simon might be hungry and thirsty and more amenable to listening if she assuaged these needs, she bought some ham rolls and a couple of bottles of water, then pushed the bike ahead of her into the quarry. She was planning what to say, how to break the news to him, as she parked the bike against the quarry wall, and began to climb the tumbled rock up to Simon's lair. She hadn't got far before he appeared above her, looking scared. The expression on his face gave way to a smile when he recognised her.

"Kel! How are you, girl?"

"Coping," she replied as she joined him in the deep fissure behind the concealing brackens. They sat side by side, leaning against the rugged wall, as she handed him two of the rolls and a bottle.

"You know what you've done, don't you?" she asked him. "I'm up the duff: pregnant! My folks are so pissed with me they've been keeping me in since they found out."

He glanced at her sideways. "Poor lass." There was no sympathy in his voice.

She scowled at the rocky walls around her, her glance catching a glint from the barrels of Simon's shotgun, at the rear of the aperture.

"What's the gun for?"

His brow beetled until his thick eyebrows almost met. "I dunno. Stay free? P'raps I ought to murder Craig."

She stared at him. "Murder him? Why? What's he done now?"

"You wouldn't understand. I lost Cat because of him."

"That was years ago."

"'Appen so, but it's stuck wi' me ever since."

She felt a twinge of jealousy. "It still isn't a reason to murder him."

"My head still aches from where he hit it. He's ruined my life. Bastard!"

223

"That's crap. Craig is nice."

He stared at her, then his eyes flicked back outside, scanning the quarry. "You don't understand!"

"But they'll lock you away forever! Who's going to look after me and the baby? My mum says you've got to pay for it. I thought we could go away together and... and get a place where we can set up our home. You can get a divorce from Victoria, and by then I'll be old enough for you to... to marry me."

He looked at her, curling his upper lip in a scornful grin, and shook his head. "Aw, come on, Kelly. Tha's joking, ent tha? Tha's not the first girl as 'as found a bun in her oven. Didn't you say you had friends at school? I only gev thee what thee wanted – you can't deny that: I never forced yer."

Her face fell and her bottom lip protruded. "You'll have to pay maintenance for our baby anyway."

He scoffed. "With what? I've got nowt."

She snuggled closer to him and picked up his hand, resting it on her flat belly. "Just think, Simon. In there is our baby. Ever so tiny at the minute, but getting bigger every day." She glanced up at him. "I've been sick every morning for a week."

"Hast tha? I told thee to get them pills."

She pouted. "I didn't think I'd get pregnant."

He almost laughed. "What do you think fuckin's for?"

She looked up sharply. "Making love, Simon. Fuckings what you do to prostitutes."

He snorted. "Oh, aye?"

She stared at him unhappily. "My parents are talking as if it's my fault."

"Looking at the paper, they're talking as if it's mine," he replied, pointing at the headline.

She took the paper from him and read about his escape from the court. The nature of the charge against him was reported, but she was not identified. She pouted with disappointment. It would somehow have made them more... connected. She leaned against him and he slipped his arm round her shoulders.

"Truth is, Kelly, it probably *is* my fault. You must think badly of me, but you know it was only because you're... you're so difficult for a bloke to keep his hands off."

As he spoke, his voice thickened with desire and his fingers began to explore her breasts. Kelly felt the beginnings of arousal.

"You've no idea, have you, of the effect you have on me?" he continued.

Kelly glanced up at his face. She rested a hand on his leg. The truth was, Simon's very earthiness drove a tidal wave of weakness and fear through her. It took away her breath and threatened to take away her control. She had become, she realised suddenly, addicted to sex with Simon. But there were limits. Now she was pregnant with his child, she was no longer content to succumb to his assaults just anywhere. He had to be taught to take more care of her.

He turned towards her and tilted her chin up so he could kiss her, but when his hand cupped her breast she brushed it away and broke the kiss.

"If you think you're having me on this lumpy old floor, you've another think coming, Simon Stalland," she said teasingly. "I had enough of rough old floors back there in the tack room. I'm carrying your child now, and I expect a bit more comfort and consideration."

"Oh, Kel," he complained.

She looked around again. "Where are you sleeping? Surely not here?"

He thought for a moment. "Can I trust you not to tell the police?"

She nodded. "I promise."

He kissed her again and whispered in her ear.

*

Jemma and Dave peered at the latest evidence they'd discovered after digging back the turf. In the middle of the curved section was something white and smooth and apparently dome-shaped.

"Reckon I'll have to get Cat to take a look," said Dave. "I'll have to phone the office as well, to see about funding. I'll get Mike and Diarmuid to strip the turf back all the way to the end of the grave cut while you concentrate on excavating the skull."

He left her to the delicate work while he tried to inveigle the Yorkshire Archaeological Service into finding the necessary funding so they could complete the excavation of the burial. Their answer was not immediately forthcoming but they seemed to be indicating that they didn't have the money. He rang Cat.

"Apart from the fact that the YAS have apparently run out of money," he added after telling her about the new burial, "we'd like your opinion on this one."

"I'll see you tomorrow."

"That's great," he said, and returned to the trench where all three students were gradually unearthing more and more of the burial Jemma had found. They looked up as he approached. His expression was grim.

"Can't she come?" asked Jemma.

"Oh, Cat's keen to come. But the YAS haven't agreed to fund her. I've had to consider other options." He looked at Mike and Diarmuid. "I'm going to sign you two off at the end of today. Sorry about that, and you won't suffer on your assessments. But I think it's more important to have Cat here to process the burial than to have you stay on another few days. She should be paid for what she does, like any of us, and the only way I can be sure of doing that is if I save your wages. Hope you'll understand."

His expression mirrored Mike and Diarmuid's unhappiness. They glanced at each other and shrugged.

"Okay, Dave. I understand," said Mike. "But you realise one of you is going to have to take over the cooking." He grinned.

"Believe me," said Dave, "I wouldn't have done this if I could think of any other way."

"We'll get as much done as we can," said Diarmuid, "then this evening, let's all go down the Mucky Duck so we can collectively cry in our beer. Well, yours, I think, Dave – shan't be wanting mine watered down." They did their best to laugh at the little joke.

*

Simon had taken the last of his money from his pocket and persuaded Kelly to go and buy them more food from the refreshment shack before it closed for the day. She came back with hot sausage rolls, burgers in buns, and two portions of chips.

In the waning light of the afternoon, they ate in comfortable silence in the quarry fissure, and drank the last of the water. When they had done she carefully collected all the wrappings. The stall-holder had left, but there was a litter bin beside it, and Simon wanted a look in it in case some uneaten food had been thrown out. When they reached it, he discovered several sandwiches, and two more sausage rolls had been dumped in the bin. He brushed them as clean as he could and put them in his coat pockets.

"Right. Let's go," he said.

"Where?" asked Kelly, who had taken the unconscious decision to stay with him. She hadn't originally planned they'd spend the night together, but she figured it would serve her parents right for trying to keep her indoors to have a night of worry about her. In her mind, she had already decided that Simon would come round to her way of thinking, everything would be all right, and he would take care of her. So, she was content to let him organise things.

"Back to Holt Carr. The stables are empty."

"I'm not laying down on the tack room floor again," she said.

"No. Reckon we can be more comfortable than that." As they approached Holt Carr, with Kelly pushing her bike and Simon carrying his shotgun, Dave Pountney's MPV burst into life on the moor top, and they crouched down as, loaded with all four archæologists, it came down the track and headed for the road.

Simon turned to Kelly. "So much the better if they're out of the way."

The kitchen light at the house was on, illuminating the yard. Simon and Kelly slipped along by the boundary wall and through the personal door in the stable block. The empty stalls gave the place a forlorn look. The end one contained a small stack of straw bales and beside them, bundles of hay. Simon indicated them.

"Hay mattresses aren't bad. People used to sleep on them years ago," he added. "Better than the tack room floor any day."

"I wish you'd thought of that before," said Kelly with feeling.

He ran his hand down her cheek. "You've got to forgive me, Kel. I know I was a bit rough, but I wanted you so much..."

She almost purred.

"Talking of wanting you," he went on, "I want you now, girl."

He guided her unresisting form towards the straw bales, one hand disappearing under the coat, finding its way under her jumper, and cupping a breast in a way which Kelly found entirely satisfactory. She busied herself with his trousers as he peeled her coat off.

*

"You still here?" Simon stood at the foot of two bales of straw on which Kelly lay sprawled, her nakedness covered by her coat. She opened one eye and looked at him in the early light filtering through the dusty roof lights.

228

"Ain't you glad?" she asked. "Nice way to wake a girl – come here and give me a kiss."

As she spoke she rolled onto her back, dragging an edge of the coat so that most of one side of her was revealed. She watched his eyes trace the shape of her leg up to her hips. He perched on the bale and leaned down to kiss her. As he approached, she watched his face and felt the heat of desire begin to rise in her belly. He threw her coat off and suckled at her breasts, while with one hand unfastening his trousers. He touched her briefly before clambering over her impatiently and ramming her full.

She loved the rough treatment he gave her, and held him tightly, locking her ankles around him and wrapping her arms round his neck. As he pistoned into her, and she responded, she felt warm and loved. It was at these moments that she had no doubts that Simon would always be around to look after her. He erupted into her and pulled away, leaving her feeling empty.

"Thanks, Kel," he said.

"Thanks? Is that what I get? Didn't we just make love?" She was indignant.

"If you like," he grinned.

"Thanks is what you say to your whore!"

He chuckled and screwed his eyes up as he looked at her dishevelment, as if he was having trouble focussing.

"You're better than any of the whores in Chapeltown," he said, referring to a notorious red-light area in the city of Leeds. It was not the sort of comparison Kelly wanted to hear.

"I'm not a whore!" she exclaimed angrily.

"Aye, tha's not," he said, "tha's allus done it willingly and for free – except for the phone, of course. I suppose that were payment in kind and it reminds me, I'm still entitled to a few more goes considerin' t' price of it."

Kelly sat up, grabbing the coat and covering her breasts with it. "Simon! Don't talk like that. I'm your girlfriend, and I'm having your baby. You have to take care of us. My mum said you'll have to pay maintenance – but if we got married—"

She stopped as he laughed aloud.

"Married? I'm already married, Kel. And I don't know that that's my kid in there, do I? You could 'a' been with anybody."

She stared at him in astonishment. "Of course it's yours. I haven't been with anyone else. I love you." It sounded hollow to her own ears.

He laughed again. "Oh, don't be daft! We've enjoyed a bit of sex. Now it's time for you to get off home – looks like your job here has finished, anyway," he added, glancing round at the empty stalls.

She stared at him, a small pool of panic inside her threatening to swell into a flood.

"You can't be dumping me, Simon?"

He got up and straightened his clothes. "I can do owt I want," he said, a beatific grin on his face. "I am a free agent: the wife's cleared off with the kids, there's just me to worry about. You were... good fun, Kelly. I want thee to know, I've enjoyed every shag we've 'ad."

She covered her face with her hands to stop him seeing her tears. She felt small and pathetic, and it did not accord well with the image she had of how she should appear. He picked up her panties and threw them at her. "Here: there's no tissues round here, you can use these." She dabbed her face with them before realising what she was holding. Angrily, she threw them away and finally gave in to her tears.

Simon let some of his irritation show. "Shut up, Kelly, I don't want to hear it."

When she didn't, he smacked her across the cheek. She screamed, but stopped crying.

"Now: get off home. I don't want you around anymore. You can have some fun thinking up what you'll call the brat."

Kelly began crying again.

"Oh, shurrup!" Simon walked into the tack room, leaving Kelly, who was slowly dragging on her clothes, still sobbing. Moments later, he emerged, wearing his waxed jacket and headed back past the girl without looking at her.

"Simon!" she cried.

He turned to find she was pointing the shotgun at him.

"What dost think tha's doing with that?"

"I want you to promise you'll help me with the baby." The barrels wobbled. "And... and I want you to be nice to me, and apologise for slapping me."

He took a step towards her, his hands in the capacious pockets of his jacket. He stopped with the barrels pressed against his chest and stared at her. She stared at him, wondering whether she had the courage to fire the thing. He reached for her and she stepped away without thinking until she felt the wall at her back. His eyes were wide and staring at her, and for a moment she thought she saw madness in them. Fear coursed through her, making her tremble. As he lunged towards her again, she shut her eyes and pulled both triggers.

There were two loud clicks. When she looked, he was holding two blue cartridges. He was grinning cruelly.

"Tha doesn't think I'd leave it loaded, does tha?" He wrenched the gun from her grip and jabbed the stock into her belly.

She screamed. The pain caused her to bend double and collapse onto the straw bale.

"Now will tha shut up about thy baby!" he said, tucking the shotgun inside his jacket and turning to leave. She got painfully to her feet and staggered after him, a sob still catching in her throat.

"Simon Stalland!" she shouted, "You've broken my heart. You shit!"

He hesitated for a moment, then strode out into the early morning without looking back.

*

"Police! Mr Jordon, open up, please!"

It was an hour later. Kelly had come over to the house and told him she was going home, sick. Craig had seen her grey complexion and not

231

argued. He'd telephoned her parents and been surprised to hear relief in their voices. They'd driven to Holt Carr and taken her home. Five minutes later, the police had arrived. PC Ackroyd stood on the threshold with another constable behind him.

"Morning Mr Jordon. We're looking for Simon Stalland. You may be aware he escaped from custody."

"Aye, it's in the paper. I haven't seen him, but you're welcome to look."

Ackroyd gave instructions to other police officers standing around the yard to search the stables and indoor exercise utility, whilst he and his colleague came into the house, assiduously wiping their boots on the doormat.

"Sorry about this, sir," he said apologetically.

The two officers visited every room in the house, including opening the loft trap and shining torches around the cellar.

Eventually, they concluded that Simon was not in the house, thanked Craig for his forbearance, and joined the others in the stables. Craig watched, suddenly surprised, when all the officers who had gone into the stables were suddenly ordered out by PC Ackroyd. He went across the yard to see what was happening.

"Looks as if somebody's been sleeping in there, Mr Jordon. I'm going to ask crime scene investigators to have a look at the place."

Craig had noticed over Ackroyd's shoulder the arrival of Susie on her bicycle, as she came round the end of the house. She stopped and looked at all the police officers.

"I'd better go and tell Susie what's happening."

PC Ackroyd turned round to see her. "Susie is...?"

"One of the girls employed to look after the horses. I've sold the stables to William Stalland. He's keeping Susie and the hacks left in there – " he indicated the stables " – while he gets things organised."

"You said one of the girls. Would the other be Kelly Frobisher?"

"Yes. She's gone home sick, only a few minutes before you all got here."

"Hmm," said Ackroyd, "That might have been her in her parents' car – we passed it on the way up." He pulled an evidence bag from his coat pocket. "Pair of dirty cotton panties. Found in the stables."

"Oh," said Craig.

"She was here earlier, sir?"

"Yes, but as I said, she had to go home. She looked very poorly. That's why I got her parents to collect her."

"I think I should pay her a visit at home," Ackroyd muttered.

Craig lifted an eyebrow before leaving the policeman and walking over to Susie.

"Hello, Susie. Don't worry, they're looking for Simon. He's not here, but they are going to have some people come to check over the stable block – it looks as though he might have been in there. Possibly with Kelly," he added.

Susie's mouth turned down in disapproval. "She's stupid for him, you know."

Craig pursed his lips. "I guess she is."

"Hope she'll be all right."

"Today she isn't. She's gone home sick," said Craig. Susie rolled her eyes. "No surprise there, then." She pushed her bike towards the stables.

*

Cat drove through the yard at Holt Carr, surprised to find police vehicles and personnel. A large police constable came over to her car when she stopped on the track just outside the yard. She opened the window. He leaned down and quickly scanned the contents of the vehicle.

"Morning, ma'am," he said, "could I ask where you're going?"

"I'm Doctor Mitchell. I'm an osteologist, and I'm on my way up to the archæological site on the moor."

The constable glanced up the slope where the top of the marquee was visible. "We're looking for a Mr Simon Stalland – escaped from custody a couple of days ago."

"Not a nice man," said Cat.

"You know him then?"

"He's been up at the dig a couple of times. Couple of times too many, in my view," she added.

"Cause any trouble, did he?"

"Nothing we couldn't handle. Can't say I was sorry to hear he'd been arrested."

"Any particular reason why you say that, Doctor Mitchell?"

She shook her head. "Ancient history, constable. Can I go now?"

"Mind if I come up to the site to have a look round?"

"Let me give you a lift."

He came round the car and lowered his bulk into the passenger seat. Cat waited until he was settled then set the car at the slope. They found Dave Pountney and Jemma crouched in Jemma's new trench, both working to expose the burial she'd found. Cat led the constable along a route to the trench that would not suffer from their footsteps. Dave looked up. "Ah, Cat... and...?"

"PC Ackroyd, sir, from Skipton Police. Looking for Simon Stalland."

"Ah, yes. Well, he hasn't been here. Have a look if you want, but please don't touch anything." Dave waved an arm in the direction of the marquee, and Ackroyd carefully followed a path leading to it.

Dave turned to Cat, who was looking at the skeleton. "Looks like a whole one," he said.

"Male," she said, running her fingertips over the brow ridges and the occipital projection of the skull, which indicated gender.

"We'll start lifting the bones in the morning, and should have them all up by tomorrow night."

"Right," said Cat. "I'll just transfer my things from the car into the marquee and come out and help." The constable completed his inspection of the marquee, and thanked Cat as she went into it, carrying her overnight bags. He set off to walk back down to Holt Carr.

*

The cream swirled in a perfect half-circle round the centre of a broad-lipped white earthenware cup. Craig set his spoon aside in the saucer and looked up into Victoria's face. She'd phoned him not long after the police had left, empty-handed, and asked if they could meet. They were either side of a table set back from the window of the coffee shop overlooking the market place in Skipton. She returned his gaze levelly over the top of her own cup which she held in the finger-tips of both hands.

"Come on, I need to know," she urged. "He doesn't seem like the same person I married. He used to be a nice man, caring of me and our children. I'm worried these headaches of his are something serious, but he won't go to the doctor's."

Craig took a deep breath. "I wondered about the headaches."

"The doctor said they were migraines when he went a couple of years ago."

"So he hasn't seen a doctor since he first hit you?"

"No."

She settled the cup in her saucer and rested her arms on the table, her wrists overlapping. She smiled up into his eyes.

"I think he had a bad experience of the Health Service some years ago – broken ribs, damaged ego, and so on."

Craig understood. "From which you rescued him."

"No, not me. The hospital fixed him and sent him home. No, if anyone rescued anyone, he rescued me." She gazed into the past, over his shoulder.

He took another sip of coffee and put down the cup. "I know you might think Simon and I hate

235

each other," he said, "but it isn't true – or if it was, it was only briefly, in the heat of the moment."

She nodded.

"It was one of those mad things young men do when they both want the same girl – very Neanderthal." He grinned wryly, remembering.

Victoria nodded again.

"But before that, we'd been best mates at school. We got along fine – sure, there was always a competitive edge, sometimes I'd beat him at something, sometimes he'd beat me. I was usually better at sciences, Simon at humanities. We both enjoyed sports, where he was better than me at football, but I could beat him at cricket." He took another sip of his coffee.

"What about now?" Victoria asked, "What do you notice that's different about him today?"

Craig thought for a moment, gazing blankly at the table-top. Outside the window, a crowd had gathered around a stall selling crockery as the stallholder worked up a pitch with a patter extolling the amazing value for money he was able to offer.

"He's more... taciturn than he used to be," he said. "Tends to keep himself to himself. But he's been okay with me, seemed to be enjoying the work." The corners of Victoria's mouth turned down. "Enjoying it more than he should!" she remarked.

Craig caught her eye. "Not really like him, is it?"

"You mean have I ever suspected him of having a thing for young girls before? No."

"Seems like his whole personality has changed recently, from what you tell me," he observed. "That's why I think he should see a doctor."

"When they catch him, I would say a medical examination is inevitable," she said.

He drained his cup. "Want another?"

She shrugged. "If you're having one."

He took the empty cups over to the counter and returned shortly with fresh ones. He sat down and glanced at her face briefly.

"How're you coping with the knowledge that he's made a girl pregnant?"

Victoria grimaced. "She's not the first innocent to be knocked up by him," she said grimly. "I think I have that honour. Am I happy that he's done it again? No, of course not. There is no excuse." She drew a shuddering breath, not meeting Craig's eyes.

"Another time, he wouldn't have given a young girl a second glance," he said, recalling what he knew of Simon. "Maybe this is more evidence of a personality change." Victoria met his gaze at last. "I hope not: if it is, then what else will he do that we can't predict?" Craig sipped the hot drink, and replaced the cup carefully. "I wonder where he is and what he's doing."

"I hope it's nothing he'll regret later."

CHAPTER 18

Sometime in the night Jemma woke up. The darkness was profound, yet something made the hairs on the back of her neck prickle. Silently, she strained to see anything in the faint moonlight filtering through the thick walls of the marquee. She sensed a movement nearby and realised a figure was standing astride Cat's sleeping bag. As she watched, frozen in horror, the figure crouched. The movement broke the spell holding Jemma complicit with the intruder. She screamed loudly and clawed at the sleeping bag to get out quickly. But the man turned towards her and swiped her hard across the face.

"Shut up, bitch!" he said.

Jemma recognised the voice. "Simon? Is that you Simon? Get away from her!" she cried.

Cat had woken in all the commotion and was trying to release herself from the clingy confines of her own sleeping bag. She found a torch and shone it into Simon's eyes, but he reached for it and she had to struggle to hold onto it. Jemma managed to wriggle free and launched herself at him, but she was no match for his weight or strength, and he shrugged her off with ease. The main light of the marquee went on, and the curtain screening off the women was pulled aside. Dave Pountney waded into the small space and grabbed Simon in a bear-hug. He pulled him over backwards and each of the women, now out of their sleeping bags, grabbed one of Simon's legs to prevent him from kicking. Between them, they managed to drag him outside. His wriggles succeeded in slackening their grip, and suddenly he was free and running for the moor. The trio watched him go.

"Thanks, Dave," said Jemma.

"Yes, thanks," echoed Cat, "and thanks to you Jem – God knows what he'd have done if you hadn't woken up and seen him."

They went back into the marquee where Cat and Dave for the first time saw the bright red mark disfiguring Jemma's face.

"Oh! Jemma! Are you okay?" asked Cat, wondering where she'd last seen the first-aid box.

"I'm fine, really," said the girl.

Cat looked closely. "No skin broken, so chances are you'll be all right."

Dave was peering at her too. "Yes – be as right as rain in no time." He still looked worried. "Should I phone the police?"

Cat glanced at Jemma's face and nodded. "I think we should. They're looking for him, and this is another serious assault on a woman."

Jemma shook her head. "No, please don't. I don't think I could go through all the questions and things. Simon's gone now, and I don't imagine he'll come back. In any case, we'll be more prepared if he does."

Dave shook his head. "I think we should phone them – but if you don't want me to... "

"We'll be all right while you're here, Dave," said Jemma, who leaned forward and kissed him chastely on the cheek. "My hero!" she breathed.

Dave's complexion began to darken in his embarrassment.

Cat leaned in and kissed his other cheek, grinning. "Mine too. You saved us from a fate worse than death."

"No – no!" he protested, "you'd already saved yourselves..."

"We couldn't have done it without you," said Jemma, enjoying, with Cat, his embarrassment.

He turned away, harrumphing and shaking his head, but both women judged from the expression he was trying to hide that he was feeling very pleased with himself. Action Man, Dave was not, and the scuffle and its outcome must have been quite novel for him. Cat caught Jemma's eye and signalled an end to their game and return to their sleeping quarters. She led the way, grinning broadly as she heard Jemma tease Dave one more time:

"Just remember in the morning, Dave, the underpants go *inside* the trousers."

"Get in here!" Cat said pulling Jemma in and closing the curtain.

"Yeah, I'm coming, I can't stand watching the smirk on Dave's face any longer." They both giggled like a pair of schoolgirls.

"You can poke fun," said Dave, "but I'm going to be right here, all night."

"Thanks, Dave," said Cat quickly, forestalling yet another jocular response from Jemma.

*

About half a mile away on the moor, Simon saw the light in the marquee go out again, as he had watched it two hours ago. Then he'd been much closer, listening through the canvas wall to Cat and Jemma talking about Craig. His headache thumped again. He pulled a half-full bottle of vodka from an inside pocket of his waxed jacket and now unscrewed the cap and swallowed a couple of mouthfuls. The night was still again. He had gone to the marquee because he'd wanted to talk to Cat. The blonde had been saying that Cat was Craig's destiny: well, Simon was not convinced. His head still ached, just where he'd struck his forehead twelve years ago. A shudder ran down his left side and he turned and limped across the moor towards the old stone quarry.

In daylight, the quarry was massive, its high sides dwarfing anyone standing on its mossy floor. Only when the sun was at its zenith in the summer did its light shine so far down. At night, Simon could almost feel the tonnage of rocks which formed the walls pressing in on him. The quarry had yielded much of the stone used to build the town of Skipton, but had not been worked for a hundred years or more. Long cracks, or fissures, had shattered the rock faces through the processes attached to cutting out slabs and blocks from the wall. He found the way up to the fissure Kelly had found him in by touch. Inside, safe from discovery unless anyone else climbed up the same narrow access way, he dragged the bottle out of one pocket and his last packet of stale sandwiches from the other. In the pitch darkness, he began to eat.

*

Cat's sleep was interrupted by moments of alert wakefulness. Every little sound, it seemed, was interpreted by her brain as indicating Simon's return. Tucked up and warm in her sleeping-bag, her brain ran newsreels before her mind's eye: Simon leaning over her, Simon angry when Jemma spoke to him and he struck her, the fury in his face and eyes as the three of them had manhandled him out of the marquee.

She remembered him in the past, not long out of school, when he'd been fit and strong, and she'd been taking her own first steps into adult relationships. She was glad now he'd not been her first lover. That brought thoughts of Craig to mind: Craig as a student, in his final year of a BSc, herself with post-graduate studies leading to a doctorate firmly in mind.

She had been so sure at the time that he was "The One". Their outlook was so similar, sometimes it seemed like telepathy, when they could anticipate each other's feelings and plans. She would go weak at the knees at the narrowness of his waist and the tautness of his buttocks. She was convinced that their destinies were entwined.

Then his job opportunity in Canada, and her own stupid insistence – she saw that now – that only in Yorkshire could she continue her studies. Of course, the archæology of Britain was more interesting than that of anywhere in the New World, where a mere four centuries was considered "ancient'. She brought her mind back to the present. Was she going to let him walk away again? She had hurt for months after his departure

241

to Canada twelve years ago: would he hurt her again? She needed to find out.

She remained in a cycle of sleep and wakefulness throughout the rest of the night. When daylight at last arrived, she was quiet enough that Jemma noticed and, after breakfast, asked if she was still upset by Simon's visit.

"Not really," she replied, arranging the small bones of a thousand-year-old hand on the trestle table. "Just brought back memories of when I knew him before. He's changed enormously. Never would have done what he did last night."

Jemma paused from removing the dirt from a thick femur with a toothbrush. "It's difficult to imagine him being the sort of man you'd have as a boyfriend."

Cat glanced up at her. "We weren't in a serious relationship, you know. That came later."

"With Craig?"

Cat nodded. "Yes."

She made a deliberate effort to concentrate on the metacarpal bones on the table. There was the right number, which was encouraging. Jemma took the hint and resumed washing the Viking thigh-bone.

"This belonged to a big bloke," commented Jemma as she carefully wielded it. "Weighs a ton even now."

Cat glanced up and smiled. "He was probably very strong and did a lot of hard work," she said. "If you look near the ends, you can see where the muscles attached. They were big and strong, too."

The remainder of her day was spent with the skeleton. At some point in the afternoon, Cat glanced down the moor to the house and noticed that Craig's Land-Rover was back in its parking bay in the old stables. After finishing with the bones she put in an hour helping Dave to tidy up the site.

"I'm going to get a shower down at the house, Dave," she said at last, leaning on a shovel. He heeled his own into the soft earth.

"I'll grab one later, but you first. We've about done here anyway." Five minutes later, her towel, toiletries and clean underclothes in a supermarket carrier bag, she walked down the track to Holt Carr.

*

Half a mile away, along the ridge which was the moor top, Simon watched her. He had watched for a while, and knew Craig was home. He guessed she was going to see him. A pang of jealousy ripped through him. He lay down in the shielding bracken and watched her hesitate on the step before knocking on the door. Craig opened it, let her pass inside and glanced around, making Simon duck his head, before closing the door. Simon found himself suddenly trembling and twitching from head to foot. Every muscle was going into spasm, and for a while he thrashed around on the ground, unable to stop. A sudden sharp pain stabbed through his brain making him whimper. The attack lasted a few minutes, then subsided as suddenly as it had arrived. Every muscle ached and the pain in his head made him screw up his eyes and beat his temples with clenched fists.

*

In the kitchen of Holt Carr, Cat and Craig faced each other across the big table.

"I've come to use the shower, if that's okay," she said.

"Sure," said Craig, turning away to stand in front of a window.

She didn't move, spoke to his back. "I gather you and Jemma have split up."

He half-turned towards her. "Apparently so."

"You don't sound bothered."

"I'm going back to Canada: she wants to pursue her studies. I guess you're more of a role model than she knows."

"What does that mean?" She put her bag on the table and went to stand where she could look up into his face.

243

"Twelve years ago, you and I were an item. When I got the job in Canada, you chose to stay and finish your doctorate."

"I know, but I didn't expect not to hear from you for twelve years, Craig. The only times I heard *about* you was when I saw your mum and dad, and I never heard anything directly *from* you. Until, of course, you wanted picking up at the airport, proving you had my email address."

He sighed. "I thought a clean break was for the best." He turned away from her so she couldn't see his eyes. "I figured we'd get over each other and move on." He turned to face her. "And, you did, didn't you? With Alan?"

"Don't tell me you've been celibate for twelve years," she retorted.

He looked over her head, not seeing anything. "We've both moved on." He focussed on her, meeting her scrutiny. "We aren't the people we used to be."

For a moment, she continued her study of him before turning away and heading for the hallway. Her jaw was clenched firmly as she fought for control of her feelings. It was obvious that whatever had once existed between them was no longer alive in his heart. She must kill any hope of its resuscitation in her own. *Move on*, as he said. She managed to get all the way into Craig's bathroom and lock the door before she allowed herself the release of tears.

*

Craig was peering through the kitchen window, his thoughts on Cat, when the shower pump burst into life. He'd noticed Cat's figure, even in the midst of his *affaire* with Jemma, and could imagine it now, hot water and rivulets of foamy gel running down it. Twelve years ago, when he had unknowingly been the first to explore it fully, she had looked terrific. Her face had needed none of the artifice of cosmetics to be beautiful, and her eyes were sharp and intelligent. Nothing, he thought, had changed there. He stared out.

In his heart he knew that the woman who had been his first real love was upstairs in the shower. There was no point torturing himself with what might have been. He'd deliberately made it easy for her, by letting her think he was well over her. That way, she'd be able to get on with her life without the kind of regrets that he was having. Anyway, it would soon be over. His bags were packed and standing in the corner of the kitchen. Cat had not commented on them, and she must surely have realised that they signified his imminent departure. If he'd had any doubts about his decision to go back to Canada, they had left him now. He glanced at the clock: the taxi to the airport should be arriving any minute.

When Cat came back downstairs, he was gone.

*

She stood in the hall doorway, slowly rubbing her wet curls with a towel, looking round for him. Something nagged at her. Something in the kitchen was different. Crossing the room, she opened the door into the yard and peered round in the gloom. No sign. She returned to the table to pick up her carrier bag, containing the underwear she'd changed out of, and was rolling up the towel to pack it in on top when her gaze travelled beyond the bag to the wall behind the hall door. That was it!

There was something in that space... Her mouth fell open as she remembered. It was not something she'd consciously noticed, being concerned to find out whether Craig still had any feelings for her, but she was almost certain there had been a couple of suitcases there. She'd heard a vehicle come and go while she'd been in the shower. Now Craig and the cases were gone, leading to only one conclusion.

She swallowed with the realisation and felt a spurt of anguish. No doubt this was another one of his so-called *clean breaks!* With a sigh, she collected her bag and trudged up the track to the marquee.

245

She didn't see Simon, squatting against the wall and camouflaged by his waxed jacket and generally dirty condition. He watched her make her way dejectedly back up the hill, the trails of tears on her cheeks reflecting the cold light of the gibbous moon.

*

In her home in the valley, Kelly lay curled up in bed, the early morning light filtering through the curtains over her window. Her arms were folded protectively around her flat stomach. She bit her lip, trying not to cry every time she felt an explosion of pain where Simon had jabbed her with the shotgun. It was her own fault, she knew. When Simon had slapped her then hit her with the gun, she had finally realised he felt no sense of responsibility, no interest, in her or the baby. She had simply been there when he'd wanted a woman. And to make matters worse, she'd actively encouraged him, thinking she held him in thrall. She'd been a fool.

The pain rolled back and she felt a gush of warm, wet blood soak through her panties. Moaning incoherently, she dragged herself out of bed and staggered to the bathroom. On the landing, she was dimly aware of her mother coming up the stairs, but she had no time to worry about that. She sat heavily on the toilet and wrapped her arms around herself. Suddenly her mother was beside her, holding her head against her and trying to comfort her with words. Afterwards, when the pain had subsided, her mother remade her bed, tucked her in and called the doctor, before sitting beside her holding her hand. Kelly chewed her lip, surprised that her mother had not been more critical, not daring to say anything in case it started her off.

Mary studied Kelly for a moment. "You realise you might have lost the baby?"

Kelly attempted a shrug. "I suppose you think that's a good thing," she replied, but instead of sounding truculent, which would have been usual

246

for her, it sounded somehow sad and pathetic to her own ears. Her mother stared unfocussed, out of the window.

"It's a gift we have," she said, looking at Kelly.

"What?"

"Women have this priceless ability to bring new life into the world. At the end of the day, it's the one thing we, and only we, can do. Men and women can be treated equally in the workplace and in society, but in this one, vital, matter, we are infinitely superior to men."

"We still need a man... " Kelly muttered.

"Of course, and we wouldn't normally want it any other way. Men are really useful, when they're properly organised." Mary lifted one eyebrow and smiled at her daughter. "We're very good at doing that, too."

Kelly smiled back. She felt strangely at one with her mother. It was a feeling she wasn't familiar with, but it was almost... She struggled for the word: sisterly.

"You should be very thankful for the fact that you won't now have to look after a child when you're scarcely more than a child yourself," Mary continued. "It's a tragedy when you lose a baby, but losing a childhood can be nearly as bad. I just hope that no permanent damage has been done." She stood up and went to the window, looking out on the moor. "I just hope they find that bastard soon."

Half an hour later, the doctor came and examined her and prescribed something for the pain. She would, he said, physically get over losing the baby fairly quickly. His manner, Kelly felt, was generally unsympathetic and she was glad when he'd gone. Mary brought her a cup of tea. It tasted, Kelly discovered, absolutely wonderful. While sipping it, she thought about Simon and how to pay him back for what he'd done. An idea came to her and brought a twisted smile to her face. That evening, she felt well enough to get up and join her family at the dinner table.

247

Her mother had cooked a hotpot, whose irresistible aroma made Kelly's mouth water. Never normally a hearty eater, she surprised her parents when she ladled her dish full and tore a handful of bread from the farmhouse loaf to mop up the gravy. Conversation round the table, chiefly between her mother and father, lapsed while the food was eaten. In a corner of the room the local evening news was on television.

Suddenly, Kelly caught sight of a photograph of Simon, obviously one taken at the police station, on screen. She froze, her fork half way to her lips.

"Police have spent the day searching the moors and remote farms in Wharfedale looking for Simon Stalland," said the reporter, "who escaped from Skipton Magistrates' Court where he had been remanded in custody on a charge of having unlawful sexual intercourse with a girl under sixteen years of age. The girl cannot be identified for legal reasons..."

Kelly felt the blood rush to her face, and looked down at her plate so she wouldn't have to meet her mother's eye when inevitably, she turned to look at her.

Much to her surprise, when her mother did respond, it was gently to slip her hand over Kelly's in a way she found reassuring. Suddenly, tears filled her eyes. She looked up at her mother and saw her concern.

Mary Frobisher got up from her chair and came round the table, to cuddle her daughter and hold her. The dam broke, and Kelly sobbed gustily against her mother's comforting warmth. Mary looked down at her daughter, her own eyes misting, and gently stroked the girl's hair, waiting until she cried herself out. Tom Frobisher, at the other side of the table, watched them in silence. He got up, pulled a paper handkerchief from a box on the sideboard, and blew his nose.

*

At the same time in the marquee, Dave Pountney eyed the small gas stove with distaste.

"What's for dinner Dave?" asked Jemma.

"That's what I was wondering," he said. "Look, shall we go out for a meal, down to the Mucky Duck? Or shall I cook something?" Neither Jemma nor Cat was particularly impressed with Dave's culinary skills following the departure of Mike and Diarmuid back to York. In fairness, he made no claim for them, and often would prefer to take the team out for a meal on the nights he was due to cook.

Cat hadn't said much after returning from Holt Carr House. Jemma saw the tear-stains on her cheeks when she returned and took her into the sleeping compartment they shared. She looked into Cat's misery-clouded eyes.

"What's happened?" she asked softly.

Cat was fighting to prevent more tears flowing. She gazed at Jemma bleakly. "Craig's gone."

Jemma stared at her. "Gone? Where?"

"Canada. For good."

They stared at each other for a long moment before Jemma put her arms round Cat and held her until she was calm. She had recovered her composure and when Dave made his offer of food, Cat looked at the last two boxes of bones.

"Look, I'd prefer to stay here and finish laying out the skeleton, if you're fairly sure that you've found all the bones?"

Jemma nodded.

"Good. So, why don't you two go and eat, and I'll knock up something for myself a bit later."

"What about Simon? What if he comes back?" asked Jemma.

"I can handle him," said Cat, "I was only hampered last night because I was wrapped up in my sleeping bag. In any case, he'd be a fool to come back here: he's on the run from the police." She looked from Jemma to Dave. "Don't look so sceptical. I did a self-defence course at uni."

Jemma rolled her eyes. "Oh, well, in that case – why didn't you mention it sooner. Come on, Dave, it's clear she doesn't want us around."

"Okay, then, if you're sure," he said.

Jemma took a couple of steps towards the women's space at the rear of the marquee. "If you'll wait a couple of minutes, I'm going to pop a few things in a bag, and when we get back, you can drop me off at the house so I can have a shower.

Fifteen minutes later, Cat was alone, cleaning the particles of moorland soil from the Viking's other femur.

*

Simon's hands clenched and unclenched. Despite the coolness of the night, sweat beaded his forehead. The blood pulsing through his head was sheer anguish: he beat his brow, he ground his knuckles into his temples, but nothing assuaged the pain. Almost blinded by it, he stumbled through the darkness towards the dig site. The bracken plucked at his clothes as he passed it by, and once, he missed the path and found himself walking across a patch of weather-worn loose particles of sandstone, outcropping on the surface. He stopped and looked round, fearful that someone might have heard. The moor was silent and empty. He pulled the bottle of vodka from his pocket and unscrewed the cap, raising it to his lips and drinking deeply. He would go back tonight and talk to Cat. He'd been going to do that before, when he'd not been given a chance. Well this time, he told himself, hefting the shotgun which he carried in the crook of his right arm, she would listen.

CHAPTER 19

The Viking femur lay in its correct position. The patella lay alongside the lower end of the femur and upper surfaces of the tibia and fibula whose abutment in life it would have helped to protect. The tibia and fibula both showed signs of trauma: breaks about halfway along, the edges of which were still fresh and sharp, suggesting the injury occurred at the time of, or just after, death.

Cat picked up the tibia and set it carefully under her magnifier, where she could examine the area immediately adjacent to the break for signs of what had caused it. There was no clear mark of external influence. She replaced the bone and slipped the fibula in its place. The tent flap behind her was carefully pulled to one side. Simon peered in and glanced around to make sure there was no-one but Cat in the marquee before slipping inside, the shotgun in his left hand, barrels pointed slightly downwards.

Cat was engrossed in her study, having found a mark on the fibula which suggested a blade could have smashed up against it, the bone itself preventing it leaving a distinct mark on the adjacent tibia, but the force shattering both bones. A mighty blow, then. Something made her look round as she finished writing a note of her findings in her rough book. Simon stood regarding her.

Her hand went to her throat. "Simon! What are you doing here?"

She dropped her hands to her sides, not wishing him to think she was scared, but conscious that her heart beat had quickened.

"Thought it was time we had a talk, Cat, put our cards on the table, and stopped messing around," he said, his words slurred so that she thought he was drunk. The marquee was lit by two electric lights powered from batteries which were charged up by a small wind turbine. One lamp was at the rear, the other, fitted with a reflector to direct the light down onto Cat's examination table, hung over the skeleton. Simon's unshaven face was only dimly lit, mainly by the lamp at the rear of the tent, but she saw his eyes glittering and wondered if one could tell from the way people stared at you whether they were mad. If so, she'd swear Simon was. A frisson of fear crawled up her spine, but she determined not to show it.

"There's nothing to say, Simon."

"Well that's good, that is," he said, moving a step closer to her, "because I'd been thinking you preferred Craig to me."

"I do," she said, pressing herself back against the table.

Simon grinned mirthlessly. "I think you can put Craig out of your mind now."

"He's gone," she said, aware that she should keep him talking. She didn't like the way he brought the gun round until his right hand was on the trigger.

"Aye, well! That's Craig for thee. Went away before, gone away again."

She shook her head, keeping her hands clasped across her stomach. It was meant to be a disarming gesture, which nevertheless left her ready to defend herself if he should come closer. The shotgun flicked upwards towards her and his chin jutted as anger flashed in his eyes.

"Cat, it's good news. He's not going to bother us again—"

"Us? Us?" she cried, "there is no "us'."

He smiled at her again in a parody of a boyish grin. "Aw, come on. No need to be coy now.

252

Victoria's gone, Craig's gone, so we can be together as we were meant to be."

"No! Victoria is simply keeping out of your way, you're still married to her—"

He waved the gun around in a reckless arc. "Well, she can go. I can divorce her." His eyes stared. "She can go to hell for all I care. I've only ever loved you, Cat. And now we can do the right thing."

"I'm not doing anything with you, Simon, if you were the last man on earth!" she retorted. Outside, she heard the blessed sound of Dave Pountney's MPV grinding up the track.

"Look, Cat, I understand, you know," Simon said in a wheedling tone. "You made a mistake once, and I want you to know, I don't hold it against you. We were all young then, and we all made mistakes – it was part of growing up. But now, you don't have to punish yourself anymore."

She summoned her courage and leaned towards him. "Read my lips: I want nothing to do with you."

He stared at her for a moment. Behind him, the tent flap opened and Dave Pountney walked in, stopping in surprise as he took in the scene. Cat glanced over Simon's shoulder. Without blinking, he turned to follow her gaze, lifted the shotgun and fired it point blank into Dave's chest. Cat pushed her way past Simon, her fear of him overcome by her dread that he might have killed Dave. She knelt by his head and forced herself to look at the bloody wound in his chest. She looked up at Simon.

"Pass me that towel, you bastard!" she shouted.

He was waving the gun around, but seemed bemused by the fact that Dave was lying on the floor with blood pouring out of him. He didn't move.

"Simon! The towel! Do you want him to die? Call an ambulance."

253

Simon shrugged, but nevertheless turned and picked up the towel near the washing-up bowl and threw it across to her.

"It doesn't matter, Cat. It doesn't affect what's between us."

She made the towel into a pad and pressed it on Dave's wound to try to staunch the blood. Dave's eyes had closed and she was terribly afraid he would never open them again.

"Dave! Wake up, Dave. Stay with me. I need you, you have to be strong now. Come on, Dave," she pleaded with him, then looked up at Simon. "There is nothing between us. Get that into your thick head," she screamed.

Dave was very still beneath her hands. Tears sprang to her eyes as she feared he was dead. Suddenly she leapt across him at Simon in hot fury, trying to remove the gun from his grasp. Simon used his superior strength to hold her off, keeping the shotgun out of her reach. His giggle as she fought with him chilled her blood.

"Eh, Cat, you're a wild one, I must say. Didn't think you had it in you," he said.

She bit his hand, drawing blood. He scowled and cracked the back of his hand across her face, knocking her to the floor. Cat's head rang from the blow and she was not able to stop Simon from crouching across her, pinning her body down, sneering at her struggles. His eyebrows arched as a new idea occurred to him and he rested the barrels of the shotgun across her throat.

"Now, keep still, Cat, or this'll hurt. Hey, now you're down there and I'm up here, shall we seal our love for each other, eh?"

He began to fumble with the buttons of her blouse, tearing some off as he pulled it aside. Cat tried to knee him, but could find no leverage for her legs under his weight. She wriggled her torso, as best she could, and had the satisfaction of seeing that he was prevented from handling her

254

breasts because he needed his free hand to maintain his balance.

The tent flap was suddenly pulled open and from the corner of her eye, Cat saw Craig enter the marquee. He took in the situation at a glance and strode across until he was close enough to punch Simon's head, hard enough to knock him sideways and off Cat. He helped her to her feet. Her head was spinning: surely, he'd gone? Meantime, Craig attempted to follow up with another punch to Simon's ribs, but this was only partly successful, rocking him further away and out of reach of another strike. Cat managed to get round behind Simon, and kicked the arm holding the gun. It flew out of his grip and hit the wall of the marquee near the door. Simon climbed to his feet and approached Craig, his eyes staring, hard and angry, his lips twisted in a snarl.

*

In the bathroom at Holt Carr House, Jemma heard a sound faintly from outside, over the music blasting from an MP3 player suspended from a hook on the back of the door. She stepped from the bath and turned down the volume. Sirens. That's what she could hear. They sounded to be heading up the track towards the marquee. Full of concern, she dried herself quickly and pulled on her clothes.

*

Simon had wrestled Craig to the ground, and now knelt on his chest, his hands pinning Craig's wrists to the floor.

"This time, I'll make sure!" he snarled.

"This time, you'll go to prison for life," said Craig. "You won't be around to see, when Cat comes away with me."

Simon moved his grip to Craig's throat, his thumbs seeking out the wind-pipe below Craig's Adam's-apple. As his grip tightened and Craig felt the pain in his throat, suddenly Cat loomed above him, clutching the massive Viking femur she had worked on so carefully earlier and smashed it down on Simon. His eyes rolled back into his head seconds before he fell off Craig and slipped to the ground unconscious. The tent flap was pulled open and PC Ackroyd followed by Stephanie Speight charged into the marquee. Moments later, Jemma arrived to find Cat kneeling on the floor, Craig beside her, rubbing his bruised throat, Ackroyd putting handcuffs on Simon before he came round, and Speight on the radio calling up an ambulance from beside Dave Pountney's bloodied body.

Jemma knelt on the other side of it, noticing that blood was still ebbing from his wound.

"He's still alive, I think," she said.

"Right," said Speight, turning to her colleague. "As soon as you can, Roger, get the first aid kit from the car, will you."

He checked that Simon was immobile and left the marquee, returning moments later with the First Aid kit, pulled the pack open and searched for pads that might be used over the wound.

"Dave, Dave," cried Jemma, tears beginning to spill down her cheeks. "Dave, wake up!" She pressed one of the clean pads on the shot-holes leaking blood.

Ackroyd in the meantime had located the shotgun and broken it open. He removed the unused cartridge and peered at it under the light. He grunted.

"What?" asked Speight, who was squatting opposite Jemma, also pressing a pad on shot-holes.

"Small mercies," said Ackroyd. "Low powered cartridges, probably used for killing rats at close range. Might not have penetrated too far, especially through the coat he was wearing." The siren of an ambulance wailed as it turned off the main road and began to come up the track.

Two paramedics were soon busy working on Dave's wound. Shortly afterward, a third paramedic arrived in a four-by-four and examined Craig, declaring there to be no lasting damage. Simon came round and found PC Ackroyd sitting on one of the folding chairs which he'd placed next to his prisoner. The paramedic who had examined Craig came over to examine Simon.

"Can I interview him?" asked Ackroyd when the paramedic had finished his preliminary examination.

"No, Constable, sorry," he said, "he's had a nasty crack on the head and lost consciousness. Think we'll have to take him to the Infirmary. You're welcome to come with us." PC Ackroyd wagged a finger at Simon and leaned forward to thrust his face almost into Simon's nose.

"And if you throw up again, you can clean up your own mess, Stalland," he muttered, "so keep your bile in!"

Simon, who was feeling sick, swallowed hard at these words. The effort of standing up to the enormous constable was just too much. The paramedic gently nudged the constable out of the way and studied Simon's eyes again.

"How do you feel?" he asked.

Simon turned his head slowly and gazed at him, his head weaving drunkenly.

"Just fine. I think the headache's eased up a bit."

There was a lump on the side of his head where a bruise was forming, the red patch of subcutaneous blood spreading far away from the point of contact with the femur. The paramedic shook his head and looked up at Ackroyd. "Sorry, I think we need to take him now. Don't like the look of him."

"Neither do I," grunted Ackroyd. "Never have done. I will come along though."

"I think you should," said the paramedic. He turned to Simon. "Think you can walk as far as the

257

ambulance?" He pointed to the vehicle, three or four metres away.

Simon looked at it, and turned slowly back. "Course I can. There ain't nowt I can't do, mate."

Suddenly his eyes rolled upwards and he keeled over. The paramedic caught him.

"Can you hold him while I get a stretcher?" he asked Ackroyd.

"I suppose so, aye." He took Simon's head carefully in his large hands. Sirens announced the arrival of another ambulance.

Dave Pountney opened his eyes to the sight of the beautiful face of Jemma Chadwick peering tearfully down into his.

"I've died and gone to heaven," he said to her. Her eyes widened and a grin broke through. She clasped his face in her hands and kissed him.

"Oh, Dave, Dave! Thank God. I was so worried."

He glanced down at his chest, which was now swathed in blood-tinged bandages. He looked up at her again. "If Mrs P had seen that, she'd be worried, too."

"We thought you were..."

"Dead?"

She nodded.

"Not yet. Though I could probably make a case for early retirement."

She chuckled.

The paramedic kneeling on Dave's other side grinned and leaned forward. "First things first. The hospital for you, Mr Pountney." He turned to where Craig was sitting on the floor attended by Cat. "Now then, sir, apart from the bruises and ankle, are you okay?"

"I'll be all right, thanks," Craig replied.

Cat held his gaze but spoke to the paramedic. "I'll take care of him," she said.

The paramedic nodded and turned to help two recently-arrived colleagues who had brought a stretcher in and between all of them, Dave was eased onto it with the minimum of jarring of his wound. "I'll pack your bag and bring it along," said Jemma as he was put into the ambulance. Moments later, the heavy vehicle turned round in the narrow area available to it and trundled off down the slope. Simon was stretchered into the second ambulance which followed the first.

Cat supported Craig out to her estate car, sat him gently in it and drove him carefully down the hill to Holt Carr House.

Jemma found the remains of the Viking femur. Sadly, the fine and hitherto perfect specimen had shattered against Simon's head, breaking into several fragments. She carefully picked them up and laid them in the proper place in the skeleton. By the time she had gathered up the contents of Dave's overnight bag, the police had finished their search of the marquee, and she was able to turn out the light as they all left.

She gave Holt Carr House, one light only burning into the night, barely a glance as she passed it. What Cat and Craig were doing and saying to each other was no longer any concern of hers. She knew what she'd be saying – and doing – if the man she loved had returned in the nick of time to effect a rescue. She grinned in the privacy of the team's MPV. Cat was no fool and would no doubt be striking while the iron was hot.

*

"I thought you were half way to Canada."

Cat and Craig were sitting on the two dining chairs set against adjacent sides of the kitchen table. She was still trying to come to terms with the shock of seeing him again after she'd been so sure he'd left. He gazed at her wryly.

"I should be. Gerry Ancrom will be very cross when I don't turn up tomorrow."

She remembered how he'd described the promotion and new job, how excited he'd been. She remembered how she'd felt when she'd seen the

259

light of ambition in his eyes. She liked that in a man. "What will you tell him?"

"That something more important turned up." He looked squarely into her eyes. She saw his darken, and felt her heart begin to beat against her chest.

"I got as far as the airport," he continued, "and you know what they're like: lots of hanging about and time to think. So I was sitting in the departure lounge feeling awful, and I remembered I had the same feeling twelve years ago."

"What was awful about it, either time? I thought you were going to do what you dearly wanted to do?"

"Oh, the job was – is – all I could ask for. But I know now what it's like living without you around. I couldn't face the thought of living without you indefinitely."

Cat felt a blush stealing into her cheeks. She didn't trust herself to speak, and simply waited for him to go on.

He cleared his throat. "Well... I realised – I suppose you'll think I'm stupid, that it took so long – I realised I didn't want to be alone; I wanted you to be with me. Once I knew that, I also knew that nothing else was more important than coming back here and trying to persuade you that we should be together."

"And you arrived back just in time," she said.

"I had a hell of a job getting my luggage back – it was already on the plane, I think. Anyway, they weren't thrilled when I told them I wasn't flying tonight after all. Anyway, they had no choice: they can't carry baggage for a passenger who isn't on the plane, so they had to find it. Took some time, though, or I'd have been back sooner."

"But you came."

"I came." He took her hand in his and grinned. "Just in time to be the White Knight rescuing the Fair Maiden."

260

"You did," she said. "Mission accomplished."

He smiled. "Yes, I did, didn't I? But it was a pyrrhic victory – he was, uh, almost too strong for me, and I am glad you got him off me."

"Let's say we're even, then," she said. "Mind you, the cost was great – one previously perfect specimen of a thousand-year-old thigh bone reduced to splinters just to save your life."

"I suppose I should be flattered?"

She smiled, looked down and shook her head. "I expect we'll find another specimen one day. I couldn't not save your life, whatever the cost." She looked up and met his gaze. "You see, I had this idea that you might feature large in my future." She grinned wryly. "What's one old leg-bone against a whole future?"

He reached out for her, and gently cupped her face in his hands. "I'm so glad – on both counts. You see, I've known deep down for a long time that you were my girl, my future," he said. "I don't regret going to Canada, but I do regret it was without you, and I'm deeply sorry I didn't keep in touch. Put it down to the folly of youth."

"I never contacted you. Talking to your parents about you was just not good enough. I should have made more effort to let you know how I felt."

He looked away, wondering how to say what he desperately wanted to. Finally he turned back and stared deep into the dark pools of her eyes.

"Cat, I might still have a future in Canada waiting for me." He gripped her hands. "But this time, I'm not going unless you come with me. I can't live the rest of my life without you, because I'm sure – one thousand percent – that I love you, and I need you in my life from now on. The bottom line is that I don't care where we live, how we live, as long as we're together."

Still blushing, Cat leaned in to him and caressed his lips with a kiss, smiling. "You're doing well. Just carry on. You have to ask me the four-

261

word question, and then you'll have to wait for the answer."

Craig's face split into a very big grin as he realised what she was telling him. He sighed theatrically and got onto one knee in front of her.

"All right," he said, "we'll do this properly, so you can tell our grandchildren." He adopted a formal tone. "Catriona Mitchell, I love you. Will you marry me? Please."

She looked back at him primly. "Why, Mr Jordon, what a surprise that you should ask."

"An early reply would be appreciated: these flagstones play havoc with one's knees."

"You sound just like Pompous Piggott," she said.

"Who the hell's Pompous Piggott?"

"The Head of my Department at the Uni."

"You wouldn't leave him kneeling on a hard stone surface, would you?"

She narrowed her eyes as if she was considering the question. "Yes."

He gazed at her suppliantly. "Please, Cat, say you'll marry me. I'm going to stay here until you do."

"What more do you want me to say?"

He rolled his eyes. "I'd like an answer to my polite request."

"You've had it." He stared at her, then realised just what her 'yes' had meant. "You will?"

"I said so," she said.

He stood up and gathered her in his arms. She pushed him away, laughing breathlessly.

"And furthermore," she added, "This time, I will come with you to Canada." He held her carefully, and kissed her. It was a long, no-holds-barred kind of kiss, involving tongues, teeth and lips. It was a kiss that weakened her and caused her to cling to him; it was a kiss which made her heart pound, and he strengthened his grip round her waist so she couldn't slide to the floor, when all her strength left her. It seemed to last hours.

She felt him bend and a moment later, his strong arm slid behind her knees and lifted her off her feet. Heat flooded her body and she was dimly aware that he was carrying her upstairs. She felt herself being lowered until her feet touched the floor, and realised she was in his bedroom. At last he broke the kiss, but only so he could remove her top. A moment later, she felt the waistband of her jeans loosen.

Her own hands busied themselves with his jeans, undoing them and opening them carefully, feeling his strength and power as she did so. She sat on the bed partly because her knees were still feeling less capable than usual of holding her up, and partly because it made it easier to slide his underpants down and slip both them and his jeans off altogether. In the meantime, he'd pulled off his T-shirt and unfastened her bra deftly, and now explored her breasts with his strong fingers. He bent and took each nipple into his mouth in turn.

A moment later, he moved her on the bed until she was laying comfortably, and she could enjoy his tender manipulations. Afterwards, she felt as weak as a rag doll. He collapsed on her, rolling off to one side. They lay together, conjoined, until she found the strength to sit up and kneel astride him.

"I guess you could lay there and think of Canada or something while I have my wicked way with you. I've waited such a long time for this!" she said.

"I shall never think of anyone – or anywhere – but you again, Cat, with me," he murmured softly. She leaned down and kissed him. He grinned and reached for her breasts. A moment later, the grin disappeared as she took control and he sucked in his breath. Tenderly but passionately, she began to make up for lost time.

*

263

"Hello, you two. You're looking happy." Victoria Stalland stood before them in Skipton's Market Place, glancing down at Cat's ring finger.

She held the sparkling triple diamond up for her to see.

Victoria admired it as it glinted in the sunlight on its white gold band. "Oh, it's beautiful," she said.

"There are advantages in having a mineralogist and petrologist as a fiancé," said Cat, grinning. Craig shuffled from one foot to the other.

Victoria glanced up, smiling. "I'm glad for you," she said to him. "Do you have time for a celebratory coffee?"

Craig glanced at Cat before accepting. A few minutes later they were seated in the window of the little coffee shop.

"Did he do the job properly?" Victoria asked, grinning.

"Oh, yes: on one knee, pretty speech, how could I have said no," replied Cat, enjoying Craig's apparent embarrassment.

"When you two have finished..." he muttered, his face red.

Cat patted his knee. "I fear you'll just have to get used to me boasting about you."

"There's so much to boast about," said Victoria, but wished she hadn't when two pairs of eyes instantly turned her way. She blushed. "I only meant, Craig's so big."

Cat lifted an eyebrow.

"Such a tall man, such broad shoulders," spluttered Victoria.

Cat nodded. "Oh yes, indeed."

"For God's sake," Craig burst out, "Can I get us another coffee, then at least you can talk behind my back and I don't have to listen." The women chuckled, accepting the offer. When he had gone, Victoria leaned forward, her face serious. "I hear there was a very nasty incident at your dig site before Simon was arrested?"

"Ah, yes. Our Site Director, Dave Pountney, was shot, fortunately with low-powered cartridges, so his injury involved a lot of blood but no serious damage. He'll live."

"Thank God," said Victoria, sounding relieved.

Cat grinned.

"Apparently, Jemma has taken to looking after him – stayed at the hospital after taking an overnight bag down for him, and Dave was enjoying her attentions – said it added enormously to his 'street cred" to have a beautiful, fit, young blonde hanging around. Mrs P. eventually arrived at the hospital and didn't see it in the same light. More or less dismissed Jemma at first sight."

Both women smiled.

"Rumour has it," Cat continued, "that since then Mrs P has been to the hairdresser's and had her perm replaced by a new style – and she's had a colour rinse with highlights. She's worrying Dave with talk of buying some new clothes, not from the charity shop this time, either, but he's either too ill or too amazed by her determination to improve her looks to object. Wait till the credit card statements start to arrive, is what I say."

"Ah, the live now, pay later society!" sighed Victoria, shaking her head in mock-disapproval. Both women laughed. "Probably do them both good," she added.

By the time Craig returned, balancing three brimming cups on a tray, they had changed the subject.

"What are your plans now?" Victoria asked.

"We're going to Canada," replied Cat.

"As soon as possible," added Craig.

"I hope you'll both be happy there."

"Thanks." Cat turned to Victoria. "Have you heard how Simon is?"

Victoria's face clouded over. "Yes. When he was taken to hospital, they gave him a complete check-up, and because of the lump on his head – " she glanced at Cat " – he was given a CT scan. They discovered he had a tumour in his head the size of an egg."

Cat and Craig stared at her, then at each other, as the implication sank in.

"That's why he became so different!" Cat exclaimed.

"The doctors say it would explain the changes in his personality."

"Poor man," said Craig.

Victoria glanced at him. "If only he'd gone back to the doctor's," she said, "there was a chance he might have been diagnosed earlier. He was convinced he was suffering from migraines."

"Will they be able to remove it?" asked Cat.

"I hope so." Victoria paused a moment. "You know, he was a nice guy when I married him," she added, "Oh I know he got me pregnant – Simon has never understood the need to use condoms – but he married me, and we were happy for eight or nine years – that's longer than many marriages last. If they can get rid of the tumour and we can get through all the things he's been charged with, I'd take him back. But the neurosurgeon says there are no guarantees, and recovery could take a long time."

She stopped, and gently stirred her untouched coffee. "I married him for better or worse, in sickness and in health: I want to stay with him," she said quietly.

Cat rested her hand on Victoria's. "I hope everything works out for you," she said.

Victoria looked up and smiled at her. "I hope everything works out all right for you two, as well. New life in a new country – it sounds really exciting." She smiled up at Craig.

"One thing I wondered about," said Cat, "and that is, how did the police know to turn up. You couldn't have phoned them, could you Craig?"

"No. I spoke to Susie – I seem to have spent hours on the phone recently – and she told me that Simon was pretty horrible to Kelly, slapped her about, and finally hit her in the abdomen with the shotgun before sending her home. Apparently, she later miscarried. What with that and his rejection of her, you can imagine, Kelly was furious. Seems she finally realised he was not the man of her dreams. Oh, I can guess there would be a lot of anger in her. Anyway, it seems she knew where he was hiding out – sometimes in the stone quarry and other times he was apparently sleeping in the stables at Holt Carr. She decided to shop him to the constabulary. They were aiming for the stables when they came, but they heard the kerfuffle going on at the marquee and went to investigate. Sound travels a long way over the moors at night."

"So it was just a happy accident that they arrived when they did?" asked Victoria.

"Yes. Very happy, though I was at that point in no danger of suffocation because my dear Cat had walloped Simon with a huge bone."

Cat turned down the corners of her mouth. "Yes. It was such a waste – it smashed to pieces on Simon's head – but fortunately everything turned out okay in the end."

"In the end?" wondered Victoria.

"Yes. Craig proposed. It was a terrible risk, I know – perfect bones like that are scarce – but I needed something to persuade Craig to say what I thought was on his mind, and it worked."

He stared at her. "That is downright sneaky," he said.

"I know," she said, her eyes cast down demurely, "but I was desperate." She grinned up at him. "You have lots of perfect bones to make up for that femur."

"And nowhere near as old," he replied.

"I'm glad to hear it. Jemma told me how young and fit you were – for your age!"

"Oh!" Craig looked away.

Cat laughed. "Of course girls talk. Especially about men. Don't be embarrassed – she said nothing to your detriment."

Victoria was grinning at his discomfort. But then her expression grew serious. "I wonder what will happen to Kelly."

Craig turned towards her. "Who knows. I expect she'll be a lot wiser now, and I imagine her mother will make sure she is protected from any more unwanted pregnancies."

"There's hope for her yet. I have some shopping to finish. Ah! There's just the matter of Holt Carr." She finished her coffee. "My father-in-law has asked me to turn it into a lodging house," she said, "for parties of pony-trekkers. I take it you're not planning to return for quite some time?"

"No. I'm sure you'll do the job well," he said.

"Thanks. I must go," she said, gathering her shopping basket. "There're some nice fresh vegetables on a stall over the road, and I want to get them before they sell out. Then there're the children to collect and Simon to visit, if they'll let me. He's guarded by a security man day and night even while he's in hospital."

Cat rested her hand on Victoria's arm. "I hope everything works out the way you want it to."

Victoria nodded and left the table. She got to the door and turned.

"Good luck to you both," she smiled and went out into the street.

Craig and Cat turned to each other. His smile was diffident. "Do you want to get married here or in Canada?"

"I expect Gerry wants you back there a.s.a.p.?"

"Yes. He was very understanding, when I phoned him, and said the job would wait another few days. I promised him I wouldn't keep him waiting a minute longer than I had to."

"Let me sample Canada for a bit before deciding. I've never been there, so I want to see what it's like. Especially your bit. I can't get away for a week, so you'll have to go ahead without me."

"How will I cope?" he asked, shaking his head.

"Same as you did the last twelve years," she replied tartly. "It could have been a month, if Pompous had had his way. Fortunately, the Vice-Chancellor has always had a bit of a soft-spot for me, and he leaned on the Professor. Because I've been on-site at Holt Carr twenty-four seven, he's decided I'm due some extra leave, which means I've only a week to work, and the rest of my notice period will be leave."

"It'll give me a chance to tidy the place up and make it more presentable," he said.

She grinned at him. "So tell me, what is your bit of Canada like?"

"My bit? It's cold, quiet and sometimes lonely except for the wildlife. But Whitehorse is a great city – still has a frontier feel to it, but with all mod. cons. as the realtors say." He paused, thoughtfully. "I wouldn't mind moving further east, say to Alberta. I don't know what need there is for osteologists in Whitehorse." She slipped her left hand over his right one, the ring sparkling in the sunlight, reflecting their hopes for the future.

"Wherever you go, I'll be with you. I want to be with you, Craig."

He put his hand over hers, clasping it warmly. "And I want to make you the happiest woman in the world, my love," he smiled.

She leaned back and looked at him evenly. "Good positions to start from, don't you think?"

He cupped her face in his hands and drew her towards him.

"Perfect," he said, and kissed her.

THE END

Printed in Poland
by Amazon Fulfillment
Poland Sp. z o.o., Wrocław